Praise for

Dolled Up for Murder

"A quick-paced mystery . . . and a wonderful peek into the not-always-genteel world of doll collecting!"
—Monica Ferris, *USA Today* bestselling author of the Needlecraft Mysteries

"A fun, frantic, and thoroughly engaging mystery set against the fascinating backdrop of doll collecting."
—Sandra Balzo, Anthony Award–nominated author of *Uncommon Grounds*

"Quick-paced and satisfying. I can hardly wait for the next one . . . A wonderful new series."
—*Green Bay (WI) Press-Gazette*

"Doesn't let up until the final page . . . Definitely a page-turner. You also learn a lot about dolls: their history and culture. Entertainment and education in one package."
—*Gumshoe Review*

"A charming cozy that brings into the light the dark side of doll collecting . . . A charming new mystery series."
—*Midwest Book Review*

"Baker has strung together not only dolls but also a sharp and entertaining mystery. Writing in true 'whodunit' fashion, she keeps us guessing right up to the end. Even readers with no expertise in doll collecting will still be drawn into this story of intrigue . . . . the lucrative and very serious business of a . . . . *Good Book*

"[A] quick-paced s . . . . olid mystery . . . Holds . . . . *views*

Dolls to Die For Mysteries by Deb Baker

Dolly Departed

DEB BAKER

BERKLEY PRIME CRIME, NEW YORK

THE BERKLEY PUBLISHING GROUP
Published by the Penguin Group
Penguin Group (USA) Inc.
375 Hudson Street, New York, New York 10014, USA
Penguin Group (Canada), 90 Eglinton Avenue East, Suite 700, Toronto, Ontario M4P 2Y3, Canada
(a division of Pearson Penguin Canada Inc.)
Penguin Books Ltd., 80 Strand, London WC2R 0RL, England
Penguin Group Ireland, 25 St. Stephen's Green, Dublin 2, Ireland (a division of Penguin Books Ltd.)
Penguin Group (Australia), 250 Camberwell Road, Camberwell, Victoria 3124, Australia
(a division of Pearson Australia Group Pty. Ltd.)
Penguin Books India Pvt. Ltd., 11 Community Centre, Panchsheel Park, New Delhi—110 017, India
Penguin Group (NZ), 67 Apollo Drive, Rosedale, North Shore 0632, New Zealand
(a division of Pearson New Zealand Ltd.)
Penguin Books (South Africa) (Pty.) Ltd., 24 Sturdee Avenue, Rosebank, Johannesburg 2196,
South Africa

Penguin Books Ltd., Registered Offices: 80 Strand, London WC2R 0RL, England

This is a work of fiction. Names, characters, places, and incidents either are the product of the author's imagination or are used fictitiously, and any resemblance to actual persons, living or dead, business establishments, events, or locales is entirely coincidental. The publisher does not have any control over and does not assume any responsibility for author or third-party websites or their content.

DOLLY DEPARTED

A Berkley Prime Crime Book / published by arrangement with the author

PRINTING HISTORY
Berkley Prime Crime mass-market edition / March 2008

Copyright © 2008 by Deb Baker.
Cover art by Teresa Fasalino.
Cover design by George Long.
Interior text design by Kristin del Rosario.

ISBN: 978-0-425-22051-1

BERKLEY® PRIME CRIME
Berkley Prime Crime Books are published by The Berkley Publishing Group,
a division of Penguin Group (USA) Inc.,
375 Hudson Street, New York, New York 10014.
The name BERKLEY PRIME CRIME and the BERKLEY PRIME CRIME design
are trademarks belonging to Penguin Group (USA) Inc.

PRINTED IN THE UNITED STATES OF AMERICA

10 9 8 7 6 5 4 3 2 1

Acknowledgments

I want to thank my first readers, Anne Godden-Segard, Peg Herring, and Lee Wolfs, for offering constructive criticism with deadly accuracy. To Cindy Church for her witty, winning title suggestion. And a special thanks to my editor, Shannon Jamieson Vazquez, for her constant guidance and support.

Gretchen Birch was still several blocks from the doll shop when Charlene Maize, better known to her friends as Charlie, failed to suck in enough air to feed her panicking brain and various other vital organs. She keeled over in the center of her miniature doll shop, Mini Maize, amid the clutter from a tipped display case. Charlie took the dive in full view of a group of Parada del Sol spectators gathered in front of the shop's window to watch Old Scottsdale's largest western parade.

No one noticed.

A marching band, passing at that precise moment, struck up the familiar beat of "Louie, Louie," and people along the parade route swayed and bopped to the music.

Caught up in the swell of humanity, Gretchen was running late, and as if enough hadn't gone wrong already, her teacup poodle, Nimrod, was slowing her down even more.

"Here comes the parade!" someone shouted as Gretchen hurried past a crowded corner on her way to Mini Maize. Nimrod, all five inches and three pounds of black puppy fur, heard his cue. He pitched his fluffy body out of Gretchen's white cotton purse, which was adorned with red bows and embroidered with little black poodles, Nimrod look-alikes. She frantically grabbed for the pup, managing to break his fall to the pavement. Then she lost her grasp, and Nimrod shot off toward the street.

Every time the miniature pup heard the word *parade* at home, he headed for the kitchen doggie door, burst through into the backyard, and trotted around the perimeter of the privacy fence that encircled the pool, barking away as though he were the grand master of a parade. It was a cute stunt at home, but out in public . . . well, she'd never expected it to be an issue.

Gretchen raced after the wayward canine, jostling past a rowdy group on the curb who had obviously started partying well before the ten o'clock a.m. parade began. One reveler almost stepped on Nimrod.

"Watch out for the puppy!" she yelled. "Don't move!" No one heard her. "Help!" she screamed, imagining the worst as she lost sight of Nimrod. "Catch him!" A few people turned and stared at her, but no one jumped to her assistance.

Gretchen burst through to the front of the parade line, knocking over a lawn chair and almost falling across an elderly couple sharing a sun umbrella. She saw Nimrod dart back into the street directly in front of the parade's lead vehicle, a Scottsdale police cruiser.

The squad car, strobe lights flashing in honor of the event, jerked to a halt, and a uniformed Scottsdale police officer jumped out.

Nimrod scampered for the other side of the street, where he was instantly enveloped in a circle of kids. Gretchen waded in, not far behind him.

"You've disrupted the parade, lady, you know that?" the cop said. "I ought to write you up for having an unleashed animal. Move back and try to stay out of the way!" He hurried back to his car, slammed the car door, and began to edge forward.

Gretchen and Nimrod ended up on the wrong side of the street, forced to wait for the parade to pass. Parada del Sol, Spanish for *walk in the sun*, was a spectacle to behold on this warm and brilliant February morning. The world's largest horse-drawn parade meandered down Scottsdale Road. Cowboys on horseback pranced by, and women in carriages threw candy into the crowd. Kids scrambled off the curb, grabbing Tootsie Rolls and bubble gum. Giant floats rambled along, trailed by clowns rolling wheelbarrows and cleaning up behind the horses.

While Gretchen watched, she had plenty of time to blame her absent Aunt Nina for teaching Nimrod such a useless trick. Purse dog trainer extraordinaire Nina hadn't anticipated problems, either.

"Don't you just love a parade?" someone said behind them. Gretchen had another tangle with Nimrod, but she was ready this time and held him back.

On the other side of the street, she saw Joseph Reiner make his way through the crowd in the same direction the parade traveled. He was hard to miss in a pink, short-sleeved, button-down shirt and yellow shorts. Joseph's Dream Dolls was one of Gretchen's favorite doll shops, but Joseph *did* tend to dress like a parrot.

He looked her way. She waved, but he continued on without seeing her. Hadn't he received one of Charlie's mysterious invitations? She was sure her mother had mentioned his name, but he was headed in the wrong direction. Odd.

Gretchen cuddled Nimrod and waited impatiently for the parade to pass. She'd be late for the party, and Charlie had stressed the importance of being on time for a grand unveiling at Mini Maize. Ten sharp, she'd written in the invitation.

When the last horse-drawn float rolled past, Gretchen stuffed Nimrod back in her purse and made for the other side, weaving among the straggling, shovel-clenching clowns. She ran right into one of them, bouncing off an enormous stuffed stomach. She fell sideways, clutching Nimrod and the purse protectively to her chest.

"Watch where you're going," the clown said, not bothering to stop or to help her up. Gretchen saw a bald head with two large patches of green hair protruding from the sides like clumps of moldy cotton candy. The clown loomed over her momentarily, and then waddled away, a purple sack slung over a shoulder and enormous red feet flapping.

"Thanks a lot," Gretchen muttered, rising and brushing herself off. What else could possibly go wrong? Today was turning out to be one of those days when absolutely nothing went right.

By the time she arrived at Charlie's doll shop, it was almost eleven o'clock, and quite a crowd had gathered in front of the store. Most of the other parade-goers along the route were drifting away from the curb to explore the shops of Old Scottsdale or head for the party at Trail's End.

"She didn't open up," a man said when Gretchen edged through and tried the door to Mini Maize. It was locked.

"That can't be right," Gretchen said, holding her invitation in the air. "I'm invited to a special celebration." She noticed a posted sign. "It says the shop opens at ten."

"We all have invitations," the same man said. "Maybe Charlie's sick?"

"She has a bad heart, you know," said a woman with an enormous straw sun hat and dimpled cheeks.

Gretchen had heard about Charlie Maize's heart condition. When the invitation arrived a week ago, her mother, Caroline, had filled her in on the doll shop owner's health situation. A recent physical had prompted the diagnosis. Immediately afterward, Charlie had arranged for the celebration at her shop, as though she worried that her time was near, and she had one last wish.

"Oh my Gawd!" A woman nearest to the window shouted.
Another woman screamed. "She's on the floor!"

"Where?"

"Right over there! In the middle of all that doll furniture. Looks like a display tipped over."

"We have to get inside and help her!"

Gretchen couldn't get anywhere near the window to see for herself. Not that she wanted to. Emergencies made her feel totally helpless. Next time she had an opportunity, she promised herself, she would take a CPR class and learn how to save people.

"Someone call nine-one-one!"

Maybe she *could* help by making the emergency call. Standing next to the locked door, Gretchen dug in her purse past Nimrod's tiny body. His head poked out of her bag, taking in the situation. She pulled out her cell phone, dialed the emergency number, and gave the dispatcher as much information as possible.

As she ended the call, a man with a full head of white hair and a white mustache that reminded Gretchen of Geppetto pushed through on his way to the shop's door.

"Bernard!" the big-hat lady called out shrilly. "I think that's Charlie on the floor inside, and the door is locked. Do you have a key?"

"Of course I do, Evie."

"Quick then. Hurry."

The crowd pushed closer. Once the door was unlocked, the entire mass surged in behind Gretchen, who was front and center whether she wanted to be or not. "Give us room, please," Bernard shouted.

"I'm a doctor," someone called from the back. "Can I help?"

"Let the man through!"

People continued to flow into the shop. Unwilling to look at the woman sprawled so close to her, Gretchen inched sideways to give the doctor space to work. She glanced around the miniature doll shop with a trained eye, taking in all the sights in the mini wonderland. Dollhouses lined one side of the shop and display cases were stuffed with every imaginable furnishing from every era: tiny Oriental rugs, little dishes, platters of food, flower arrangements, pictures for small-scale walls, and of course, miniature dolls.

Her eyes roamed to the floor involuntarily. She caught a glimpse of one of the fallen woman's legs, splayed at an awkward angle. The toes of Charlie's sandaled feet were motionless. Sirens wailed in the distance, growing louder.

The doctor, crouching beside Charlie, changed position, blocking the woman from view. Gretchen edged away. The doctor spoke to someone, but she couldn't make out his words.

Evie, the big-hat woman, let out a piercing screech. "She's dead. Charlie's dead!"

There was a collective gasp from everyone inside the shop followed by a moment of silence. No one knew what to say or what to do next.

Gretchen stepped around several pieces of dollhouse furniture, heading for the door, desperately needing fresh air. She cast her eyes to the floor, so she wouldn't step on any of the scattered items.

Gretchen stopped abruptly and stared down.

One of the items . . . it couldn't be.

But it was.

Gretchen was looking at a miniature axe with a dab of red paint along the blade. She stepped gingerly around it and made for the exit, feeling nauseated.

A Scottsdale police cruiser pulled up to the curb.

"What's going on here?" the cop said, unfolding from the squad car. He squinted at Gretchen and then frowned.

"I know you. Is trouble following you around, or are you starting it?"

Just my luck. It was the same cop who had threatened her with a ticket at the start of the parade.

"A doctor is inside," she said with a catch in her voice. "Charlie Maize is dead. She had a bad heart."

"Stay put," he said, heading inside. "I'll need your name and a statement."

An ambulance rounded the corner and stopped on the street, lights flashing and siren wailing. The sound died away, but the colored lights continued to rotate. Two paramedics jumped out, pulled equipment from the back of the ambulance, and hurried inside.

The cop came out of Mini Maize a few minutes later, as another squad car arrived. He shook his head when two female officers joined him. "You," he said to one of the officers, "get in there and contain the crowd."

"Shop was all locked up," he said to the other cop. "And what do they do? They find a key, unlock the door, and storm in. Must be fifteen of them inside, touching everything, kicking little pieces of furniture around. Nobody, not one of them, ever thinks they might be contaminating a crime scene."

He shook his head again and fiddled with the top of his holster as though the possibility of a rapid draw was always on his mind. "I have them all backed up against the far wall with their hands in their pockets. I need assistance. The doctor who examined her doesn't think it was her heart. We're treating it as a crime scene unless we find out differently."

Gretchen stood next to the shop's window, watching and waiting while the officer rushed in. The cop from the parade glanced through the window. She thought about the tone of authority he'd used. When other emergency vehicles arrived, he was the one who gave them directions. Equipment was carted past her: cameras, a tripod, video recorders, and something that looked like a large toolbox.

Gretchen slid along the side of the shop, planning to make her escape unnoticed. The cop turned as if on cue and stared at her. "Come over here," he said. Gretchen eased off the wall.

"Let's hear your side of it. And you," he nodded to the officer who remained outside, "go inside and make sure none of them get away before we have a chance to talk to them. Handcuff them, duct tape them up in a big ball if you have to. Whatever it takes. And tell them we'll arrest anyone we catch touching any of the dolls. Touching anything, for that matter." He looked back at Gretchen. "Well?"

"I was running late. I don't know any more than you do."

"Did you know Charlie Maize?"

"She was a good friend of my mother's. Charlie sent us an invitation to a party at her shop. It was supposed to be at ten o'clock this morning."

"Do you have the invitation with you?"

Gretchen dug in her overfilled purse. Nimrod licked her face.

"Here it is." She handed him the invitation. While he read it, she noted the name on his uniform. Officer Brandon Kline.

He looked up from the invitation. "It doesn't say what the celebration's about."

"I don't have any idea either," Gretchen said.

"Where's your mother? Inside?"

Gretchen shook her head. "She's out of town."

"Why was your mother on the invitation list?"

"We are doll restoration artists. We repair and restore dolls for collectors. My mother knew Charlie through her work."

"Do you believe in the chaos theory?"

What a question. "I'm not sure." Gretchen hesitated. "Why?"

"If I can create order from this chaos, it'll be more like a miracle."

He flipped out a notebook and started writing. "Name," he said.

"Gretchen Birch."

"Driver's license." She handed it over.

"Well, Gretchen Birch, you're in the thick of it now." Officer Kline returned her license before handing her a clipboard with a form attached to it and a pen. "Fill this out and stay right here. Since you're the expert, I may need you."

She stared at him. "I don't think I can be of any help."

"Well, I don't know a damn thing about dolls. And you do," he said, catching her look of dismay. "Stay put," he warned her before heading back inside.

Gretchen sighed. She was smack-dab in the middle of a police investigation. She glanced at her watch. High noon.

• 2 •

Bernard Waites can't pull his eyes from the fallen woman. How many years has he known her? Twenty? Fifteen, at least. They are . . . were a team. He built dollhouses to perfect scale, and Charlie designed the miniature furniture and room details.

They are . . . were a good team.

His eyes swing to the dollhouses displayed on shelves along the far wall. He'd built every one of them with his own hands and his own tools. He lifts a veined and knarled hand and studies the back of it. It shakes slightly.

Bernard is proud of his craftsmanship. His favorites are the American farmhouse, a Victorian cottage, the English Tudor, and especially, the Queen Anne mansion. He looks at the dollhouse pieces lying on the floor, furniture catapulted everywhere. His eyes shift back to Charlie's body. Two EMTs are loading her onto a stretcher.

"Careful," one of them warns the other.

The one doing the cautioning is a female, as are several of the cops in the room. In his day women didn't do this kind of work. They knew their place just like the men knew theirs. The world is a changed place, and Bernard isn't sure he likes it.

Will they cover Charlie's face before carrying her past the gawkers outside the shop? Look at them out there, straining to see through the window from their positions on the other side of a line of cops, all hoping for a good view of something horrible. Anything will do.

And the ones inside don't give a hoot about Charlie Maize. Nosy gossips, the bunch of them. If they craned their necks any farther, they'd look like geese. Bernard watches the EMTs prepare Charlie for the ambulance, strapping her in.

Once, long ago, Bernard had been an emergency medical technician himself, back before all the governmental licensing requirements and insurance restrictions. He knows what death looks like. He knows it in all its forms. Grow as old as he is, and you watch friends and family drop one by one. The curse of old age. All his friends gone and not much family left either.

The two EMTs heave Charlie up between them and carry her out. It was hard to see what was happening before, such a cluster of people swarming around her and him forced back into a corner with the rest, like a herd of cattle. Yellow tape used as fencing strung everywhere.

Camera flashes going off. Someone is making one of those newfangled movies of the shop. Not good. Several more cops arrive. They begin interrogating everyone inside the shop. Let them. His turn is coming, and he is more than ready. The key weighs heavy in his pants pocket.

Bernard is puzzled by one of the boxes on the floor. *Why did she build a room box herself? Why didn't she ask me to do it?*

Bernard knows Charlie must have made it herself, because it isn't exactly perfect. Not even close. The edges are rough, the sides don't fit together like they should. A craftsman would have done much better. This one was amateurish.

Looks like she used a jigsaw and fiberboard to construct it. He glances around and sees the ones he made. His practiced eye skillfully measures each one, calculates the dimensions: nineteen inches by twenty-six inches by fourteen. Large room boxes, crafted to Charlie's specifications.

He wants to pick up the one she made and study it, but the cops are attentive, watchful of the so-called "witnesses," treating them more like suspects than concerned friends of Charlie's.

"Are you the one who unlocked the door?" a cop asks him. Bernard stares at his badge.

"Yes, Officer Kline. I have a key." He keeps his voice low and respectful.

"What are you doing with a key?"

"I've had one since the day Charlie opened the shop. She gave out keys like candy." He hopes his hand isn't shaking noticeably when he points at the dollhouses. "I made those." He sees the tremor running along his index finger and quickly closes the finger against his palm.

The cop's indifferent eyes slide up to the dollhouses. He writes something down in a notebook.

"Name."

"Bernard Waites."

"When was the last time you saw Charlie?"

"Yesterday," he lies as pat as a slice of butter, or so he imagines. The cop eyes him with a piercing stare, but Bernard stays calm and pierces him right back.

"Let me see the key," the cop says.

Bernard dutifully presents it.

"Same key fit the back door?"

Bernard nods.

"Did you ever think you might have destroyed evidence by letting all these people in here?"

"I had to see if she needed help. How was I supposed to know she was dead?" Tears form in his eyes when he says the word *dead*. He allows his sorrow to show.

The cop closes the notebook and hands Bernard a piece of paper. "Fill this out. At the moment, we're using every clipboard, thanks to the free-for-all. We have an entire room full of potential witnesses who haven't seen a thing." The cop looks frustrated. "You'll have to find something firm to write on."

Bernard looks around the room with satisfaction. People are filling out paperwork left and right. They're hunkered over the questions as though this is a written exam, and they want to get all the answers correct.

"And stay on this side of the room," the cop cautions him.

"What about my key?" Bernard says.

"We'll get it back to you."

A woman enters and approaches the officer, "I have to leave," she says. "I have an appointment."

She's good-looking, about thirty, give or take, wild hair, buxomy. Bernard always liked his women full-figured. Most Arizona women look like toothpicks, like they'd snap if you squeezed them. Not this one.

He notices the dog. It looks like a black dust ball.

"You can go," the cop says to her. "I have your number, if I have any more questions." She nods, stands in the entrance searching through her purse. Must be chock-full of whatever women carry with them, because it takes her a while. That dog is in there, too. She draws out sunglasses and puts them on, then swishes out with her bowwow dog.

But first she touches the palm of her hand to the doorframe.

Fingerprints.

The more, the merrier.

· 3 ·

In the early 1900s, candy shops sold tiny bisque dolls. These half-inch, miniature dolls could be purchased for a penny—the same price as a piece of candy. Many of the penny dolls wore crepe paper dresses. Others were nude except for shoes and socks, so little girls could design and make their own clothing. The first penny dolls had mohair wigs or molded and painted blonde hair, and their eyes were painted bright blue. The smallest dolls were made with no movable parts. Larger dolls had wire-strung joints and heads that moved. Today, penny dolls are fun to collect and are still affordable, although they cost much more than a penny.

—From *World of Dolls* by Caroline Birch

Gretchen held a penny doll in her hand. A four-inch doll-house doll with finely painted features, it wore a pale blue silk gown and a matching hair band in its blond molded hair. It had belonged to Charlie. The doll shop owner had asked Gretchen's mother to repair a damaged arm, and she had. Gretchen had planned to return it at the party, but the doll had been forgotten in her purse. Until now.

"The Scottsdale cop asked me if I believed in the chaos theory," Gretchen said to her aunt from a stool at her work-table.

Aunt Nina removed a pile of doll clothing from a chair

and scooted lightly onto it. The bows in her hair matched perfectly with the pink and green swirls on her capris.

Nina's precocious schnoodle, Tutu, also sported matching pink and green bows. The spoiled pet was bent on destroying the possibility of a long, pampered life by angering Wobbles, the three-legged cat who chose to live with Gretchen. Wobbles, Gretchen had found out early on, belonged to no one.

"The chaos theory," Nina said, "is a mathematic theory about finding order in chaos. I wonder if he's a New Ager like me."

Gretchen bent over the doll, still studying it. "I reached Mom. She's canceling the rest of her book tour and coming home tomorrow. I told her one of Charlie's display cases tipped over, upending a number of room boxes, and she's insisting she's going to restore the room boxes to their original forms."

Gretchen heard a hiss from Wobbles and a yelp from Tutu. Nimrod, the teacup poodle, was sound asleep in his bed, oblivious to the disagreement. Nina lunged from her seat and distracted the two warriors. She shooed Wobbles out of the workshop, closed the door, and fussed over her darling pet.

Nina reassured herself that Tutu had survived her brush with death. "Okay," she said, "where were we? What are these room boxes you were talking about?"

"They're usually little displays that contain a miniature scene. Like those dioramas kids make from shoe boxes, but much more sophisticated," Gretchen explained. "A living room with all the furnishings, for example, or the inside of a store, like a pet shop. All with very realistic miniature scale details."

"You mean like rooms in a dollhouse?"

"Not exactly, but close. Each room box is self-contained

and can be an entirely different setting with no relationship to any others. What makes them really unique are all the tiny pieces of furniture and accents that go inside the room boxes. Some hobbyists are extremely creative and make their own furnishings."

"Humph . . ." Nina leaned on the worktable, flashing her polka-dotted pink and green nails. How long would it have taken to paint on all the little polka dots? Probably hours, Gretchen thought.

"And your mother wants to fix them?" Nina asked.

Gretchen shrugged. "It all depends on the police investigation. If they aren't sure Charlie died from natural causes, who knows when they will be through with her shop?"

"If putting the room boxes together helps Caroline through her grief, I'll be there to help my sister."

"Oh, right."

Aunt Nina didn't know a thing about dolls. She trained miniature dog breeds to travel in their owners' purses, teaching them to duck down and hide if they entered an unfriendly environment like a restaurant or grocery store. It was a perfect career for her. She had no competition and no real overhead costs. Nina had created her very own exclusive service industry, and she had more clients than she could manage.

But dolls?

No way.

Her aunt kept herself busy training dogs, perfecting her psychic abilities, and matching her accessories to her outfits, not necessarily in that order.

"Don't forget I've been hanging around with doll collectors," Nina said, as though she knew exactly what Gretchen was thinking. "I love to decorate, and you and Caroline know everything there is to know about doll repair. I'll be able to tell you where all the pieces go. We'll be a great team. I'm getting a psychic message right this minute." Nina's long fingers connected with her forehead in a telepathic pose. After listening hard, she said, "We were meant to do it."

In Gretchen's opinion, Nina's psychic abilities were entirely trumped up. None of her aunt's otherworldly announcements had ever amounted to anything.

"I don't know if we should," Gretchen replied. "What about all the work piling up right here?"

"Between the three of us, it won't take long," Nina argued. "I'm sure April would like to help, too. That would speed it up."

April was the Phoenix Dollers' favorite doll appraiser. She wore tent-sized muumuus, drove a banged-up white Buick, and lived in a dilapidated house in Tempe. She didn't care for any material possessions except for her prized collection of miniatures. Gretchen chuckled to herself every time she envisioned the large woman engulfing a mini doll in her chubby hands.

"April," Nina repeated the name acidly. "She's always hanging around. This should be just family."

"But April collects miniatures. She'd bring a lot of experience to the project."

"She should stick to appraising dolls."

"I thought you liked April."

"I do. We've just been seeing too much of her."

Gretchen glanced sharply at her aunt, who had been uncharacteristically catty lately. If she didn't know better, she'd think Nina was jealous of the time Gretchen spent with April.

Gretchen lifted the dress on Charlie's penny doll and noted the stamp on the doll's back. "Charlie's doll is fascinating," she said. "See the stamp on its body? It was made in Germany some time in the very early 1900s, one of the more expensive penny dolls. April could tell us more."

Nina scowled at another mention of April's name.

"Wait . . ." She paused dramatically. "I feel something coming in. Yes, you need a reading."

"A reading?" *Oh, no. I have to keep my aunt away from New Age shops.* Over time, Nina had progressed from analyzing colored auras to communication with spirits. Now what? Readings?

"I bought my first set of tarot cards," Nina said, "and I'm practicing. You might discover your true self."

"I've found my true self. See, here I am."

"You're such a pragmatist."

In spite of all her aunt's hype about her special ability as a psychic, she hadn't managed yet to impart anything unusual, helpful, or remotely close to remarkable.

"I still don't understand why Mom wants to put the room boxes together," Gretchen said.

"Maybe Caroline needs the closure." Nina studied the little colored dots on her fingernails. "Besides, it might give you an opportunity to see more of a certain man." She glanced slyly at Gretchen. "Detective Matt Albright's divorce is almost final. But, of course, you know that."

Gretchen pretended disinterest by shrugging her shoulders.

Buff, hunky, masculine Matt. Separated, living alone, but technically still-married Matt. The *M* word bothered her tremendously.

Matt's mother Bonnie was president of the Phoenix Dollers Club and the biggest blabbermouth on planet Earth. If she found out Gretchen had gone out on a date with Matt, his soon-to-be ex would find out, and that could create all kinds of serious problems for the detective. And for her.

They had to slow way down and keep their relationship casual while he waited for his divorce to be finalized. Nina knew about her niece's attraction to the detective, but Gretchen didn't want the rest of the doll community to know.

What if he went back to his wife? If they reconciled, wouldn't she feel foolish if everyone knew? You bet. But her decision to avoid Matt made him that much more intriguing and sexy. She hadn't been able to get him out of her mind.

"Don't pretend indifference with me," Nina said.

"I like to travel light," Gretchen said, repeating her old mantra. "And he comes with a lot of baggage."

"Look who's talking? You spent seven years with a cheating man."

Steve. The years she'd wasted with the self-indulgent attorney! How naive she'd been. All those "business trips." She'd still be buying his line if one of his little "distractions" hadn't called and spelled the entire thing out for her.

The discovery that Steve had been unfaithful had felt like Camelback Mountain boulders crushing the air from her body. She'd thought she'd never breathe again. But she had.

"You make it sound like I knew he was playing around all along," Gretchen said. "The minute I found out, I ended it. No baggage here."

Nina peered at Gretchen's face as though hoping to read her mind. "One lunch date with Matt, and you've been dodging him ever since. What happened? Did he forget to use utensils? Did he make lewd and inappropriate sexual advances to the waitresses? What?"

Gretchen shrugged. "He was interesting, comfortable to be with, considerate—"

"Those certainly are serious flaws in his character. I can see why you're avoiding him."

"You're too pushy. Give me some time." Gretchen felt a twinge of guilt for speaking so harshly.

"Is his wife still stalking you?" Nina asked, not even noticing Gretchen's tone had become brisk and impatient. "Or rather, his soon-to-be ex?"

"Once in a while I spot her. That's another good reason to stay away from him."

"She's a nutcase, all right," Nina agreed. "You know, Bonnie really wants you to get together with her 'Matty.' I bet she's the one who spilled it to Kayla. His own mother is making his life impossible." Nina clasped her hands together. "But why think depressing thoughts? What do you think about restoring the room boxes? Let's do it. Say yes, and I'll teach Nimrod more tricks."

"I'll say yes if you promise *not* to teach him any more tricks," Gretchen said, remembering the parade fiasco and her horror when he'd dashed into the street after hearing his "parade" command.

"It's a deal." Nina looked quizzical but was too caught up in her own drama to ask for an explanation. "But you aren't going to mention our plan to April, are you?"

"She'll find out," Gretchen said. "How do you think that will make her feel if we've excluded her?"

"But—" Nina started to say.

"No buts."

"Well, if you insist." Nina rolled her eyes theatrically.

Gretchen worried about what was going on with her two buddies. She'd hate to see anything come between their friendships. Maybe working on Charlie Maize's room boxes would bring them back together.

Gretchen put Charlie's penny doll in the top drawer of her worktable, really hoping that the bloody miniature axe she'd seen on the shop floor had nothing to do with the room boxes her mother wanted to restore.

Saturday evening's festivities were in full swing along the streets of Old Scottsdale. Parking was at a premium. Gretchen and Nina found a parking space several blocks from Mini Maize. Gretchen wasn't sure why she found herself drawn back to the shop, but here she was.

"Let's go in this shop," Nina suggested, "or this one."

"Come along," Gretchen ordered. "We aren't here to spend money."

"You lured me with promises of great shopping."

"*After* we peek in Mini Maize."

Nina trailed behind with prancing Tutu. Nimrod rode in Gretchen's purse. He seemed as excited as the children who wore cowboy hats and rode ponies around in circles. Better yet for the tiny pup, everyone who encountered the miniature teacup poodle wanted to cuddle him. Nimrod was his own showstopper. Gretchen felt like his personal bodyguard.

She couldn't pry Nina from the window displays, so she reconciled herself to a slow, halting pace.

"How about this shop," Nina whined. "Let's go in. Just this one."

"After."

Old Scottsdale was one of Gretchen's favorite places to browse. They strolled past western-style shops filled with Native American pottery and Navajo rugs. Art galleries, antique shops, trading posts, and jewelry stores lined the busy streets.

Gretchen admired a turquoise and silver bracelet in a window. She wished she could afford to buy it, but at the moment, she was saving for her own apartment.

"It's beautiful," Nina said, stopping to admire the same piece of jewelry. "Turquoise and silver are the hottest combination this year. Let's go in. You have to try it on."

"I can't afford to even think about it," Gretchen said wistfully.

Nina groaned and pulled Gretchen's arm. "Come on. Just try it on."

"No, once it's on my wrist, I won't be able to take it off."
Gretchen stood firm.

"Why fight it?" Nina insisted. "You're saving so you can
move out of your mother's home, but Caroline is hardly
there since she started her book tours. Stay there as long as
you want. Besides, the repair workshop is right there at the
house. How much more convenient could it be? You don't
want to start commuting to work."

"She's coming home tomorrow," Gretchen reminded
Nina.

"Because of Charlie. After that, poof, she'll be gone
again. Say after me, buy jewelry."

"I need my own place. Ever since moving across the
country, I've lived with my mother. Not that I'm complaining about the circumstances, it just doesn't feel grown-up."

"You lived by yourself in Boston, and you were horribly
lonely."

"What makes you think that?"

"Psychic analysis."

Gretchen turned from the tempting bracelet and continued walking in the direction of Charlie's doll shop. Nina
and Tutu scurried to catch up.

"I love my work," Gretchen said, stopping to let a little
girl pet Nimrod. "But I'm new at it. When I agreed to the
business arrangement with Mom, I didn't anticipate going
it alone. It was supposed to be a partnership. Two of us.
Dos." She held up two fingers.

The doll restoration business she shared with her
mother had taken off, but so had her mother. Once
Gretchen had agreed to help with repairs, Caroline had
handed most of the real work to her and was now traveling
extensively to promote her new doll book, *World of Dolls.*
In her spare time, she hunted for treasures to add to her collection or to sell at the doll shows that Gretchen attended.

Nimrod's most recent admirer gave him a kiss on the top of his head and waved goodbye.

"Caroline is having the time of her life," Nina said. "Having you in Phoenix has been so good for her. She can pursue her writing, thanks to you. She needs you as much as you need her."

Gretchen strode along, considering the years of trouble that had plagued her family: her father's death in a car accident, followed rapidly by her mother's battle with breast cancer. She'd almost lost both of them.

She realized Nina wasn't beside her. She stopped and turned.

"You're walking too fast," Nina huffed from behind, eyes darting to catch every window display. "Slow down."

"You're a shopaholic," Gretchen called out.

Nina glanced into an art gallery. "Let's go in and check out the paintings."

"Mini Maize is right here," Gretchen said, pointing to the next shop.

"I'll be along soon." Nina darted into the gallery with Tutu at her heels, leaving Gretchen standing alone in front of the doll shop.

Here I am. Now what?

Gretchen peered through the window. A light had been left on over the main counter. She could see the display case lying on the floor. The room boxes and scattered doll furnishings still remained where they had fallen earlier in the day. From her position, she could even see where Charlie Maize's body had been found.

Then she saw movement. A woman came out of the back room and approached the counter. With her back to Gretchen, she straightened a stack of magazines on the countertop.

Gretchen tapped on the window to get her attention. The

woman's head snapped around. Gretchen motioned to the
door. The woman met her there and unlocked it. As she
stuck her head out, Gretchen could see the wariness in her
eyes. "The shop is closed."

"I know. I'm Gretchen Birch. I was here this morning
when Charlie's body was discovered. I wanted to come
by." That sounded foolish. Why *had* she come to the shop?

"I was her best friend," the woman said without opening
the door any wider. "I'm Britt Gleeland. I made most of the
miniature dolls on display in the shop."

"I'm surprised I haven't met you before."

"I'm not a member of the Phoenix Dollers."

Gretchen knew that there were two distinct doll
groups: doll collectors and miniaturists. They each had
their own clubs and shows, so it wasn't unusual that she
hadn't met Charlie's friend before. Of course, there were
always crossovers like April, who loved all aspects of the
doll world.

"I'm sorry for your loss." Gretchen said.

"Thank you." Britt Gleeland had dark hair in a tightly
rolled French twist with a fringe of long bangs. She was
about forty-five years old and wore a crisp white blouse,
dark skirt, and businesslike heels that matched the professional expression on her face.

"Can I come in?" Gretchen asked.

"It's not a good time."

"I won't keep you long." Gretchen couldn't believe how
quickly the police had wrapped up their work at the shop.
How long had it been? Less than twelve hours?

"Very well," Britt said, reluctantly standing back.

Gretchen moved past her and noticed a shopping bag on
the floor next to the counter.

"I'm collecting some of my dolls," Britt said. "Charlie
had them on consignment, so they belong to me. I don't

know what's going to happen to the shop now that she's gone, and I was concerned about retrieving them."

"I hope you left the display pieces."

"Why?"

"My mother will be restoring the display case and would like everything to be just as it was. Please don't remove anything just yet."

"I didn't hear anything about that," Britt said. "But it doesn't matter. I've only gathered up the dolls that Charlie had on consignment." Britt squatted and picked up a room box. "I don't know what I'll do without a best friend. They take years to acquire." She glanced up, her eyes teary.

Acquire? What an odd thing to say. It sounded like she was talking about a doll collection rather than a human relationship.

"Charlie sent me an invitation to attend a party after the parade," Gretchen said. "Do you know what we were celebrating exactly?"

Britt rose and shrugged. "She liked to invite people to the shop, hoping they'd make purchases. And she'd been working on a new display she wanted to show. I had a migraine this morning, or I would have been here when it happened. I might have been able to save her."

Gretchen walked over to the display case on the floor. The display case had wooden partitions, each with slightly larger dimensions than the room boxes.

The case was surprisingly light. She righted it, then saw an inscription on a small metal plaque attached to the top. *In memory of Sara Bellingmore.*

"Who's Sara?" Gretchen asked.

"Charlie's younger sister," Britt said, running her fingers over the letters.

Gretchen retrieved one of the room boxes and tucked it into a display panel. It fit perfectly. "The room boxes must have been in the window," Gretchen guessed, noticing a red table covering in a heap near the window. "That's why the area around the window is empty now."

"Yes," Britt said rather stiffly.

Wasn't it unusual that the authorities would open up Charlie's shop so soon after Charlie's death? Wouldn't they want to keep people out? "Did the police give you permission to come in and take the dolls?" Gretchen asked.

"Of course. Officer—now what was his name?"

"Kline?"

"That's it."

"You have your own key?"

"We were best friends." Britt started to bristle. "You have no authority to question me. You're acting like *I* did something wrong. I'd like to see proof that *you* have permission to be here."

"I didn't mean to imply—"

"I have to ask you to leave now." Britt escorted Gretchen and her travel companion, Nimrod, out of Mini Maize.

Gretchen joined her aunt on the street of Old Scottsdale.

"I can't believe some people," Nina said. "That crabby gallery owner threw us out. No dogs, the guy said."

"Join the club," Gretchen muttered. She felt sufficiently chastised. Why had she questioned Charlie's friend?

Who do I think I am? Jessica Fletcher?

· 4 ·

"Peanut flour," April Lehman exclaimed early Monday morning while jiving to the beat of "Wake Up Little Susie." Her heavy frame heaved from the exertion, her legs pounded away on the gym mat.

"Peanut flour?" Gretchen asked.

Curves was packed, as usual. "Change stations now," the programmed voice commanded, as it did every thirty seconds all day long. The women moved in a large circle, climbing onto different machines or creating their own moves on the square platforms spaced at intervals around the exercise equipment.

The doll collectors, who all gathered at Curves to exercise three times each week, were keeping a steady stream of conversation going. Gretchen looked around at the familiar group: Rita, the Barbie enthusiast; Karen, the kindergarten teacher who liked Lee Middletons; and April, the club's doll appraiser and Gretchen's friend. April always seemed on the verge of collapsing after the first pass around the circle.

"Peanut flour?" Gretchen repeated.

"Peanut flour?" echoed Ora, the Curves manager.

Bonnie Albright hurried in before April could expand on her peanut flour comment. Bonnie was not only Detective Matt Albright's mother, she was president of the Phoenix Dollers Club and the biggest gossip of the group. She wedged into the circle between April and Gretchen.

"Where's Nina?" Bonnie asked, her red wig slightly skewed. She had applied lipstick in a shaky line around her mouth.

"She's picking up a client," Gretchen said. "Enrico is back in training."

"The Chihuahua?"

Gretchen nodded. "He needs a monthly refresher course." Enrico didn't forget what Nina taught him; he simply refused to cooperate.

"How's your mother?" Bonnie asked.

"She came in late last night. She's still sleeping."

"Let me get back to my story about Sara Bellingmore," April said. She plopped on the thigh abductor but didn't attempt to work the hydraulic machine. She wiped her face with her sleeve.

When Gretchen had mentioned the inscription on Charlie's display case, April had pounced on the chance to hold center stage.

"You remember Sara," Rita said to Bonnie. "She was Charlie's sister."

"The name doesn't ring a bell." Bonnie ran in place on a platform.

Gretchen smiled to herself. Bonnie's version of running amounted to a few sloppy arm swings and small heel lifts.

The mechanical voice interrupted, and everyone moved to the next position in the large circle.

"You knew her, Bonnie," April said. "She was a miniature collector. She also collected antique penny dolls and must have had several hundred of them. She had a table at one of our shows a few years back, brimming with those tiny little dolls." April sighed wistfully. "I should have bought all of them. I love penny dolls." Gretchen's friend was a serious miniature doll collector, but cash was always tight for April.

"Now I remember her," Bonnie said, looking thoughtful.

"The miniaturists keep to themselves, but so do we," she acknowledged.

"Sara Bellingmore died last year," April said. "She ate a slice of banana bread made with peanut flour."

"Don't you mean peanut butter?" Bonnie said.

"Peanut flour," April emphasized. "It has a very mild peanut flavor. Sara died from an allergic reaction to the nuts. Her throat swelled up, and she suffocated to death."

"What an awful way to go," Gretchen said. "Peanut allergies are dangerous, especially severe ones."

Rita piped up. "I have a friend who gets sick if she eats anything that's been prepared in a pan that contained peanut oil, even if the pan is washed out first."

April leaned over to catch her breath after the first turn around the machines. Gretchen worried she might pass out, but, after a few seconds, April straightened up. "I need to lose some weight, and exercising isn't doing it."

"You have to stop putting all that food in your mouth," Bonnie scolded, throwing tact to the wind. "I've never seen anyone eat so much."

"Try the Curves diet," Rita suggested. "That's how I lost all my weight. And you get to eat a lot of food."

"A new diet class is starting up," called Ora from the front desk. "Want me to sign you up?"

April shook her head. "I have it all figured out," she said. "I started a submarine sandwich diet yesterday. I can eat as much as I want and I'll still lose weight. Besides, I love subs."

"Dumbest thing I heard today," Bonnie muttered, loud enough for everyone to hear.

"I think the sub diet is worth trying," Gretchen said. After a few days of nothing but submarine sandwiches, April would be so tired of them she'd stop eating altogether and start losing weight.

"At least I have one supporter in this group," April huffed.

"Get ready for a ten-second count," the mechanical voice said. The women stopped exercising and pressed fingers against their necks and wrists.

"Sounds like Charlie and Sara shared a love of miniatures," Gretchen said, turning the conversation back to the miniature shop owner's death.

"Charlie really loved her sister." April left the circle and sat down in a chair. "My heart rate is over the chart. I need a rest." She slung an arm over the back of the chair. "Charlie always thought Sara had been murdered, but she couldn't prove it. Charlie wouldn't stop talking about it. When she wasn't working at the shop, she was investigating Sara's death."

"What did the police say?" Gretchen asked. "Surely they would have looked into her claim."

April dug her reading glasses out of her pocket and perched them on the end of her nose. She looked at Gretchen over the top of the lenses. "Nothing came of it."

"The police are investigating as though Charlie's death could be murder," Gretchen said, remembering last night's interrogations and the technical equipment used at the scene.

Bonnie perked up. "Maybe my Matty knows something," she said. "You could call him, Gretchen. Wouldn't that be romantic?"

"Matt's with the Phoenix police," Gretchen reminded her. "Charlie died in Scottsdale, in a completely different jurisdiction."

What a break for me. The last thing she needed was Matt Albright coming around, asking her questions and sending signals her way. More than once, she'd caught him watching her with those intense, dark eyes. She had to stay away.

"Charlie probably had a heart attack," Gretchen said, hoping the doctor at the scene had been overly cautious.

"Love Potion Number Nine" came on the boombox and livened up the group. Bonnie sang along.

"Maybe we'll find out more when we go over to her shop this morning," April said. "Did you call and get permission?"

"I did," Gretchen said, still surprised at how easy it had been. Her mother had supplied the name of Charlie's only surviving brother, now an MS patient in a Florida assisted-living complex, and he had granted them access. In return, Gretchen promised to clean up the shop and send photographs of the room boxes to him.

"Permission for what?" Bonnie asked.

April stood up slowly. "We're going to restore Charlie's room boxes. Hopefully, they will be ready in time to display at her funeral." To Gretchen, she said, "I'll see you at Mini Maize at ten."

She was almost out the door when she turned. "I almost forgot the most important part of my story. Charlie was convinced that Sara had been killed because Sara always had a big supply of epinephrine on hand in case she had an emergency attack. She had prefilled injections that she could give herself. But when she died at home, all alone, there wasn't a single epi dose in the whole house."

"My," Bonnie said, eyes shining with the possibilities.

"And . . . ," April paused for dramatic effect, "the police never discovered where the deadly banana bread came from."

Gretchen parked in front of Charlie's miniature doll shop at nine thirty and sat in the car waiting for Officer Kline who, after conferring with Charlie's brother, had volunteered to meet her with a key to the store. She had asked Nina and April to meet her at Mini Maize at ten o'clock to begin their restoration work. Gretchen wanted to talk to the officer, settle in, and make a few quiet observations before her band of merry women arrived with all their accompanying bells and whistles.

While she waited, she gazed at Nimrod, asleep on the seat next to her. She couldn't imagine life without him. Her opinion of dogs had changed for the better over time, thanks to Nina, who had pressured her into taking Nimrod when his former owner abandoned him. And the feline Wobbles tolerated the fur ball, which was uncharacteristic of the sinewy tomcat.

A blue Chevy pulled up behind Gretchen's car, and she groaned when she looked through her rearview mirror and saw who it was.

Just great.

She'd been avoiding Matt Albright lately for several very good reasons. Aside from her own mixed-up feelings for him, Matt's wacko, estranged wife Kayla was capable of just about anything.

And here they were, together, out in the open.

Gretchen stuffed a groggy Nimrod in her purse and got out of the car.

She peered around for signs of the Wife.

This guy comes with way too much baggage. Keep telling yourself that.

She didn't see Kayla's black Jetta anywhere on the street, but that didn't mean anything.

What could he possibly be doing in Scottsdale right outside of Charlie Maize's miniature doll shop? This had all the signs of big trouble.

Matt hadn't closed his car door before he was flashing his dazzling smile. "What are you doing here?" he asked, beating her to the question of the day. He didn't look at all like a cop. Sandals, shorts, T-shirt, body builder's physique.

Undercover and armed, she was sure. Making him even more mysterious and sexy.

"I was going to ask you the same thing," Gretchen said.

"I'm meeting—" He stopped midsentence and laughed. "I should have known."

"What?"

"That it was you."

"What?" Gretchen's heart did a little backflip.

He grinned wolfishly. "I'm meeting a doll repairer here at the doll shop at . . ." he checked his watch. "Nine thirty."

Gretchen stared at him. "Where's Officer Kline?"

"Busy. And he really isn't a street cop. He's a detective, too."

"He fooled me—parade work, uniform, the squad car." That explained his air of command.

"That's what our superiors do to us when we cross them. They give us traffic."

"I thought that was only in the movies."

"There's a thin line between fact and fiction." Matt moved closer.

She could smell his Chrome cologne. Her favorite male scent.

He grinned, wide and exceptionally friendly. "The departments are collaborating on the cases."

"Why? Wait . . ." Gretchen paused. "Did you say cases? Plural?"

"Charlie's sister died last year in my jurisdiction, and we're taking another look at the circumstances surrounding her death."

"I heard she died from an allergic reaction."

"That's right."

"And Charlie had a heart attack?"

"I'd like to tell you more, but you're friends with my mother. If she gets wind of it, the entire state of Arizona will be alerted to classified information. I won't look too good."

"You know you can trust me. Come on."

"All I can say right now is that we are looking into it," Matt said, the grin not quite as wide. "I seem to get every one of these types of cases." His eyes went to the doll shop window.

Gretchen knew Matt's secret: he had pediophobia, a fear of dolls. The big, hunky specimen of a man was afraid of dolls.

"Yes, I can see why this case would be hard for you." Gretchen's lips quivered, and a chuckle escaped.

"See," he said, good-naturedly. "You find my soft spot, and what do you do? You make fun of me. Do you think I *want* to be this way?"

Gretchen rearranged her face to show concern. "Of course not. I'm sorry I laughed."

Matt looked toward the doll shop. "These are itty-bitty dolls, not enormous killer dolls. I'll be fine."

"I have confidence in you."

"We should go inside," Matt said, droplets of manly moisture appearing on his brow.

"When was the shop released from police custody?" Gretchen asked to confirm Britt's permission to be in the shop last night.

"We finished up yesterday. It's all yours." Matt handed her the key. "You first."

"After you."

"I'm being polite. Ladies first."

"Yoo-hoo," someone called from down the street.

Gretchen turned to see Nina hustling down the street from the north, Tutu in the lead. The dog wore a large ruffled pink collar and matching bows clipped to her ears. When Nina drew closer, Gretchen could hear Enrico, the ornery Chihuahua, snarling from a Mexican tapestry purse slung across her aunt's shoulder.

"Yoo-hoo," she heard from the opposite direction. April thundered at her from the south.

They all converged in front of Mini Maize as Gretchen unlocked the door.

· 5 ·

Room boxes offer an excellent way to create a scene that is smaller than the traditional dollhouse. Art in miniature has been around since ancient Greece and still has an avid following today. Use your imagination to create your very own. Either purchase a room box or build one out of cardboard, plywood, or fiberboard. Then let the fun begin. For enhanced realism, you can build false walls with windows or doors and display scenic photographs behind them. Make window treatments from shelf edging, shades from mailing tape, or Venetian blinds from wooden coffee stirrers. Paper napkins make excellent bedding, after dunking them in a mixture of glue and water. Gift wrap becomes wallpaper, and refrigerator magnets turn into wall hangings. Common household objects will take on new significance as the hunt begins for new and creative ways to furnish your very special room box.

—From *World of Dolls* by Caroline Birch

"Why is that hunky detective still outside?" April said, waving at Matt from inside Mini Maize. "I thought he was over his doll problem."

"Apparently not," Nina said, roaming through the shop and picking up one item after another. She glanced at the floor. "What a mess. This place looks like Gretchen's workshop."

Gretchen slid Nina a look before finding several empty

containers in the back room and distributing them to her crew. She picked up a five-inch porcelain ballerina doll from the countertop, encircled it with bubble wrap, and put it inside one of the containers. "Help me pack these up," she said to the two women. "He won't come into the shop until the dolls are out of sight."

"Why didn't you say so earlier?" April said, rushing to help. "Let's not keep him waiting any longer than we have to."

Enrico watched slyly from his purse hanging on a doorknob, waiting for just the right opportunity to escape. Nina held up a finger in warning as if she could read his thoughts. "Stay," she said in her dog-training, authoritarian voice. Then she turned to Gretchen. "You don't really think you can put away the entire room of dolls, do you?" she said.

"Just these on the counter and nearest the door."

April was really moving.

"Okay," Gretchen called out the door a few minutes later. "Coast is clear. Just don't look inside the display cases around the counter. I don't have time to put away every one of them. After all, this *is* a doll shop."

Matt's head popped around the corner, his even tan a few shades lighter. He had a cheesy grin on his face. "I've been called away," he stammered. "I'll check back later and see how it's going."

Gretchen watched him scramble for his unmarked car. "Coward," she muttered under her breath.

April was on her hands and knees, examining miniature furniture pieces. Nina, casting around for something to do other than actual physical labor, chose to entertain the canines with a walk around the block. She came back with new and improved managerial skills.

"April," she said, "You need to sort the pieces and do groupings based on the type of furnishings."

"I know that."

"Gretchen," Nina said, "where are the mini dolls that go into the room boxes?"

"Haven't found any yet."

"April—" Nina began.

"Stop," April said, raising her arm to Nina, palm out like a cop stopping traffic. "You don't have to manage me. I'm capable of handling this without supervision."

"Some sort of order would help. And we know Gretchen can't do it."

A direct shot at Gretchen's lack of organization skills. Wait until Nina found out that Gretchen had locked her keys in her car. She'd discovered the lockout when she tried to get in to retrieve her toolbox. Peering through the tinted window, she had seen her keys hanging in the ignition. If there was any way of keeping Gretchen's mistake from her aunt, she'd try it. At least they had all arrived in separate cars. She'd call for help later.

"Why don't you take the dogs for another walk?" April suggested to Nina from the floor.

"I just got back. Why would I . . . Wait a minute . . . Is that sarcasm I hear in your voice?"

"If you can't find anything to do, go outside and practice your hocus-pocus," April retorted. "Why stick around if you aren't going to help?"

"I'm giving valuable advice."

"Will you two quit crabbing at each other?" Gretchen said, taking Nina by the arm and leading her to the counter. "See all these accessories and accents?"

Nina looked at the things Gretchen had scooped from the floor: tiny lamps, pictures, and knickknacks.

"You're our interior decorator," Gretchen said. "Your job is to help figure out which ones go together in the same room boxes."

"How am I supposed to do that?"

"We're partners, remember? Your skill, you said, was in decorating and deciding where all the pieces should go."

"I don't remember saying that."

"I recall it as though it just sprang from your perky lips."

"I thought I'd take care of the dogs while you worked."

Gretchen frowned at her aunt. Why did Nina offer to come if she wasn't going to pitch in? Ah . . . she got it. Gretchen's cunning, calculating aunt didn't want her spending time alone with April. Gretchen had to find a way to stop this childish rivalry. "See what you can do," she said, leaving Nina alone at the counter.

"There are some creepy miniatures scatter—" April began to say.

"Here comes Caroline," Nina announced, cutting her off.

Gretchen's mother walked in wearing sunglasses. When she didn't remove them, Gretchen guessed that she was hiding red-rimmed eyes behind the shades. Throughout the night, Gretchen had heard her mother crying over the loss of her friend.

"Just in time," Gretchen said, giving her a hug. "You're the expert. We await your orders."

"First, we'll pick up all the scattered pieces." Caroline said, digging right in by walking to one corner of the shop and searching the floor.

Gretchen retrieved an empty room box, admiring its tiny painted walls. A rendition of a church loomed in the background. Charlie had captured the essence of it in her painting: the stonework, stained glass, and a slender tower with a cross at the top.

Gretchen slid the room box into a display case partition along with the one she had placed there when she met Britt Gleeland. This one must be a bedroom, she guessed, based on the floral pattern of the wallpaper.

Gretchen's practiced eye scanned the boxes. A standard one-inch scale equaled one real foot, so she estimated the room it represented at about fourteen feet by twelve feet.

She bent down to pick up another box that had landed facedown. Gretchen turned it over and gasped.

"What happened?" April sprang from the floor.

"I'm not sure what this scene is supposed to represent, but that looks like blood all over the ground," Gretchen said, picking up the room box in her arms and turning it so April and Nina could see it. A wooden structure towered behind a high wooden fence, Charlie's brushstrokes barely visible. The base of the room box was painted brown with small worn tufts of grass jutting along the sides of the fence. "Not real blood, of course, but I'm sure that's what it's meant to be."

"A courtyard?" April said. "Covered with blood?"

"Some courtyard," Nina said. "It looks slummy to me."

Caroline joined them and studied the box. "Well, I think it's a backyard."

"Here's a street sign," April said, shuffling through a pile of items. The little green street sign mounted on a green post reminded Gretchen of a signpost from the Department 56 Dickens Village that she and her mother assembled every Christmas.

"Hanbury Street," Gretchen read.

Caroline placed the room box on the counter. She squinted to read the small numbers that Charlie had painted on the street sign. "Twenty-nine Hanbury Street."

Gretchen searched through the growing pile of miniature furniture and accents on the counter. "I saw a bloody miniature axe on the floor right after we found Charlie. I wonder where it went."

"What?" Nina said. "An axe?"

It wasn't on the counter. Gretchen bent down, peering

around the area where she had seen the axe when she had left the shop. An object had been shoved under a display case. She knelt down and pulled it out. "Here it is."

"One item now in its proper home," Nina said, taking the tiny axe and placing it next to the painted blood in the backyard scene.

"Creepy," April said. "Why would Charlie create a gruesome room box? There's nothing cute about the background scenery, nothing charming about an ax with red paint all over the blade. What was wrong with her?"

"It's probably my fault." Caroline leaned against the counter, removed her sunglasses, and rubbed teary eyes. "Charlie was totally obsessed with Sara's death. She talked about it incessantly. I suggested she instead focus on creating some room boxes, to give her something to do besides grieve for her sister. I never imagined this."

"The other room boxes are fine," Gretchen said. "One is set in a meadow with a church in the background. And this one . . ." Gretchen lifted another room box. ". . . is a Victorian dressing room or something like that. Maybe Charlie had a bad week or two and decided to express herself in a more base way with the axe scene."

Nina picked up the last room box. "This one looks unfinished," she announced. "It can't be part of the same grouping. But, no blood."

The room box Nina held was shabby next to the others, like it had been constructed hastily. The sides didn't fit together properly, and the walls were bare except for an uneven piece of full-sized wallpaper glued to the back of it and a rough sketch that resembled a sink.

"Am I doing the right thing," Caroline said, "by insisting that we restore Charlie's last project?"

"Absolutely," Gretchen said, realizing her mother needed to do this.

"We're wasting time standing around hypothesizing," April said. "Each of us needs to go to a corner of the shop and work outward. Let's gather every single item before we start guessing what Charlie had in mind."

The team paused for a lunch of submarine sandwiches, which April insisted was the answer to her years of obesity. She remained convinced that her new diet plan would transform her into a sexy, curvy shell of her present self. Nina refused to cooperate, stomping down the street in search of "real food." She returned with a salad.

"Detective Albright should be back soon," April said, munching on a foot-long sandwich while she looked out the window.

"Fat chance," Gretchen replied.

"I completely understand his phobia." April placed a few tiny articles of doll clothing into one of the bins. "I have my own fears, you know."

"We know," Nina said with a hint of distaste. "Clowns."

"Half the world's population is afraid of clowns," April said, defending herself. "And you know it."

"Yes," Nina agreed. "The half that's under four years old."

Gretchen couldn't believe what she was hearing. It wasn't like Nina to be so spiteful. "Isn't it potty time for the dogs?" Gretchen said to break up the next round of pointed barbs before one of them was fatally stabbed.

Nina checked her watch, then stuffed the pups in carrying totes. She slung Enrico over one shoulder and Nimrod over the other, ignoring Enrico's throaty growl. She clipped the pink leash to Tutu's collar and disappeared down the street.

"What's with her?" Caroline said. "I've never seen her behave like that before."

"I'm not sure what her problem is. April, just ignore it,

if you can." Gretchen sat down, removed her flip-flops, and wiggled her feet.

"I'm going for a walk," Caroline said. "Maybe it will perk me up."

Gretchen watched her classy mom walk down the street in the same direction her aunt had chosen and wished she had inherited more of her features. Beautiful shoulder-length silver hair, delicate nose, green thoughtful eyes, and a slim body, even at twenty-six years older than Gretchen.

"I found something interesting," April said, digging in her pocket. "I thought I'd wait until we were alone to show you." She held up a miniature dagger. The tip had been dipped in red paint.

"Terrific. Another piece for the backyard scene."

"And . . . ," April paused. "There's a smudge of red on the floor of the Victorian bedroom, but I'll try to clean it off if you think it will upset Caroline."

"Let's leave everything as it is for the moment," Gretchen answered. "You don't seem upset by all these flashes of blood."

"Blood doesn't scare me."

"But clowns do?"

April nodded. "If I even see a clown in the distance, I get all sweaty and dizzy, and I worry that I'll pass out. It's a hor-rible feeling. I know it's irrational, but I can't control how I feel."

"I think you have to work through it," Gretchen said, sorting through some of the tiny pieces of furniture. "Maybe it would help if you exposed yourself to your fears more often, like Matt's trying to do." She didn't mention what a bad job the detective was doing.

"I've tried that, but clowns are *not* nice people. They scare kids, and they're ugly and evil. Have you ever seen a clown helping a little old lady across the street?"

Gretchen thought it over. Actually, she hadn't.

"See?" April said, reading the expression on her face.

"I ran into a clown yesterday at Parada del Sol," Gretchen said, remembering the green-haired clown and her fall to the sidewalk. He hadn't bothered to help Gretchen up.

April grimaced. "That's exactly why I didn't go to the Scottsdale parade. Clowns are my absolute worst nightmare." April looked around as though they might be overheard. "That's not all I'm afraid of, but don't tell Nina. Promise?"

"Promise." Gretchen felt childish.

"Ventriloquists scare me to death, too. And sometimes in the dark, I'm afraid that something is lurking under my bed."

"I used to think something scary was under my bed," Gretchen said, remembering how afraid she was, almost paralyzed with fear. But that was when she was a kid.

She headed for the back room to search for boxes to separate and temporarily store the pieces, once they determined where each of them went. Gretchen rummaged through several small boxes, removing their contents and stacking the items neatly on a shelving unit. When she came back into the shop, she spotted something behind the storage room door.

She bent down and picked up a tiny pistol.

· 6 ·

Britt Gleeland stands across the street and watches the women through the shop window. She remains motionless, arms crossed.

Almost five o'clock, and the sun slowly edges over the desert horizon, casting long shadows on the sidewalk. By six it will be dark.

Her daughter, Melany, comes out of a trading post, carrying a shopping bag, a gift for a friend.

Twenty years old and talking about abandoning the family business and finding a new life someplace else. Out of the blue with no warning signs at all. Hasn't Britt groomed her daughter to take over for her in a few years? Perhaps it isn't the most profitable business, creating exquisite miniature dolls, but it has its own rewards.

Britt works her own hours, in her nightgown if she wants to. She's her own boss, answering to nobody. And, most importantly, she has the respect of the local *miniature* community.

Apparently these perks aren't enough for her daughter.

Let her go out in the world and slop burgers for minimum wage. That will cure her of her wanderlust.

But what about this "person" she's moving out east with?

Britt knows exactly who the man is, and she doesn't like him one bit. Melany is going to "live in sin," as Britt's mother would have said in shock if she were still alive. Whatever you call the arrangement, it's still shacking up.

Young people and their relationships. Who can figure them out? "Going out" they call it. Going out used to mean going on a date. Not anymore. Now it means something much more serious. What does she know?

More importantly, what will Britt tell her acquaintances? "My daughter's attending an Ivy League school out east"? Yale, maybe? Yes, that could work. Britt could make it sound like a wonderful opportunity. And who is she to hold her daughter back? After all, there is the scholarship. *Ooh. That's good.*

"One more stop." Melany scowls as though she's angry and disappears into a bookstore.

Another twenty minutes of waiting, for sure. The girl loves books.

Britt fidgets with her French twist and fluffs her bangs. Who will do the miniature faux flower arrangements if her daughter moves away? Britt feels the crevice widening between them, the enormous, cavernous divide. And the fear that she won't cope well with aloneness.

If only Charlie were here. What will she do without Charlie *and* Melany?

She sees someone come out of the doll shop and approach a car parked at the curb. It's the same woman who barged into the shop when she was collecting her dolls. Gretchen something. She had been spying on Britt, she was sure of it, questioning her loyalty and her right to be in Charlie's shop. The nerve!

What's she up to now?

The nosy woman has a wire hanger in her hand that she is bending to change its shape. After a furtive look back at Mini Maize, she tries to stick it in the top of the car's closed passenger window.

Breaking into someone's car? Not likely in the middle of the day right outside the shop.

No. That must be dear Gretchen's own car, and she is locked out of it. Britt smiles smugly to herself while she watches Gretchen move to the driver's window and twist and pry with the wire hanger.

No luck. The snoop tries again, both sides, determined. After the second try, she goes back inside. Harder than it looks, isn't it?

Britt cringes at the thought of strangers in the shop, rifling through Charlie's things, her things. The work she has put into her miniature dolls! She's a professional artisan, not some hack. Twenty years in this business, and she is the best there is. Sculpting all her tiny creations, no kits or premade molds for her. Firing them in her very own kiln. Then wigging and dressing the darlings to be exact replicas of anything your little heart desires.

Charlie, for example, wanting those tiny dolls, each with specific requirements regarding sex, size, and age. And for what? That was the question Britt kept asking her friend. And Charlie just smiling. "You'll see."

Well, she had.

Yes, she had.

Britt's eyes try to penetrate the window. If only she could hear what is being said in the shop, and if only she had a clearer view. What do they hope to accomplish by putting a silly display back together?

The one with the pretty gray hair is familiar, she's been around before. Her name is Caroline Birch, another of Charlie's friends. She must be Gretchen's mother. Her friendship with Charlie wasn't nearly as close as the relationship Britt had with Charlie.

Britt feels such physical pain at her loss.

She thinks of Ryan Maize, Charlie's drug-addicted,

pathetic excuse for a son. Ryan is somewhere in the city of Phoenix, panhandling with other homeless, empty-eyed derelicts. Poor Charlie. She had actually tried to help the ingrate. How many rehabilitation centers before she finally gave up? How much money down the drain?

Britt stares at Gretchen's car. What luck that she has a few sharp sculpting tools in her purse. She glances at the bookstore where Melany is roaming the shelves, delving into possible purchases. She'll be a while longer.

Britt steps into the street, using the shadows for cover.

· 7 ·

From the sidewalk in front of Mini Maize, Gretchen watched the Scottsdale squad car pull to the curb. After a long workday, the others had gone their separate ways. One went north, another south, finishing the day as they had started, as polar opposites.

Caroline had waited around until Gretchen shooed her off. Her mother had enough on her mind without dealing with Gretchen's problems as well.

They never suspected that she had managed to lock herself out of her car. At least it hadn't been running. She'd done that once, too.

It was a good thing she had a little extra puppy food in a plastic container in her purse, or Nimrod would be complaining loudly and insistently by now. Come to think of it, she had a little of everything in her purse. Except the proper tools to break into her car.

Gretchen could imagine her aunt's reaction if she knew about the lockout, especially with Nina in such a snit. She would have had to listen to a long lecture about the condition of her workshop, and her purse, and who knew what else.

Officer Kline stepped out of the police vehicle with a long rod in his hand. "Not you again," he said, wryly. "Tomorrow, when I transfer out, the department will have to hire another full-time officer to deal with you."

He had a twinkle in his eye. What a ham.

"Rumor has it you're impersonating a traffic cop," she said with a smile.

"Never trust a Phoenix detective. He'll expose you every time."

"How did you know Matt told me?"

"Albright is like my Siamese twin. I can't get rid of him no matter what I do. We're attached at the brain."

"Ah, two with the mental capacity of one."

"Do you want help, or should I leave you standing on the curb?"

Gretchen moved aside.

He inserted the long metal tool through the top of the driver's side window. The lock popped open. "There you go," he said.

"Thank you so much. I'm embarrassed."

"Don't be. It happens all the time. It was your karma for the day. Couldn't be changed." He stepped back and took a good look at the car. "Look at that."

Gretchen followed his gaze. The tire was flat.

He pushed on it. "Not much air left. You must have driven over something, a piece of glass or a nail."

Gretchen scanned the street for the Wife. It was exactly the kind of thing Kayla Albright was capable of. The woman had been stalking her since the moment Gretchen had met Matt. She'd been relatively harmless, until now. This was getting much more serious.

"Can you tell if my tire has been tampered with?" she asked.

He shrugged. "Hard to say. Maybe an auto mechanic would know."

"Now what?"

"Now you wait for the service truck, which I'm going to call for you."

"Can't you change it for me?"

"Puh-leeze," he said. "What you citizens expect."

Gretchen stared at the tire, then out at the street. She saw Matt Albright trot across Scottsdale Road midblock and step onto the curb, his dark hair wind-tossed, his face handsome and tanned but taut. Edgy.

Then he spotted her and smiled. "What's going on?" he said, approaching.

"Do you know how to change a tire?" Gretchen asked, pointing at the flat.

"Hey, Kline," Matt called out to the Scottsdale detective, who was digging in the squad's trunk. "I'll handle it from here."

"You don't know what you're getting yourself into."

"She's that bad, huh?"

"You know it." The Scottsdale detective hopped into the police vehicle and drove off.

Matt leaned up against her car and crossed his arms. The tension she had seen on his face when he crossed the street was gone. He smiled at her.

"I hate to spoil your day," Gretchen said. "But your wife punctured my tire."

His smile slid sideways. "Are you sure?"

"Not exactly. I mean, I didn't see her do it, but who else would do something so vicious?"

"You're awfully suspicious, considering she hasn't done anything to you up until now."

"Stalking me doesn't count?"

"She followed you a few times, I threatened to lock her up, she said she wouldn't bother you again."

"I can see the warning was effective," Gretchen said, pointing again at the tire.

"You probably drove over a nail." He bent over the tire to examine it. "I tell you what. I'll change it for you. Do you have a spare?"

Gretchen nodded, opening the trunk.

"And I'll buy a new one to replace the flat. How's that?"

"You're agreeable tonight."

"I hate to admit it, but it looks like someone *did* slash your tire. See here." He ran his fingers along the tire. Gretchen bent down. Sure enough, there was a long slit in the rubber.

"We can't be sure Kayla did it." A sparkly smile as he stood up, his dark eyes locking onto hers. He was only a few inches taller than Gretchen's five eight. Just the way she liked a man. "But I'll buy you dinner, too," he said, "as compensation." He reached to give Nimrod a pat on the head. "We'll drop Nimrod at your house first."

"He still knows his 'hide' command." The detective was standing way too close.

"Is that a yes?" Matt moved to the trunk and pulled out the spare tire.

"It's a maybe. I'm worried about the rest of my property. I wouldn't want my house to burn down while we were dining unaware."

"I thought you had nerves of steel. What happened? Don't you like a little excitement in your life?"

"You'll have to assume responsibility for her actions."

"I always have. Is that a yes?"

"Um . . ." Gretchen grinned. "Entice me some more."

She watched him jack up the back of the car, muscles rippling, not an ounce of fat anywhere.

"I have information about Charlie. I'd like your take on it."

He knew just how to reel her in. She pretended to waver. "Okay," she said, ignoring the sensible, barely audible little voice that was trying to remind her that he was still married, and his wife was certifiably nuts.

"What are you looking for?" Matt said, after watching her dig through her purse.

"My sunglasses. I don't remember where I left them."

"They're on your head."

Gretchen lifted a hand to the top of her head. Sure enough, there they were. She pulled the glasses down over her eyes, then realized the sun had almost set.

Matt Albright could really rattle her cage.

"Okay," Gretchen said, over after-dinner coffee beside her swimming pool. "I've waited long enough."

Caroline walked past the patio door and peeked out, giving Gretchen a thumbs-up. Gretchen pretended not to notice.

"I didn't want to spoil dinner by talking shop," Matt said.

"Understandable. I've already promised to keep anything you say confidential, so tell me."

"I'm telling you for a specific reason. You absolutely must keep it to yourself. No one needs to know how she was murdered until after we've had time to investigate. I won't go into gory autopsy details. The results were clear, though. Charlie Maize was poisoned."

Gretchen blinked. "Poisoned?"

"We almost missed it."

"A poison showed up during the autopsy?"

"Almost didn't. Nicotine leaves the body quickly. The report might have been inconclusive, except for the suspicions of the doctor at the scene. According to the ME, we got lucky."

"I don't understand."

"Like I said, giving you graphic details isn't necessary." Matt leaned back in the patio chair, crossed his ankle over his knee, and gazed out at Camelback Mountain.

"I'm tougher than you think," Gretchen said. *Yeah, right. This from the woman who faints at the sight of an insect.*

Matt's gaze shifted from the mountain to her. "The poison

was in her coffee. We analyzed the dregs from a cup in her shop. Charlie's fingerprints were all over it, and the coffee was loaded with nicotine."

"Nicotine? In her coffee?" Gretchen stared at her own cup of coffee. "Nicotine is poisonous?"

Matt nodded. "She had a lethal dose, well over the sixty milligrams necessary to kill somebody."

"But how? I've never heard of anything like this before."

"A few drops of pure nicotine can easily kill a human being. It's more deadly than arsenic or strychnine."

He took a sip of coffee. Gretchen pushed hers away.

"According to the medical examiner, it's tasteless. Once Charlie drank it, she would have had difficulty breathing. Then she would have begun to have convulsions. Her diaphragm would have been paralyzed. Then death. All in pretty rapid secession. The whole process could have taken less than five minutes."

Gretchen made a gurgling sound.

"Sorry," he said. "But you wanted to know."

"Who would do something like that?"

Matt shrugged. "She could have poisoned herself, according to the medical examiner."

"You think it was suicide?"

"No. There are much more pleasant ways to kill yourself."

"Then you think she was murdered."

"Looks that way to me."

Nimrod flew through his doggy door, ran past them, and dove into the swimming pool. Matt jumped up and followed him to the edge of the pool. He looked back quizzically at Gretchen and kicked off his sandals. "Do I have to jump in to rescue him?" he said.

Gretchen laughed. "Poodles are water dogs. My biggest challenge is keeping him *out* of the pool."

Nimrod paddled in circles before swimming to the pool stairs and climbing out. He trotted over to Matt and shook water on his legs.

"He's also a hunting dog," Gretchen said.

"What does he hunt? Ants?" He laughed at the tiny puppy.

"He's a ferocious hunter. Rubber balls, socks, my cat Wobbles."

The tomcat sat in a window overlooking the pool. While they watched, he rose from his position and stretched.

"He gets around well on three legs," Matt said. "You never told me his story."

"I was crossing a street in Boston when it happened. A pickup truck swerved around the corner and hit him, then it took off. I rushed him to the vet, but I never found out where Wobbles lived, although I put up posters and called the animal shelters. We've been together ever since the accident."

Matt slipped his sandals back on and sat down. "How are you adjusting to life in Phoenix? Do you miss Boston?"

"I don't miss it at all. I love the mountains and the desert air. February is wonderful."

They sat quietly for a moment. Gretchen had called Boston home for most of her life. But with her mother and aunt in Phoenix, and after a bad breakup with her long-term boyfriend, Steve, Phoenix had seemed like the perfect solution.

Matt sipped his coffee. "I want you and the others out," he said quietly.

"Out?"

"Out of the shop. Stay away from Mini Maize."

"That's ridiculous. Charlie's brother gave us permission."

"I'm insisting."

"You sound just like Steve. He was a control freak, too." Gretchen narrowed her eyes. Who did Matt think he was?

"This isn't about control," Matt said. "I'm concerned about your safety. Do you know about Charlie's sister and how she died?"

Gretchen felt herself growing angry. *He isn't Steve,* she tried to remind herself. "Sara died from a peanut allergy," she said. "She ate banana bread that was made from peanut flour."

"Sara wore a Medic Alert tag as a precaution. Strange, don't you think? That she went to all the trouble of wearing the tag, but she forgot to stock up on epinephrine? Not a single dose anywhere in her home."

"You think the deaths are related?"

"Yes. Want to hear the specifics of Sara's death?"

Gretchen shook her head. "Not really."

He continued anyway. "Shortness of breath, serious drop in blood pressure, swelling of her tongue until—"

"That's enough," she said. Was Matt's theory correct? Had the two women really been murdered—one poisoned, the other . . . well . . . poisoned, too, by someone who knew about her severe peanut allergy?

"I can help," The same woman who fainted over bugs was about to offer to go up against a creature deadlier than any black widow spider. Gretchen heard the stubbornness in her voice. "I'm in a unique position. I can question doll collectors and dealers without drawing suspicion to myself. I'm one of them. And while we are restoring the room boxes, I'll pay attention. Something might turn up."

Like tiny bloody weapons!

"This isn't one of your reality shows," Matt argued. "This is real life, and it isn't that canned."

"I'm going to do it."

She had let a man define her once. It wouldn't happen again.

"You're impossible," Matt said lightly, but Gretchen noticed the tension in his facial muscles as he worked his jaw. "The more I insist, the more you're going to resist. Am I right?"

Gretchen smiled like Mona Lisa.

Tuesday morning Gretchen and Nina sat on patio chairs outside the cabana, sipping coffee, eating chocolate croissants, and admiring the warm February morning. The sun glowed, illuminating the red clay of Camelback Mountain.

Caroline joined them.

"You look well-rested," Nina noted.

Caroline smoothed back a few strands of silver hair, the aftereffects of chemotherapy in her battle against breast cancer. When her hair had grown back, it came in this amazing color. Six years and counting since her last treatment. Gretchen's mother was one of the success stories.

"Perfect weather at last," Gretchen said, looking into the sparkling blue pool water.

"February is the month of love in Phoenix," Nina said somewhat slyly.

"Is that your way of telling us you have a man in your life?" Caroline asked her sister.

"Don't be silly. I'm talking about Gretchen and Matt Albright." Nina stretched her arms over her head, reminding Gretchen of Wobbles right after a long nap. Nina was very much like a sleek cat. Today, she wore a crinkled ivory peasant skirt and a floral tank top. Tutu wore a scarf around her precocious neck. It matched the material in Nina's top.

"You're making too much of a simple dinner," Gretchen said. "It was strictly business." Which was true. She'd gone about the business of putting Matt Albright in his place. He had treated her like a ditzy female who couldn't take care of herself. She would show him.

Nina squinted at Gretchen with her penetrating hazel eyes. "You have a secret. I can feel it."

Caroline laughed. "Sis, you never fail to amaze me with your intuition."

"But she's wrong," Gretchen protested.

Caroline leaned back, holding her coffee cup with both hands.

"Tell," Nina demanded.

Gretchen looked at her aunt in amazement. "What makes you think I'm keeping something from you?"

The information Matt had shared with Gretchen was bursting to explode. Had her aunt sensed it? Or was it Gretchen's feelings for him that her aunt was picking up on? This was crazy!

"My psychic abilities are at their peak today," Nina insisted. "A good night's sleep and two cups of coffee do wonders for my powers. Now, tell."

"Last night Matt told me to quit," Gretchen said. "He wants us to stop going to Charlie's shop."

"But why?"

"It's that whole guy thing," Gretchen said, wondering if Nina would "see" through to the secret Matt had shared about the deaths of the sisters. *What good is having a secret if no one knows you have it?* "You know how it works," she continued. "Power plays begin right at the beginning."

"The beginning! Does that mean you've decided to have a real relationship with Bonnie's son?" Nina jumped up and did a little jig. "Wait until the Curves group hears about this."

"They'll do backflips," Caroline agreed.

"*NO!* Please don't tell them," Gretchen said loudly and

firmly. "After Matt's demanding attitude, I'm considering writing men out of my life. They're not worth the effort."

"What rubbish," Nina said.

"I'm through with men for . . . um . . . for a year." Gretchen said impulsively. She liked the sound of that. A year to get her life in order, a year to heal and regain faith in men. Her conversation last night with Matt had her doubting her ability to establish a real relationship. If it meant kowtowing to some man's demands, forget it. She'd been there, done that.

"I give you six months," Caroline said.

"Three tops," Nina wagered.

"Is that a challenge?"

Her mother laughed, a throaty, husky chuckle just like Nina's. "Not at all. You and Matt are cute together. I'm rooting for him. Stop comparing him to that jerk, Steve. How could you have known he was cheating? He fooled all of us."

Unfaithful, conniving Steve. Gretchen couldn't understand what she saw in the loser with a capital *L* in the first place. Time had brought out the worst in him.

"Your strength has certainly been tested in the last year," Caroline said. "Life throws curve balls. Look at what happened to me? A malignant tumor. I thought I'd die, but I didn't. You'll come back even stronger."

Gretchen bit into a chocolate croissant and thought about Matt Albright. He was a little too sure of himself, a little too arrogant for her taste. And what *was* her taste in men? After seven years in a stagnant relationship, did she even know? She wasn't about to rebound with the first man who walked by.

"That isn't your true secret," Nina singsonged. "There's more. Come on," she said, egging Gretchen over the edge. "I'll tell you what I found out, if you tell me what you know."

"You have a secret, too?"

Nina nodded smugly.

The best part of having a secret, Gretchen decided on the spot, was sharing it with someone else. What could it hurt? Besides, her family members should know all the details so they could decide for themselves if they wanted to continue working on the room boxes.

"Promise not to tell anyone," Gretchen said. But she had also promised to keep the information confidential and here she was, about to blab. But this was her aunt, she reasoned. And her mother. Family.

"I won't tell a soul," Nina said, crossing her heart.

"Ditto," Caroline echoed.

Gretchen gave in to temptation but spoke gently, in consideration of her mother's feelings for the dead woman. "According to Matt, Charlie was murdered. She was poisoned with a concentrated dose of nicotine. A lethal dose was in her coffee."

Nina gasped dramatically. "Nicotine can kill just like *that*." She snapped her fingers. "I've heard of dogs eating nicotine patches and dropping dead."

"Matt said nicotine is more poisonous that arsenic."

"I think it's used as a pesticide," Caroline said, her face pale.

Nina drummed a fingernail on her chin. "Charlie's murder had to be premeditated."

"I hadn't thought of that. You're becoming quite deductive." Gretchen could see a hiker climbing steadily up Camelback Mountain and suddenly wished she were doing the same thing instead of discussing murder.

"Do you think the killer wanted her to die during the parade right in front of all those people?"

"You're the psychic. You tell me."

Nina shrugged and didn't answer. Her aunt's powers short-circuited without any advance warning.

Nimrod flew through his doggie door, ears flapping wildly. He leapt into the pool, paddled in circles, climbed out, and shook water all over the women's legs.

"Watch what I taught him," Nina said, clapping her hands to get his attention. Gretchen knew she was trying to restore a lighter mood. "Come, Nimrod, let's show Momma your new trick." Nina moved her right hand in what must have been a sit command, because Nimrod sat down and dutifully watched her for the next order.

"Smile," Nina commanded.

Nimrod pulled his lips back, exposing his teeth.

"That's a pretty grotesque smile," Gretchen said, giggling.

"He has nice teeth, though," Caroline observed cheerfully, but Gretchen could see tears welling in her eyes from the recent news of the circumstances surrounding her friend's death.

"Good boy." Nina gave him a doggy treat. "We're still working on the smaller details."

"We're still waiting for your secret, Nina," Gretchen said. "Share."

Nina fluffed her hair and cleared her throat, preparing for her stage entrance. "Bonnie, as you know, lives for gossip and spends most of her time tracking it down. She overhead her son speaking on the phone." Nina paused. "I can just see her, slinking around, listening at doors, can't you?"

"And?" Gretchen said.

"He thinks the two deaths are related. Charlie and her sister, Sara."

That was it? The extent of Nina's information? "I already know that," Gretchen said.

Nina raised a perfect eyebrow.

"I forgot to tell you. Seriously," Gretchen said. "I wasn't holding out. I forgot."

"You two are way ahead of me," Caroline said, sitting up straight. "Why kill both of them? And why wait a year to murder the second one?"

"The killer will turn out to be a family member," Nina said. "A nut . . . ooh . . . sorry about the unintended pun. You know, nut and all. Anyway, it must be a family member who is crazy and has some knowledge of poisons."

"That person is heartless, brutally so," Caroline said. "Both women must have suffered terribly before they died. Poor Charlie."

"That was the intent," Nina said. "Don't you think? To make them suffer."

"It appears so," Caroline agreed.

"I'm sure the police are doing everything they can." Gretchen looked at her mother, worried about her.

"I have more to tell you." Nina leaned forward. "Bonnie has sharp ears. She heard Matt talking about a miniature peanut butter jar."

"Peanuts killed Sara," Caroline said.

"Exactly. Anaphylactic shock," Nina said. "Her entire body went into a serious allergic reaction."

Gretchen was surprised at Nina's knowledge. Her aunt wasn't exactly the medical type.

"I looked it up on the Internet before I came over," Nina said. "Don't look so surprised."

"I'm not," Gretchen fibbed. "Tell me more."

"The peanut isn't actually a true nut. Did you know that?"

Gretchen and Caroline shook their heads.

"It's really a legume, and a ton of people are allergic to it. Some people can have a life-threatening reaction just by inhaling the odor of a peanut."

"You sound like a walking encyclopedia," Caroline said.

Nina looked flattered. "See? I'm good for something."

Gretchen stood, leaned over her aunt, and gave her a big hug. "What would we do without you?"

"I ask myself that every day."

"Where did Matt find the miniature peanut butter jar?" Gretchen asked.

"I thought you'd never ask," said Nina. "Brace yourself." She paused for effect, her jeweled fingers fluttering. "The police found the little jar under Charlie's dead body."

Gretchen stared at her.

"Maybe the killer is leaving a calling card," Nina hypothesized. "Or he wants to be caught."

"Gretchen, dear daughter," Caroline said. "Matt might be right. It could be very dangerous to go there."

"Both sisters are dead," Gretchen reasoned. "There's no reason to believe anyone else will die."

"Maybe the brother killed them?" Nina suggested.

"Not likely," Caroline said. "He has serious health problems. Charlie had a son, but they were estranged. I wonder if he knows about his mother's death." She paused in thought. "When Sara died, the police determined that the banana bread must have come from a farmer's market. Sara went to various markets every Saturday morning. The authorities looked for a vendor who might have sold it to her but never found one."

"If you want to abandon the room boxes, I'll understand," Gretchen said. "Or we could move the project to our workshop where we'd feel safer."

Caroline sighed heavily. "Charlie worked hard on the room boxes," she said. "They were her final artistic endeavor. I want to restore them more than ever."

Gretchen took a sip of coffee. It tasted bitter when she thought of Charlie dying after drinking poisoned coffee. "Should we move everything here?"

"No," Caroline said. "There's more elbow room at the

shop. And with all of us working together, we can wrap it up quickly."

Gretchen remembered the authoritative way Matt had ordered her away. She hadn't planned to quit, no matter what her mother and the others decided. She wouldn't let him win.

Over my dead body, she thought.

• 9 •

Some doll collectors believe the eyes make the doll. Googly eyes are big, round, side-glancing eyes that are much larger than the doll's other facial features. They usually have large, exaggerated eyelashes, as well. Flirty eyes move from side to side, giving the doll a watchful appearance. Paperweight eyes are curved glass eyes that give a doll a very natural look. Sleep eyes close when the doll is laid down and open when she is upright. One of the most complex doll repairs involves working with eyes. They have to be placed just right, with no room for the slightest error.

Look into your doll's eyes. Are they gateways to the mystery of her life? What would she tell you if she could speak?

—From *World of Dolls* by Caroline Birch

Gretchen stared at the tiny penny doll's painted eyes as if she might find the answer to Charlie Maize's death. Why had the woman constructed room boxes containing bloody stains? Why furnish them with killing objects? Had that been her way of finding peace within the boxes' confines?

The answers eluded her, and the penny doll's eyes didn't give up any secrets.

"The keys to Mini Maize are on the kitchen table," Gretchen said to Nina, who buzzed into the workshop with her canine entourage. "I need to spend a few hours working here. I've promised to complete several dolls before the end of the day. I'll join you as soon as I can."

"Where is Caroline?"

"Mom's running errands," she answered. "She'll be at the shop as soon as she can."

Gretchen scanned her basket cases, those dolls that needed extensive reworking, the real fixer-uppers. She'd made a commitment to repair a basket case for a customer today.

"I can't start without you," Nina said with a small whine. "I wouldn't know what to do."

"Do the same thing you did yesterday. Figure out where the pieces go. The sooner we put them together, the better for Mom."

"We?" Nina complained. "Is there a mouse in my pocket?"

"I won't be far behind you."

"What about the danger? You know, the killer?"

"We decided last night that we're perfectly safe working at Mini Maize."

"I thought we would stick together."

"Make sure you lock the shop door behind you. I'll call Detective Kline and ask him to keep an eye out for suspicious characters."

"How old is this Detective Kline?"

Gretchen glanced at her aunt. "Why?"

"Just wondering."

"He's tall, intelligent, has a good sense of humor. He talked about karma last time I saw him."

Nina perked up. "Is he married?"

Gretchen searched her memory. "I don't know." If he was single, she'd hook Nina up with the Scottsdale detective. Wouldn't that be fun?

Her aunt packed up. Nina carried as much doggie

equipment as a family with twin babies carried baby equipment. "Are you sure I'll be okay?"

"If you're that worried, call April and ask her to go over instead." Gretchen picked up a German dolly face doll and looked at the work tag attached to its arm. "Go on home and let her handle it."

Gretchen glanced at her aunt. *That wasn't very thoughtful. Why did I say it like that?*

Nina's eyes turned into narrow slits. "I have to pick up Enrico first, then I'll go to Mini Maize. I can manage just fine by myself, thank you very much."

Gretchen sighed. "What's going on with you and April?"

"Nothing's going on. I don't need her. After all, I'll only be there alone for an hour or two. Right?"

"Maybe less."

"And I'll have Tutu."

"The guard dog."

"And I'll keep the door locked and won't let anyone in."

"Great." Gretchen bent over the German doll, and a few minutes later she heard the door slam.

Quiet at last. Sometimes she wondered why she became so claustrophobic when she was around other people for any length of time. No one else seemed to have that problem. Nina, for example, thrived on hordes of humanity; the thicker the brew, the better.

Gretchen looked longingly out the window at Camelback Mountain. She was too busy for a hike up the mountain, but she needed fresh air and Arizona wildlife to maintain her equilibrium. She felt the stress building. Repairing dolls was another perfect escape from the crowded planet. Dolls didn't talk back. No complaining, no arguing, no whining.

She placed the basket case doll on the worktable and picked up Charlie's penny doll again. She had used small stringing elastic and her tiniest stringing hook to attach a new arm. It looked good as new.

Gretchen tackled the German dolly face doll, which needed an eye repair. This one had glass sleep eyes with hair eyelashes. When Gretchen laid the doll on its back, the eyes remained open instead of closing as they should. She removed the head from the body, lifted the wig, then washed the doll's head and cleaned the eye-rocker unit. Time seemed to stand still while she immersed herself in her work.

The doorbell rang, bringing Gretchen back to the present. She glanced at the clock and was surprised to see that more than an hour had gone by since Nina had left for Charlie's shop.

Nimrod flew out of his bed and shot for the door, barking a shrill warning.

"I heard it, too," Gretchen called out to him. "You're supposed to warn me *before* the fact, not after."

As she walked down the hall, Wobbles slid around the corner, intently watching the commotion.

"Bernard Waites," said an old man when Gretchen opened the door. He looked vaguely familiar. He held out a small paper bag. "You left this at Mini Maize on Saturday."

She took the offered bag and used her foot to gently keep Nimrod from bolting through the opening in the door. She edged out, closing the door behind her, and looked inside the bag. "My checkbook," she said. "Where did you find it?"

"Right by the entrance. You must have dropped it when you left."

She remembered digging through her purse before she left the Scottsdale shop. It must have fallen out, and she hadn't noticed. "Please come in." Gretchen moved to open the door.

"No, I don't want to come in," he said, gruffly. "I need to get going."

"You can tell how much money I have in my account by the fact that I haven't even missed my checkbook in the last four days," Gretchen said, realizing he must have seen her balance. She would have peeked if she had found a lost checkbook. Her bank balance wasn't much to look at, slightly embarrassing.

Bernard gave her a hint of a smile, like he wasn't listening. "I found your address on the checks," he said.

The old man wasn't any too steady on his feet. Brown suspenders, a full head of white hair, and a long white mustache. He looked kindly but crotchety. "Shame about Charlie," he said.

"I saw you at the shop on Saturday. You were the one who opened the door and let everyone in."

"The police didn't like that one bit."

"Yes, I know."

"I made all the dollhouses in that shop," he said. "Last year I won Phoenix's Best Dollhouse Design award for the Victorian dollhouse on the shelf above the counter. It's not for sale, only for show. I'm keeping it."

"That's wonderful, a very prestigious award. I'll have to take a look at it when I go back to the shop."

His car was parked in the driveway, a white Ford pickup truck. Worn out, like the man before her. Bent and dented, the outer layer of paint peeling away, lumber in the back of the bed, poking over the top of the tailgate.

"What will happen to Mini Maize now?" Gretchen asked. "With Charlie and her sister dead, will the shop close up for good?"

"It could continue on," Bernard said. "Sara used to make most of the miniature dolls in the shop. When she passed, Britt Gleeland picked up the slack. Life goes on no matter what. Everybody thinks they're indispensable, but no one really is." He turned his head and looked out at the street. "I've been thinking about taking it over myself. Half of the stuff in there belongs to me anyway."

How old was this guy? At least eighty, maybe older. Gretchen had to admire him for his ambition. Of course, the opportunity to own the shop could also be a motive for murder, couldn't it?

"I hear you're working in Charlie's shop," Bernard said, leaning against the door frame for support, a slight tremble in both hands. "What's going on?" His eyes were watchful.

"We're repairing Charlie's last display in her honor, the room boxes she was going to present the day she died."

"Funny that," he said.

"What do you mean?"

"Charlie always asks me to make the display cases and room boxes for her, then she decorates them up. This time . . . funny . . . she did one of them herself. This is a first for her." He used the present tense like Charlie was still alive.

Bernard must be talking about the room box they had decided wasn't part of the display.

"Thanks for returning my checkbook," Gretchen said.

"Not many people like me left," he said. "Doing good deeds."

Gretchen stood in the front yard while he slowly pulled himself into his truck cab and eased away from the house. Strange old man.

She was just about to turn back into the house when a woman in trendy workout clothing strode briskly down the street toward her house. The walker wore a leopard print sport tank, matching shorts, and dainty white walking shoes. A matching choker clung to the woman's long, slim neck.

All she needed to complete the ensemble was a whip and a divorce decree. It was Matt Albright's crazy, stalking, soon-to-be ex.

Gretchen marched to the street, hoping she looked more ferocious than she felt. The woman was certifiable and had no business anywhere near Gretchen's home.

"What are you doing here?" Gretchen demanded.

Kayla Albright came to an abrupt halt.

"Exercising. Something you could use a little of." The Wife closed a cell phone and tucked it in a fanny pack around her waist. The fanny pack was made of matching leopard print material. "No law against keeping fit," she said, tilting up her perky little nose.

"Stay away from my house."

"Stay away from my husband."

The women faced off. They both took a step closer.

"You slashed my tire," Gretchen said.

"You stole my husband."

"So you admit it."

"Admit what?"

"That you slashed my tire."

"I don't know anything about your tire."

"The police are dusting for fingerprints," Gretchen said. What a stupid thing to say. As far as she knew, a tire had *never* been checked for fingerprints. Ever.

"That's ridiculous." The Wife snickered. Okay, she was smarter than Gretchen assumed. Crazy and smart and beautiful.

Gretchen looked down at her own rumpled T-shirt. Nail polish peeled from her toenails, and stubble sprouted all over her legs. She felt like a tarantula.

Leopard Lady was absolutely perfect. She looked like a blonde Barbie doll: an impossibly shaped thirty-nine–eighteen–thirty-three. At the moment, Gretchen hated her and every single sleek and trim Arizona woman. "Get off my property," she said.

"You don't own the street."

They glared at each other.

A siren wailed in the distance. It grew louder. Kayla smiled a nasty, cold smile. A police car turned the corner and stopped in front of Gretchen's house.

A Phoenix police officer rose slowly from his squad car and hitched his pants. "What's the problem? I got a call for a disturbance at this address."

Gretchen's mouth fell open in surprise when she saw the smirk on her adversary's face. Kayla had called the police herself. The call she was finishing when Gretchen spotted her! What nerve!

"That's right, officer," the Wicked Witch Wife said, adjusting her face from smirk to faux fear. "I was walking along, and this woman . . . "—she pointed at Gretchen— " . . . ran out of this house . . . "—another point—" . . . and started saying the most awful things to me. Crude and vulgar language like I've never heard before. There must be a law against verbally assaulting helpless women."

Helpless!

Where was Matt Albright when she really needed him? Where was a good man when she needed one? The male standing right in front of her was smiling at hotsy Kayla. His shoulders straightened when the Wife gave him the helpless routine. He sucked in his gut.

After tearing his gaze away from her, he bent into the interior of his car and pulled out a clipboard. "Okay," he said, flicking open a pen. "Let's get started."

He smiled again at the curvy Barbie doll, a big, toothy, drooling grin.

"I don't believe it," Gretchen said to the teacup poodle inside her purse. She stood on the sidewalk looking through the window of Mini Maize. Nimrod peeked into the shop from the purse, ears perked as though he understood her mutterings.

Inside, Britt Gleeland and Nina were huddled together behind the counter, giggling like schoolgirls.

From her position on the street, Gretchen saw no sign that anything productive had been accomplished in the last two hours. The same piles of mismatched dollhouse furniture still cluttered the countertops in the same haphazard, unsorted mess. Except for a space in front of the happy duo that had been cleared away to make room for Nina's latest hobby. Instead of digging in and working, Nina had her tarot cards scattered on the counter where the work in progress should have been.

Gretchen had been fending off an insane, evil woman and a love-struck, Barbie-admiring cop, and here sat Nina, doing nothing. Tarot cards. Geez.

Calm down, Gretchen told herself, taking a deep breath. *You're just a little stressed from your brush with Arizona's legal system.* At least the smitten cop had been more interested in Kayla's address and her leopard halter top than in taking any real action against Gretchen or following up on the alleged assault. His eyes had never left the Wife's ample chest.

Gretchen needed to clean up her act. Dress better, slim down, figure out how to manage her unruly hair. Sleek. That's what she wanted. To become a true Arizona woman. A little suntan wouldn't hurt, either. Her skin looked like a polar bear's. White as Elmer's glue.

"Yoo-hoo." Gretchen turned to see April getting out of her car, arms filled with submarine sandwich bags and a large bottle of soda.

"It's not my day," April huffed, laboring onto the curb. "I had a doll appraisal way over in Glendale, and after that I had another fender-bender."

April was prone to frequent but minor accidents.

"Anyone hurt?"

"Naw."

Gretchen glanced at April's car. Her old Buick's bumpers, front and back, were crumpled like accordions. "Looks the same as always to me."

April nodded in agreement just as Caroline walked briskly past April's car. "Sorry I'm late. The traffic was awful. What's new?"

"As far as I can tell, no progress at all inside the shop," Gretchen said, "but it's my fault for coming so late. I had a confrontation this morning right outside our house, and you'll never guess with who."

"Tell us." Caroline said, moving aside to let pedestrians pass.

"Matt Albright's wife."

"Whoo-wee!" April screeched. "That must have been something."

"It sure was."

Gretchen gave them the sordid details. April almost dropped her bags when Gretchen told them how Kayla had called the cops. Caroline had her hand over her mouth, speechless.

"I wish I had been there." April shifted her bags. "I would have fixed her wagon."

"Not only that, the cop gave me a warning."

"Let's ask Matt to step in," Caroline said. "She's going too far."

Right. Let Matt step in and rescue her. And prove how helpless she is.

April snorted. "No kidding. She's going too far. Boy, she's slick. Crazies usually are."

"I don't want this to get back to Matt or the Curves group," Gretchen said. "If Bonnie finds out, she'd tell Matt, and I just want to forget that it ever happened."

"I'd watch my back if I were you," April warned. "That woman is loony." She hefted the bags in her arms. "I brought lunch."

"I ate before I came. Thanks, though," Caroline said. Then, "Why are we standing on the sidewalk?"

"I can't eat another submarine sandwich," Gretchen said, opening the shop door. "Don't buy them for me anymore."

"You only had one for lunch yesterday, and you're done already?" April said. "You should be me. Breakfast, lunch, dinner, and all the snacks in between. I'm *really* sick of them."

"King of pentacles," Nina said to Britt as they entered. She had the tarot cards' instructions open on her lap and read a passage from the booklet. "A successful leader with business sense, strong character, intelligent, a loyal friend."

Britt clapped her hands together. "And you're my new friend. Wait until you see how loyal I can be."

They both giggled. Gretchen found it amazing that a woman dressed as severely as Britt could even accomplish a giggle. She wore another stiff-collared blouse, and every hair in her French twist was tucked where it should be.

Gretchen started to speak, but Nina held up a finger in

warning. "I'm almost done," she said, picking up another card. Gretchen looked over her aunt's shoulder. The picture on the card depicted an angel with red wings pouring water between two challises.

"Temperance," Nina read from her book. "Accomplishment through self-control, patience, bringing together into perfect harmony."

"I love that one," Britt said.

Finished, the two gypsy women finally looked up. Britt leveled a withering stare at Gretchen; the incident at the shop the other night hadn't made them best buds. But for Nina's sake, Gretchen had to make an effort. "Let's start over," she said to Britt. "I think we got off on the wrong foot."

"Of course," Britt said, but her body language remained tense.

They gave each other a stiff handshake.

"We've met before," Caroline said to her. "You were one of Charlie's dearest friends. I'm so sorry about what happened."

"Thank you."

"And this is April," Caroline said when Nina remained silent, refusing to be the one to bring April into the conversation.

Gretchen cleared her throat and addressed her aunt. "How are the room boxes coming along?"

Nina shuffled the cards in her hands. "I was going to start without you," she said. "Honestly I was, but Britt came along, and we really hit it off." She bent down to pick up a card that had fallen to the floor.

"That's a weird card," April said.

"The hanged man," Nina said. "See how he's hanging upside down? And he fell right by your feet, April."

April snorted. "Hogwash. I don't believe in that stuff. I

suppose you're going to tell me that I'll be hanging from my toes."

Nina consulted her instructions. "The hanged man means it's time for rest and reflection. You should stay at home more." She picked up the remaining cards from the table and flashed the same card she had read earlier. "King of pentacles is a great card, Britt."

"We need to get back to business," Caroline reminded her sister.

"Do any of the pieces on the counter look familiar to you?" Gretchen asked Britt.

Britt stood up and wandered along the counter, picking up a piece here and there.

She shook her head. "Not really," she said, one hand fluttering to check her French twist, tucking an imaginary stray hair back into the tightly wound locks. She re-arranged her bangs.

April's thick fingers combed through the piles. "It's a strange brew," she said, holding up a Victorian dresser. She picked up another object with the other hand. "Here's another street sign. And another."

Gretchen took the signs from April. None of the street names were familiar to her.

"A broken-down wooden bench," Nina said, joining in the inventory. "A mahogany wall mirror. How do all of these fit together?"

"They don't," Caroline said. "Each box is unique. The differences in time periods and social settings will make putting them together easy."

Britt still fidgeted with her hair. "Bernard made the room boxes."

Gretchen glanced up at the shelves lining the upper part of the wall. Bernard's dollhouses. And the Victorian he had mentioned. She stepped closer.

When Bernard had said he'd designed a Victorian, Gretchen had assumed it would be an English Victorian with dormer windows and window boxes filled with petunias and ivy. Her second guess would have been a Victorian farmhouse with a wraparound porch. Instead, she faced an enormous three-foot-high French Victorian with two sloped roofs, wrought-iron balconies, and molded cornices. The steep vertical slopes to the roofs and the heavy faux stonework gave it a sinister undertone.

April came up beside Gretchen. "It looks like a haunted house," she said.

"It sure isn't a painted lady," Gretchen agreed. "No vibrant colors and trendy painted trim work on this Victorian."

"It won an award," April pointed out, reading from a mounted plaque next to the dollhouse. "Designed and built by Bernard Waites. Kind of scary-looking, but the details are amazing."

"Bernard looks like a cuddly teddy bear," Britt called from the other side of the room, "but he has a dark side."

"What do you mean?" Gretchen asked.

"Bernard is always in the background like he's waiting for an opportunity to seize control," Britt said. "He's been hanging around Charlie ever since she retired last year."

"It looks like he contributed quite a lot to the shop." Gretchen selected a miniature blue velvet hat from one of the piles.

"He built the dollhouses mounted on the walls. But what about everything else you see?" Britt grabbed a container. She had a firm set to her jaw. Determination. Gretchen recognized the box as one that Britt had been packing up when they had met at the shop. She'd forgotten all about it.

Britt opened it up. "Come over here. Feast your eyes on

my contribution, and then tell me if you think that old man has done the most work."

All four women leaned in.

The box was filled with the smallest miniature dolls Gretchen had ever seen. Britt picked one up with the tips of two fingers and held it out for everyone to admire.

"A Shirley Temple doll," April said, excited. "It can't be over a half inch tall."

"Not a bit of detail was sacrificed," Britt bragged. "The mouth, the eyes, the fingers—all as perfect as the original doll."

Nina reached out with a jeweled forefinger and touched the Shirley Temple doll's blonde, curly locks.

They all leaned in again and peered into the box. Dozens and dozens of exquisite, dainty, mini-miniatures were lined up in padded rows. Tiny beds of bubble wrap cushioned them from breakage.

"You can't imagine the work that went into these," Britt said. "Now I'll have to find another miniature shop to sell my creations."

Gretchen looked over at the room boxes. "Did you make any of the dolls for Charlie's special project? For these room boxes?"

"Charlie asked me to make some for her." Britt's face brimmed with self-pride. "And I obliged. She had very specific instructions on what she wanted. A clergyman sculpted at a precise height, a married couple for the Victorian era. She said she wanted to dress them herself, so I dropped them off here the day before when we had dinner together, before she . . ." Britt's composure slipped, and she worked to restore it.

"Where are the room box dolls?" Gretchen hadn't seen any miniature people other than those with price tags in some of the other display cases.

"She must have them in the back room. Maybe she didn't have time to arrange them before she died."

"They were part of the display then?"

"Apparently," Britt said.

"You don't know for sure?" Gretchen watched Britt fuss with her French twist.

"Of course, I know. Don't be silly. We were best friends." Britt's nervous fingers played over her bangs.

· II ·

Matt appeared on the sidewalk outside of Mini Maize but refused to enter the doll shop. "I'm taking Gretchen to lunch," he said, doll phobia sweat shiny on his forehead.

April tittered. Nina and Caroline looked on expectantly. Gretchen swung outside before her aunt had time to push her out.

"I thought you were in therapy," she said, as they walked down the street.

His humor came back as soon as they left the storefront. "I am. Can't you tell?"

How could she be interested in a man who was afraid of her life's work?

They found a restaurant with an outdoor courtyard and sat down at a small, round table. A waiter took their orders—tortilla soup for Gretchen, who was watching her weight since her morning resolve to become a hot Arizona babe, and enchiladas for Matt.

Gretchen kept one eye peeled to the street and sidewalk. But chances were that the wacko wife wouldn't appear and cause trouble now. She'd wait in the background until he was gone.

With the doll club members' passion for gossip, her altercation with Kayla wouldn't stay a secret for long, unless April was more dependable than Gretchen when it came to confidences.

"What are you looking for?" Matt asked, following Gretchen's gaze down the street.

"Nothing," she answered. "Can I ask a personal question?"

"You're interested in my personal life?" He had laugh crinkles around his eyes. "I bet it's because I've put extra effort into my grooming today. I've showered, brushed my teeth with extra whitening toothpaste, and I used a manly scented deodorant called Wild Beast. Just for you."

That sexy grin. Gretchen hid her amusement.

The waiter brought tortilla chips and salsa.

"Why isn't your divorce final yet?" Gretchen picked up a chip and broke it in half. "I don't have much experience with the process, but friends of mine have gone through them in much less time."

"Ah, I see you're getting impatient?"

"Please tell me."

"Kayla has pulled every trick in the book." No smile now. "Several appearances have been rescheduled at the last minute, she's changed attorneys three times, she's appealed to the court for more time due to one problem after another, it goes on and on. Sometimes I think I'll never be free."

"What about Detective Kline? Is he single?"

Matt gaped at her. "You don't waste time, do you?"

Gretchen laughed. A jealous streak? This was interesting. "I'm inquiring for my aunt. That *did* sound terrible, though."

"He's single. And looking for a serious relationship. So now I have a question for you."

"Okay."

"Why were you at the shop today? After what I told you last night, I had hoped you would reconsider and stay home."

"Hoped? You ordered me away."

"Order seems a little strong. I gently suggested it."

"Gently suggested it?" Men really were impossible to deal with.

"You're right. I don't want you anywhere near Charlie Maize's shop. But since you refuse to listen, please tell me that you're almost done."

"We're sorting through the pieces, deciding which room box each of them goes into. It wouldn't take long if my mother and I were the only ones working on it. Instead, the shop is filled with small animals and several people who are in the way more than they are helping."

"Well, there's more safety in numbers. Keep it that way. All I'm asking is that you remain alert."

"You're making too much of it."

"That's my job. To expect the worst."

The food came, temporarily distracting them.

"Anyway," Gretchen said between mouthfuls, "none of us knows what the room boxes represent. Based on the detail pieces that go into them, they're all from different time periods. There doesn't seem to be a common theme."

"Are you trying to read too much into them? I heard that Charlie was a bit odd toward the end. It might just be a hodgepodge."

Gretchen remembered the miniature street signs. She had shoved them into her purse, thinking she would ask around or check a phone directory later. Now she drew them out.

"We found these on the floor. I was meaning to ask mom if she recognized any of them, but then I became distracted." *By him!*

She handed over the tiny green street signs. "At least the signs are all the same, green with yellow lettering. They're the only things in the group that are consistent."

"Twenty-nine Hanbury Street." Matt read each one aloud.

"De Russey's Lane, Seventeen seventeen Elm Street, Number Ninety-two Second Street. Four room boxes?" His eyes pierced hers. "Each with a street sign?"

"Five room boxes, actually. But we aren't sure the fifth one is part of the display."

Matt handed the tiny signs back. "I know every corner of this city. None of those addresses are familiar to me."

"Any suspects yet?"

"We're working on it. Nobody claims to have seen Charlie on Saturday morning. Britt Gleeland had dinner with her the night before and saw nothing unusual in Charlie's manner. Britt's daughter went by the shop to drop off some miniature flower arrangements, but it was locked up. She looked through the window and saw nothing unusual."

Gretchen watched Matt carefully. She saw concern etched on his face.

"Wrap it up soon," she said.

"That's the plan."

"I could hardly wait for the two gigglers to leave," April said from a stool at the Mini Maize checkout counter. "They went out for a late lunch, and I don't expect them back anytime soon."

Gretchen released Nimrod from her purse, and he trotted off, sniffing around the edges of Charlie's display cabinets.

"What a pair," Caroline said from a seat at a card table that Gretchen had set up after finding it folded in the corner of the storage room. Piles of room box furnishings covered the square table.

Nina's friendship with Britt Gleeland certainly had come on fast and furious. Gretchen hoped her aunt wouldn't share any confidential information with Britt. She regretted opening her own big mouth. Now the secret about Charlie's poisoning threatened to spread like valley fever.

The two sisters had both died in agony. It gave Gretchen the creeps just thinking about what they went through. She was glad that April and her mother were still at the shop to keep her company.

"April and I decided to take pictures of the room boxes," Caroline said. "Before and after photographs."

"But neither of us can figure out how to use the camera part of our phones." April chuckled. "You're the only one of us that isn't technology challenged."

Gretchen pulled her cell phone from her purse. "Smile." She took April's picture, then showed it to her friend.

April sighed. "I've lost five pounds, but you'd never know it. I have another hundred to go."

"One day at a time. Smile, Mom."

Caroline turned away from the camera's eye. "Not me! The room boxes."

Gretchen took pictures of the empty room boxes. After each snapshot, she checked it for clarity on the small phone screen.

"Joseph Reiner stopped by while you were gone," April said, wiping grime and footprints from a little mahogany bed frame. "He was extremely upset by Charlie's death. He broke down and cried twice in the short time he was here."

"I'm sorry I missed him." Gretchen had lost a convenient opportunity to ask the Joseph's Dream Doll shop owner about his presence at the parade. She still wondered why he hadn't been at Charlie's doll shop with the rest of the invitees.

"I have the room box pieces separated as best I could," Caroline said. "It wasn't as hard as we originally thought it would be. The different time periods helped. But I still have a small pile of unknowns."

On one corner of the card table, Caroline had placed Victorian pieces. Gretchen studied the grouping, gently touching the fabrics. A miniature mohair sofa, wooden bedstead, mirrored dressing table, a woolen floral rug. And all the articles that would complete a setting from the late 1900s.

Gretchen glanced sharply at her mother.

"I know," Caroline said softly. "I see it."

"What?" April said, hurrying over.

"Flecks of blood on the sofa," Gretchen said. "Not too much. Just a little. And more on this painting. A spot or two."

"It almost looks like an accident," April said. "Like Charlie spilled red paint."

"What about the red paint on the edge of the axe and knife? Those weren't accidents." Gretchen went through all the pieces on the card table, one by one.

"What in the world was Charlie thinking?" Caroline rubbed her eyes. "This one is a Victorian household, That"— she said, pointing at a different pile—"is a farmland setting with a church in the background. Little crab apple trees, a bale of hay, not much else."

April held up two tiny steps. Decrepit, worn, a touch of blood on the first stepping-stone. "From the backyard pile. Mini windows with small panes, some broken, a wooden door."

Caroline gestured toward another group of items. "This is also a bedroom, but from a later era and much more luxurious. An Oriental rug, mahogany bed and dresser, fan-back chair. Look at the precious Martha Washington bedspread."

"And the pile of unknowns." Gretchen looked through

the leftover pieces. Tiny sheets of old plywood, bits of paper, things that might not have anything to do with the room boxes.

"It sure would be fun to make my own miniatures sometime." April picked up another item and wiped it with her cloth. "I'd never be as accomplished as Britt, though. Few doll makers are. It's extremely detailed work. You need a lot of patience."

"Was Sara's craftwork as good as Britt's?"

"At least as good, maybe better," her mother answered.

"Where *are* the dolls Britt made for the room boxes?" Gretchen asked.

"We haven't gotten that far," Caroline said. "Now that we've cleaned up and organized the room furnishings, we'll place those where we think they go and move on to finding the dolls."

April sucked soda through a straw. "I'd like to give Gretchen an award," she said, presenting Gretchen with a small wrapped box. "I'm so proud of you. I thought you'd like a little memento of your accomplishments since coming to live in Phoenix."

"But why?" Gretchen said. "I haven't accomplished anything."

"You will."

"And that isn't true, Gretchen," Caroline said, watching from the table. "You're very talented."

Gretchen opened the cover and peeked in to find a gold badge. It had a shiny gold finish and was shaped like the sun. The inscription read Best in the West.

"Let me pin it on you." April scooped up the badge.

"Best in the West?" Gretchen asked, laughing. "Best what?"

"Best restoration artist," Caroline called out.

"But that's you."

"There." April finished pinning it on and stood back to admire it. "You look great, real professional. The gold matches your hair. And I have one for Caroline, too."

April handed another package to her mother.

Gretchen turned to check her reflection in the window and was startled to see a man peering in. He wore a dirty sleeveless T-shirt, and a black do-rag covered his hair. A silver ring pierced his lower lip, and a tattoo like barbed wire wound around his right arm.

He stared at Gretchen.

April shrieked.

"That's Charlie's son, Ryan Maize," Caroline said softly.

He was young. About twenty. Wiry with dirty, ill-fitting jeans that dragged on the sidewalk. Black running shoes that had seen better days. Ryan's eyes shifted nervously to the badge pinned on Gretchen's chest. His eyes grew wide and frightened. When Gretchen moved closer to the window, he darted out of sight.

Gretchen slammed out the door, breaking into a run. "Wait," she shouted. He disappeared around a busy corner. She raced behind him onto the sidewalk bordering Scottsdale Road.

So this was Charlie's son. But why was he running away? Why did he look so frightened? Gretchen was used to jogging and hiking. Camelback Mountain and the desert air were perfect conditioning tools, and though she wanted to lose a few pounds, Gretchen considered herself aerobically fit. She'd been a runner her entire life.

Ryan Maize, however, was younger and very quick, weaving among shoppers, never looking back. He shoved someone out of the way. Gretchen heard gasps and squeals from those on the sidewalk as she chased after him. She threaded through the crowd and leaped over a dropped shopping bag, running as fast as she could.

What was she doing? What was she going to do if she actually caught up to him? What if he had a gun or a knife? She'd karate kick the weapon out of his fist. Sure, right. Brucaleen Lee.

Ryan pulled ahead. Gretchen was fast, but she wasn't fast enough. He was getting away.

Stop, she thought, *let him go.* No, she wouldn't give up.

The loose soles of his shoes were his downfall. Gretchen saw him stumble. She picked up speed, giving it all she had. Did he know about his mother? That she was dead?

Gretchen was using all her energy to catch him. She didn't have the breath to speak. She reached out, and her fingertips almost touched his back.

He pulled away. And tripped again. This time she got a firm hold on the back of his shirt. She heard it rip.

· 12 ·

Ryan Maize ducks down and tries to twist out of the woman's grasp. She has him by the back of his shirt, and she's incredibly strong, like the lioness of Babylon.

He hears the cloth tear.

If he wasn't bingeing at the moment, she wouldn't be catching him.

Too much alcohol and crack cocaine in his past.

Whatever he's on, he can't remember taking it. That worries him.

It isn't his fault that he's in a weakened condition. Everything goes wrong for him. People don't help him enough. Like his mother. If she hadn't refused to help him out, he'd be doing really good. Healthy, happy, and rich. All he needs is a little support from the people around him. He needs just one little break.

Life sucks, and then you die. That's his motto.

He twists again, trying to break her grip. She's on him like the evil witch she is.

Shapeshifters masquerading as cops. What's next?

He's coming down, slowly descending from an alternate reality.

She's a real cop. He'd seen the badge. That's what he gets for going back to the shop, for wanting one last look.

"Stop running and listen to me," the female cop says. Words staccato through the air like breaks in the time continuum. Moments lost.

For him, it isn't lost moments, it's lost years. All gone.

Twenty-one going on dead.

The cop's breath is labored, or is that his?

He whirls and catches another glimpse of the badge.

You can't even tell the law from the rest of society. A fake woman has him in her power. A Matrix society, and he alone realizes the truth.

Ryan karate-chops the hand.

No reaction.

She must be undercover.

Then why the badge?

A voice inside of Ryan's head answers him. It always does. It's dependable, like nothing else in his life is.

Ego. Power. They're all alike, even the women. Especially the women.

Ryan jabs her hard with his elbow, and he feels the release.

Freedom.

Run!

If she catches up again, he'll sucker punch her.

Anything to get away. Anything at all.

"Your mother is dead," the woman says, and Ryan is slammed up against the side of a building. She must know all the martial arts. A trained assassin. Who would have guessed by looking at her?

He thinks he will throw up because of the heat pouring through the cracks of the street. He sees serpents twisting out of the poured concrete, coming for his soul.

She repeats the statement. *Dead, dead.*

Ryan makes a fist. He puts everything he has behind it, everything he has.

The punch connects, and the woman goes down. Surprisingly fast.

His strength and power must be growing.

She doesn't move.

Ryan thinks about the concept of remorse but doesn't feel any. He rarely feels anything.

A being with silver hair comes at him, followed by one the size of a wrestler. He recognizes them from his mother's shop. Ryan saw them there, talking to the woman cop.

The enormous woman glares at him but is winded and bends over to widen her airway, to make room for her precious air. She glares up at him, then grimaces without saying a word. The other one is filled with anger but hesitates a moment too long. Her eyes flick to the woman on the ground.

His feet pound the pavement, and it sounds like thunder of the gods to him. They have decided to protect him from harm, to champion him for his abilities.

He is one of them.

· 13 ·

Miniature dolls, also known as dollhouse dolls, are an intricate part of a small-scale scene. Collectors find miniatures in all the usual places: doll stores, online shops, and auctions and doll shows. But for the most fun and versatility, why not try making your own? You can begin by purchasing a basic doll-making kit from a miniature shop or order one through an online catalogue. Kits contain porcelain parts, patterns for making the doll's costume, materials for jewelry, wigging supplies, and easy-to-follow instructions. In no time at all, you will want to cast molds and design your own line of costumes from fabrics and ribbons. You'll be creating hats and shoes from card stock patterns and designing handbags from binder clips. Welcome to the fascinating world of miniature doll making.

—From *World of Dolls* by Caroline Birch

Wednesday morning the women at Curves hopped to the beat of "Build Me Up Buttercup."

Gretchen tried to ignore the pain in her temple where Ryan Maize had struck her. One punch from that scrawny kid, and she'd fallen hard, like a rock from a mountain ledge. Her mother and April, miraculously arriving just as Gretchen dropped to the sidewalk, had strong-armed a street vendor into parting with a cup of ice. Their quick thinking had kept the swelling to a minimum.

A couple of ibuprofen tablets this morning, and her head no longer felt like it had a built-in subwoofer. And her hair covered the ugly purple bruise.

"I hear you were clobbered good last night," Bonnie said, her red wig stiff with hair spray. Lip liner was drawn in an exaggerated arch around her lips. "Are you okay?" She trotted in place on a small platform, swinging her arms above her head as the music changed to "Chantilly Lace."

"I'm perfectly fine," Gretchen replied, trying not to wince when she bent over. She had a huge headache and two more hours to go before she could take more pain relievers.

Nina, working the abductor machine, piped up, speaking around her niece as though she wasn't present. "Gretchen is too impulsive for her own good. Imagine chasing a tattooed, body-pierced, crazy man through the streets of Scottsdale. What was she thinking?"

Gretchen shrugged. She didn't have a good answer and secretly agreed with Nina.

"Where's Caroline this morning?" Bonnie asked.

"Trying to catch up on our repair work," Gretchen said.

"I should do a reading for you." Nina bounced a large pink ball while running in place. "The tarot cards complement my psychic predictions," she said. "You really need a reading."

"Maybe later."

"I'll take one," Bonnie said.

"I'll watch," April said.

Nina smiled. "Okay."

Gretchen noticed a definite clearing of the air around Nina and April. Nina's new friendship with Britt had something to do with it. And Nina seemed grateful that April had helped rescue Gretchen and then cared for her after the blow to her head. April was doing her part by showing interest in Nina's tarot cards. Gretchen knew how hard that was for her.

April sweated over the shoulder press. "What do you make of the miniature peanut butter jar?" she asked Gretchen. "How does it fit in?"

Gretchen looked questioningly at her aunt, remembering the promise Nina had made to keep the jar's existence confidential. Nina's eyes shifted to Bonnie, who had originally shared the information with her.

Bonnie grinned conspiratorially. "I had to share a teensy bit of police work with my favorite group." She held up her right hand and pressed two fingers together to show how minuscule her sharing really was. "But remember, no talking outside our little circle."

"Change stations now," the programmed voice commanded, and everyone shifted to the next station in the circle.

"After all, you are my best friends." Bonnie's arms swung to encompass all Curve's members working out, even two women who had signed up that very morning and had only introduced themselves moments before.

Her "best friends" nodded enthusiastically.

"That's right," said Rita Phyller, the Barbie collector.

"That's right," Ora, the Curves manager, echoed. "We're buddies."

"Does anyone have a theory about the jar?" April asked.

"I do. I do." Bonnie shouted, waving her right hand like a kindergarten student. "Charlie always thought her sister had been murdered. Matty is looking into it again."

"Wouldn't that be something if Sara really had been murdered," Rita said, shaking her head. "Too bad Charlie's ticker gave out before the investigation was over."

Gretchen glanced over at Nina. Other than law enforcement officials working the case, the true cause of Charlie's death should only be known to Gretchen, Caroline, and Nina. This was the moment that would tell her how reliable her aunt was.

No one said anything. Charlie's suspicious nicotine overdose was still under wraps.

Nina glared at Gretchen as though she knew that her niece hadn't trusted her, and Gretchen gave her an I'm-sorry look.

April huffed loudly and paused in her workout to rest. April had chased Gretchen and Ryan down the street yesterday. Today, she couldn't get through a ten-minute circuit, working slow. *April's adrenaline must really spike when she gets excited, turning her into superwoman*, Gretchen thought.

"I think someone scared Charlie to death," Bonnie said. "Literally. Her heart gave out."

"That's impossible," Rita replied.

"No, it isn't," April said. "That son of hers was pretty scary-looking. His face could frighten a person enough to bring on a heart attack."

"I wouldn't go that far," Gretchen said. In spite of Ryan's grungy appearance, he had seemed young and frightened.

"I almost fainted from fear after looking into his eyes." April shivered. "He's lost his grip on reality; that's obvious."

"If Sara was murdered, I'd put him first on the list of suspects," Ora said. "Look how he hurt Gretchen."

"What if Charlie was murdered, too?" Rita called out.

"That kid's a drug addict, you know," Bonnie said. "Crack cocaine, pot, booze, you name it. He's been in and out of rehab centers, and nothing works. What if he killed his mother in a fit of rage? Maybe she wouldn't give him money for more drugs, and he was strung out. An addict without drugs will do anything to get them, even if it means killing his own mother."

"There wasn't any sign of a struggle," Gretchen said before the exercise group got too carried away. "And no marks on Charlie's body."

"Does your detective son know about Charlie's son?" Rita asked Bonnie.

"Of course, Matty's onto him like lint on Velcro." Bonnie grimaced. "That isn't a very good analogy."

"Like toilet paper on a shoe?" Nina offered.

"Like a flea on a dog?" April said, laughing.

"I'm out of here," Gretchen said, heading for the stretching area.

Nina followed her over. "I'm having breakfast with Britt."

"Sounds good," Gretchen said, bending at the waist and touching her toes while the inside of her head pounded on her skull. "Don't worry about coming to the shop. Mom accomplished so much yesterday, we might wrap up the project today."

"I'm your chief problem solver," said Nina. "I'll be there. After yesterday's excitement, I'm staying close by. Who knows what disaster will happen next?"

Matt Albright's unmarked blue Chevy passed Gretchen's car going the opposite way. The detective waved, not a friendly hello wave, but rather a trying-to-flag-you-down sort of wave. Gretchen recognized the hand gestures but ignored him. She gave him her best smile and wiggled her fingers as if to say toodle-oo.

Matt wasn't much of a team player. He worked alone and kept his progress to himself. He didn't take her seriously enough, so today she was following his example and working alone.

Gretchen turned onto Central Avenue, wondering what

the detective was doing in this neighborhood. Central Avenue divided the city into two grids. Numbered streets ran north and south on the east side of Central. Numbered avenues lined the west side. Gretchen drove slowly up First Street, crossed Central, and cruised down First Avenue.

Gretchen was looking for Nacho and Daisy, two destitute characters whom she'd become friends with. She had to find time to help out more at the homeless shelter, but life had been busy. Soon, though.

Nacho, an alcoholic who lived inside his mind most of the time, appeared to enjoy his life of freedom from the heavy responsibility imposed on others by what he thought of as a tyrannical society.

Daisy, a would-be actress, was always on the lookout for Hollywood talent scouts; and considered herself an honorary member of the Red Hat Society and dressed accordingly.

Gretchen had tried to change the two derelicts with limited success. She'd opened her home to Daisy in hopes that a normal environment would improve her roving ways. Occasionally, Daisy stopped in for a bath and a soft bed. But then, to Gretchen's frustration, she would be gone again, back to the streets and her own circle of friends.

Gretchen drove past Saint Anskar's soup kitchen without spotting them. The streets were quieter today than usual, less foot traffic, fewer homeless with all their possessions stuffed into plastic garbage bags or shopping carts.

When she turned onto Central Avenue for one last look, she finally spotted Daisy, wearing her purple sundress and a red hat adorned with a large feather. The homeless woman was pushing a cart that brimmed with junk. "Today's my lucky day," she said with a big grin after Gretchen stepped out of the car. "I can feel it in my bones and in my heart."

Daisy's purple dress was crumpled, and her best hat

showed signs of wear. Gretchen thought she saw a smidgen of pigeon droppings on the brim. Daisy's secondhand sandals exposed dirty feet.

"It's time to take a break from the street," Gretchen said. "Why don't you come home with me for a few days and get some rest?"

Daisy shook her head. "Not today. I'd miss an important opportunity to break in to the biz. I'm trying out for a part at Orpheum Theatre."

Gretchen hid her frustration. "Where are all your friends?" She didn't see any of Daisy's usual acquaintances. Even the pigeon-feeding ladies were missing from their designated bench.

"On vacation. I stayed behind for the audition."

Gretchen almost laughed out loud. Daisy must really be delusional today to think all the street people were away on vacation. "Where did they go?"

"San Francisco." Daisy adjusted her dress, and Gretchen caught the faint scent of the perfume she had given to her, among other odors. "How do I look?"

"Like a million bucks. You're kidding, right? About San Francisco?"

Daisy shook her head. "No. Nacho heard that San Francisco closed the homeless shelters. Instead, the government is handing out money every month. If you're homeless, you get dough. And they can't tell who's a resident and who isn't, because none of us carry identification. Slick. We're like a secret society. Like Masons."

"Did Nacho go, too?"

"He led the pack," Daisy said. "I tried to tell him that the grass is always greener, but he has to find out on his own. California, here he comes."

"How long are they on this . . . ah . . . vacation?"

"Just long enough to pick up some cash and tour the

city. Speaking of cash, when is your aunt going to need my services again?"

"I'll ask her."

Daisy was a natural with animals, connecting with them in a way she couldn't with people. Daisy occasionally helped out with the purse dog training whenever Nina had more business than she could keep up with.

Matt Albright's blue Chevy swung around the corner, two blocks down. Gretchen had been expecting him. The man never gave up. She was running out of time. Gretchen kept an eye on the unmarked car. "I'm looking for a drug addict named Ryan Maize. Do you know him?"

"We stay away from the druggies," Daisy said. "They're insane. Totally over the top. And they steal from us." She looked down at the shopping cart filled with her possessions, then up at the blue car pulling to the curb.

"Wait here," Gretchen said to her. She stepped off the curb and rounded on the driver's side. "Please stay in your car," she said.

Matt paused halfway out of the car and gave her a dazzling, toothy smile. "You're telling me to remain in my vehicle?"

"Correct."

His eyes swung to Daisy, who had her hands on her hips and didn't look pleased to see him.

"She's never going to talk to me if you're part of the conversation," Gretchen explained.

"What are you two talking about?"

"This and that. Now please stay in your car."

"Okay," he said and climbed back in.

"What's *he* doing here?" Daisy wanted to know.

"You remember Matt Albright. His mother is the president of the doll club. He's a friend."

Daisy glared at his car. "A cop is a cop. I know you like

him, but I wouldn't trust a cop as far as I could spit, and I can spit a long way. He'll be nice and friendly until he gets what he wants."

That wasn't news to Gretchen. That pertained to all men, not just cops.

"I need to find Ryan," Gretchen said. "Can you help me?"

Daisy tilted her head, considering the request. "I'm not sure," she said. "Try Twenty-fifth and Van Buren, pink stucco house. But be careful. Those druggies are dangerous." Daisy shook her head and clicked her tongue before adding, "This city ought to clean up its streets."

14

"Come with me," Gretchen said to Matt after Daisy had wandered out of range.

"Where are we going?" Matt said with a suggestive grin.

"Have you found Charlie's son yet?"

"Almost," Matt said.

"Almost doesn't count. If you want to talk to him, I'll take you there."

"I'll follow you over."

"Come with me. It will give me a chance to tell you about my first impression of him."

"My mother already told me. But I'd like to hear it from you."

He slid in beside her. Gretchen related the story of yesterday's chase down Scottsdale Road. Matt sat next to her, gripping the sides of the car's seat.

"You can trust me," Gretchen said, noting his clenched fists and braced posture.

"I've heard that before," he quipped.

Gretchen had never driven with a cop in her car. She drove as carefully as she could, obeying every traffic sign, coming to complete stops, using her directionals properly.

What a pain! Twenty-five miles an hour was much slower than she thought.

Out of the corner of her eye, she had the feeling he was watching her every move. She was relieved when he answered a call on his cell phone. Business kept him occupied until they were close to their destination.

Gretchen made a turn onto Van Buren and slowed to look for the house.

"This must be it," she said. "It's the only pink stucco." She pulled to the curb.

"Wait in the car. I'll be right back," Matt said.

"Not in a million years. This is my gig. You're tagging along for the ride. I'm the one who found him."

"You're impossible. I knew driving over with you was a bad idea when you suggested it. We should have taken my car." Matt didn't look like he meant it. Or maybe he did, but his lips had that amused turn to them. "What next?" he said. "Should we surround the house and go in with guns drawn? You can cover me. Oh wait, you don't have a gun."

"Shush."

They both stared at the house. Chipped pink stucco. A broken window boarded up with plywood. Discolored blinds, all drawn.

"Stay here," Gretchen said.

"*What?* I'm the law enforcement official, in case you haven't noticed. You're stealing my line. *You* stay here."

"No way. I'm the one who found this address. If you weren't so busy following me, you would have found Ryan by now."

"I haven't been following you."

"I'm going in."

"I happen to be the detective in charge of this case. I don't wait in cars."

She gave his garb an appreciative glance and wondered if he'd look as good in a uniform. He wore one of his social causes T-shirts, a white one that proclaimed, Running Strong for American Indian Youth. She'd seen him wear several with different motifs. This one had teepees against a backdrop of soaring eagles and an orange setting sun. "You look like a cop," she said.

"No, I don't. That's the whole point of working undercover. So I don't look like a cop."

"He won't even open the door if you go up to it."

"He isn't going to open it either way."

Gretchen was already making her way up a broken sidewalk. Wilted shrubs framed the house. It looked deserted. She knocked softly and listened for movement inside. Nothing. She banged loudly. Then banged again.

Gretchen could smell Matt's Chrome cologne floating on the breeze behind her.

She thought she heard something inside. A scurry sound like a mouse. Or a rat. The place was probably crawling with rodents and insects. The door opened a crack, and an eyeball peered out.

"I'm looking for Ryan Maize," Gretchen said. "Is he here?"

"Who wants to know?"

"Gretchen Birch. I'm a friend of his mother's."

"No, you're not. You're a cop."

"I'm not a cop."

Gretchen heard a chuckle behind her.

"Do you have a search warrant?" the person inside asked.

"No. I'm trying to tell you, I'm not a cop."

The minuscule opening in the door began to close. Matt's arm shot out to stop it. He flashed identification with his other hand. "I'm the cop," he said. "Don't make a bad choice. Open the door and talk to us."

"Don't you need a warrant?"

"Not to ask questions about a death."

The door swung open, and Ryan stepped hesitantly out onto the porch wearing the black do-rag. He squinted and rubbed his eyes. His shoulders slumped with an air of defeat, like he expected life to keep disappointing him.

Classic drug addict's philosophy, Gretchen thought. They blamed their circumstances on bad luck and the actions of others, instead of taking control and making different choices.

"I don't feel too good," Ryan said, leaving the door ajar. "I think I'm sick."

Matt gave him a cold stare.

The porch was covered with cigarette butts and round burn holes. Gretchen tried to look past Ryan into the house, but the interior was dark. The sunlight blinded Ryan. He covered his eyes. "Make it quick," he said. "I gotta go. I'm gonna be sick."

Gretchen tried not to look at the silver ring piercing his lower lip.

Matt leaned against the stucco wall, outwardly relaxed and appearing casual. But he wasn't. "First, I have a complaint. You assaulted this woman."

Ryan glanced at Gretchen. "She chased me down the street and grabbed me. I was looking through the window, and she started yelling and coming after me."

Gretchen squirmed. He wasn't lying. When he said it like that . . .

"You struck her and knocked her down."

"She started it." Ryan said, a kid's whine in his voice.

"Let it go," Gretchen said to Matt.

"But he assaulted you. Don't you want to press charges?"

"No."

"Why not?"

Gretchen didn't know why not. All she knew was that she felt sorry for him. She'd worked with the afflicted before, serving meals and donating money when she could spare it. Ryan, although not exactly destitute, had a certain helplessness about him. He brought out the maternal side of her, as weird as that sounded.

Go figure. She felt sorry for the guy who'd slugged her.

She looked up at the crumbling pink stucco and wondered how many drug addicts lived inside. "I only wanted to talk to you about your mother," she said to Ryan. "You didn't have to hit me."

"I really think it's important that you press charges," Matt said.

"No."

"Can I go now? I'm really gonna be sick."

"Not yet," Matt said. "How did you learn that your mother died?" He didn't say *murdered*. Ryan was too messed up to wonder why he would be questioned if his mother had died from natural causes.

"One of her friends came by and told me."

"When?"

"Saturday . . . um . . . like afternoon."

"Who?"

"Britt somebody."

"What did she say?"

"That my mother had a heart attack."

"What kind of relationship did you have with your mother?"

Gretchen studied Matt. Cool, crisp, and professional but with the appearance of casualness. Even though he wasn't taking notes, she was sure he'd remember every word of the conversation.

"Not too good, but it was her fault. She didn't approve of my lifestyle. Wanted me to be more like her, like everybody else." Ryan's eyes were bloodshot, and his face was pale.

Who would want to look and feel this bad every day?

After several more questions, Ryan hunkered down on the side of the porch and retched.

Gretchen and Matt looked at each other.

"We'll have more questions later," Matt said to him.

Gretchen wasn't sure Ryan heard.

She stepped off the porch with Matt right behind her. "I don't understand you at all. I thought we were in agreement," he said in a low voice. "Wasn't the whole point to bring him in for questioning? The assault was a perfect opportunity. His mother was murdered and . . . I don't know why I'm even trying to explain it to you."

Gretchen frowned at him. Men! Talk about miscommunication. Or more like no communication. Other than a few Neanderthal grunts, none of them had the ability to express themselves. "I wish you had told me you were going to threaten him," she said, looking back. Ryan had disappeared inside.

"I wish you had told me what you wanted."

"You need to drop it," Gretchen said, wanting the last word. "I'm not pressing charges."

This time Matt scowled at her.

"What's going to happen to him?" She meant it philosophically, but Matt took her literally.

"If you aren't interested in pursuing charges? Nothing. I really want to know why he's been hiding. And why he struck you." Matt stopped by her car. "Why did he think you were a cop when he opened the door?"

Geez. Did she really have to go into this? She stopped and dug through her purse.

Matt leaned forward and peered inside. "Where's the little fluff ball?"

"He's with Nina. We're meeting at the shop. Here it is." She held up the Best in the West badge. "April gave me this and had pinned it on right before Ryan looked through the window. He saw it and automatically assumed—"

"So yesterday he thought he was punching a cop?" Matt shook his head.

The situation seemed to be getting worse.

Without waiting for a reply, Matt turned and started out down the street, whistling a tune.

"Where are you going?" Gretchen called after him.

"Back to my car."

"I'll give you a ride."

"I'm a terrible passenger."

"My driving was that bad?"

"I'm really just a bad passenger."

"We're miles away from your car."

"One point four miles, to be exact. Don't worry about me. If I need help, I'll call for a squad."

Look who's the impossible one now?

"Wait up." She trotted to catch up.

"I'd love company," Matt said. "But the logistics are complicated. For example, who'll drive your car?"

"You can give me a ride back."

"This gets sillier by the second."

"You started it." Using the same tactic Ryan had. Blame it on the other guy.

Matt raised his arms in a gesture of surrender. "Okay, let's go."

Gretchen looked around at the boarded-up houses and litter in the yards. "This isn't the best neighborhood to leave my car. Or to be walking."

"Anyone bothers us, I'll shoot them." He flashed that great smile, swung his head to check for cars, and jay-walked across Van Buren. Gretchen trailed him across, then quickly fell in next to him.

They silently cut around a slow pedestrian, and Matt's arm brushed against hers. She sucked in her breath, feeling young and foolish. Not a bad feeling. Not at all.

Matt glanced at her. "Are you finished at Mini Maize?"

"Probably today." Should she tell him about the miniature bloody weapons and the tiny, painted stains on some of the furnishings? Wouldn't he know about them from the crime scene analysis? "We found interesting things in the display cases. Weapons, fake blood on some of the furniture."

He nodded. "We assumed that was part of some crazy doll collector's scene." Another grin. "Charlie's prints were the only ones on them. They have nothing to do with her murder."

"I disagree," Gretchen said. What else was new? They disagreed on so much. Matt might send jolts of electricity through her entire nervous system, but his wattage wasn't entirely compatible with hers. Kind of like putting cables on the wrong battery terminals.

"Let's have your take on it then," Matt said. "As if I'm not going to hear it anyway."

"I think she realized that she'd been poisoned and tried to make it to the door. She took the time to knock the display over as a clue, in case she didn't survive. There's something strange about the display. I can't put my finger on it though. Oh, I know—" Gretchen stopped, snapped her fingers as though she just thought of it. She waited for him to stop walking, too. "Maybe it's because of the miniature peanut butter jar. You know the one? It was under her body."

His jaw dropped open. "Where did you get that information?"

"I know who I *didn't* get it from."

They approached Matt's unmarked car. Daisy was nowhere in sight. She must be at the audition, if the audition was real. It was hard to tell what was reality and what was fantasy when it came to the homeless woman.

Gretchen looked at Matt. She had thrown out a hasty

theory, but it made sense. "I'm sure you're right," she said. "The display case has nothing to do with Charlie's or Sara's murder. Nothing at all."

"You can't fool me. I hear the sarcasm in your voice. I'm not your ordinary insensitive male, you know. I have feelings." Matt opened the passenger door for her. "Hop in."

15

"Nina and I had breakfast at a dog-friendly restaurant," Britt said, laughing. "Can you believe it?" Britt and Nina were back at work at Mini Maize. If you could call it work.

Nina laughed, too. "The restaurant had a patio with a fire hydrant fountain and our waitress served mutt muffins. Not to us, of course, but the dogs loved them. Britt and I had coffee and people muffins."

"I'll be talking in my sleep again tonight," Britt said laughing along. "Or barking."

"You really should see a hypnotist," Nina relied. "You have to be losing lots of sleep."

Nina, Gretchen decided, could benefit from a little hypnosis herself. Her aunt put all her attention and affection into animals. She needed a male companion to ground her. Although she certainly looked content enough at the moment.

Tutu and Nimrod played at their feet. Enrico watched from the safety of Nina's leg, peeking out beside her painted toenails, snarling a warning whenever the other dogs came too close.

April swung through the door, carrying her usual bag of subs. "I lost another five pounds," she announced, setting the bag on the counter.

"Five pounds a day is incredible," Gretchen said, not really believing it was possible. But April *did* look thinner.

"Caroline can't come," Nina said. "She has a tip on a

collection of antique dolls that's for sale. She's driving to Fountain Hills to look at them."

The piles on the card table were still as they had been yesterday. After Gretchen's encounter with Ryan, all work on the room boxes had ceased for the day. "Let's each take a room box," she said, "and see what we come up with. I think we can wrap this up in a few hours."

They settled in. Gretchen was continually amazed at Charlie's gift for interior design with the tiny, detailed pieces, the unity of her composition, and the precision of the scale.

Gretchen paused from her work on the backyard scene to watch Britt and Nina. Britt had chosen the Victorian bedroom scene, carefully placing each item where she thought it might have gone. By the hint of a smile on her face, Gretchen could tell she truly enjoyed working with the miniatures.

"I'm finished," April called, proudly showing them the orchard and church scene. "I found a blue velvet hat in my pile. I'm going to add it to the leftovers, since I don't know where it goes. I think it was made from a cardboard pattern. Isn't it cute?"

"Charlie used simple household supplies for many of her projects," Britt said to April, who hung on every word. "She was very creative."

"Making minis would be fun, especially making the little dolls," April said. "I'd love to try it."

"I'm starting a baby sculpting class soon. Why don't you sign up?"

"Count me in."

"Here comes someone I'd like you to meet," Britt called out, looking toward the door. "My daughter, Melany."

Britt's daughter was in her twenties, slightly overweight, and wore no makeup, not even mascara. She was frumpy next to her mother, who bustled over to give her daughter a kiss on the cheek. Gretchen couldn't see much resemblance—Britt with her tailored blouse and immaculate French twist, Melany in rumpled shorts and a top that was way too tight.

"Bernard's been taken to the hospital," Melany said to her mother, an almost hostile expression on her face. "I thought you'd want to know."

"What happened?" Britt clutched her throat.

"A jar of bug juice exploded."

Had Gretchen heard her correctly? Bug juice? It sounded like an insect killer, or a name for summer camp juice drinks.

"Bug juice is a concoction Bernard uses," Melany said when she noticed the other women's lost expressions. "It turns new wood a grayish brown. He uses it to age wood details for his dollhouses."

"I warned him several times about mixing chemicals," Britt said. "Is he going to be all right?"

"I think so, but his arm was injured." The coldness was back in her voice. "The bug juice hit like shrapnel from a bomb. I had stopped at his house to deliver the miniature orchid bouquet for a wedding display, and his neighbor told me what happened."

"How awful," Britt said.

"What is this bug juice made from," Gretchen asked, "that it has the capacity to explode?"

"To get the effect he's looking for in the wood, he uses an old-timer's recipe," Britt explained. "He puts rusty nails in a glass jar, then pours vinegar over them. He's supposed to put the lid on loosely and leave it for a few weeks. If the lid is too tight, it can produce a gas, and the pressure builds."

"The poor old man," April said.

Britt picked up her purse and slung it over her shoulder. "Melany and I will check on him," she said. "We'll let you know."

After Britt and Melany left, Gretchen told Nina and April about the visit to Ryan's house.

"Do the police think he murdered his mother?" Nina asked.

"I don't know. We'll have to wait and see what happens, but I assume he's a prime suspect, especially because he's an addict."

"Let's take a break and drive over to Joseph's Dream Dolls," April said. "I love that place, and Joseph could use some company. He was so distraught when he came by."

Gretchen picked up a miniature lamp. "Joseph was at the parade on Saturday, but he wasn't here at Charlie's. Mom said he had been invited, so why was he walking in the opposite direction when I saw him? I'd really like to ask him a few questions."

"Let's finish here first," Nina suggested.

Twenty minutes later, they had completed the room boxes. Gretchen looked at the finished scenes: a Victorian bedroom and sitting room, a man's dressing room and bedroom, an orchard near a church, and a dilapidated backyard. How did the tiny peanut butter jar found under Charlie's body fit in? Gretchen glanced over at the fifth room box, at its hasty construction. She wondered how it would have fit in with the others. If only Charlie had had time to finish it.

After taking pictures with her cell phone of the completed settings, Gretchen tucked Nimrod into her purse.

Nina had her hands full with Tutu and her current client, Enrico. Enrico watched the action suspiciously from his Mexican tapestry purse, ready to defend himself from the entire world if necessary. *Short-dog syndrome,* Gretchen thought. Like short-man syndrome. A Napoleon complex.

Not that Matt had that problem, although he wasn't very tall. Gretchen, at five eight, could look right into his dark and stormy eyes without tilting her head much at all. Why was she thinking about him? *Geez. Get over it*. Did every thought have to lead back to the detective? Did it?

"I'll drive," crash-prone April announced.

"I'll drive," Nina said immediately.

"Let's go with Nina," Gretchen said. No one in their right mind would drive with Fender Bender Mama.

Nina darted through traffic in her red vintage Impala. She'd had the chrome polished recently, and it glistened in the warm Arizona sun.

Gretchen found herself wedged into the backseat with the canines. Between the three dogs, they'd managed to streak and smudge both back passenger windows. Gretchen's clothes were covered in dog hair.

She had given up on keeping the dogs from racing across her lap. Any minute now she expected Enrico to lunge for her throat. He stared at her with his beady little eyes, waiting for her to make a wrong move.

Why am I the one in the backseat?

April glanced back. "Sorry," she said to Gretchen. "But I really don't fit back there. Maybe in a day or two when I lose more weight."

"No problem," Gretchen said, not meaning it.

"I think we could solve this case," April said. "Break it wide open. Let's do a little digging and see what happens."

"We're the Mod Squad," Nina said, veering around a slow car ahead of them.

Gretchen slid sideways. Enrico snarled.

"Charlie's Angels," April said.

"Without Charlie," Gretchen joined in.

"Detective Matt Albright can be Charlie," Nina said.

"No," Gretchen said. "He can't." She saw Nina and April give each other a glance.

Nina checked her rearview mirror. "Oh, no," she said, slowing down.

"Yikes," April said, glancing in her side mirror.

Nina changed to the right lane and came to a stop along the curb. Gretchen looked back and saw a Phoenix squad car pull in behind them. "Were you speeding?" she asked Nina.

Nina shrugged. "I wasn't paying attention." She shuffled through her purse, rolled down her window, and stuck her driver's license out.

The cop bent down and studied each of them through Nina's window. All three dogs watched out the back driver's side window. Enrico growled. The cop shot him a no-nonsense look. "Do you know why I stopped you?" he said to Nina.

"I'm not sure, but I know I wasn't speeding," Nina said, smiling her widest and brightest. "I can see an orange aura surrounding you, Officer." Nina used a long, polished nail to draw a circle in the air around his torso. "That means you're confused. This is all a misunderstanding."

The officer frowned. "I need your identification, too." He looked right at Gretchen.

"As you can see, I wasn't driving. I'm in the backseat. Why do you need mine?"

"Hand it over."

Gretchen did as he asked. He stared at her for a minute, then studied her license. "Yours, too," he said to April.

"I'm calling my attorney," April replied.

"Call whoever you want," he said. "After you show me some identification."

"I don't have any," April said.

"Wait here," he said.

"Auras don't lie," Nina called out the window. "You'll see."

"What are you doing?" April said to Nina. "Stop with that mumbo jumbo, or he'll lock us away."

"Or worse," Gretchen said. "He'll think you're drunk."

"Should we tell him we're undercover?" April said. "Charlie's Angels don't get tickets."

Nina tittered, and that started April off. Hee-hee. Haw-haw.

"This isn't funny," Gretchen said. "Why did he want my license?"

"And what's this attorney thing?" Nina said to April. "You don't have a lawyer."

"I wanted to intimidate him."

"Shhh, here he comes."

"Your brake light isn't working," he said. "Step out of the car, please. You, too." He looked at Gretchen.

"How about me?" April said. "Should I come?"

"Yes, ma'am. And take the dogs with you, especially that one." He looked at Enrico. "Leave your purses where they are."

Another squad car with lights flashing and siren wailing pulled in ahead of Nina's Impala. The women stepped out, Gretchen carrying Nimrod and Nina clutching Tutu and Enrico. April had her cell phone pressed to her ear before the car doors slammed shut. Another squad car arrived.

"This isn't good," Gretchen said. "Something's seriously wrong."

April gave someone on the phone their location. "Hurry," she said before hanging up.

"Come with me," the first Phoenix police officer said.

He walked them to his car and opened the back door. "You can wait in here."

They crawled in, first Gretchen, then April. Nina squeezed

in. The cop slammed the door and walked away. Gretchen tried to open the door on her side. "It's locked," she said, although she already knew that.

"We're trapped," Nina said, holding Tutu and Enrico on her lap.

"We weren't going to make a run for it, anyway," April said. "This is unnecessary brutality. Look! They've left the windows open an inch. How nice. They're treating us like animals."

"Who did you call?" Gretchen asked.

"You'll see."

Gretchen fought against a wave of claustrophobia. The women looked through the cage separating the front from the back of the squad car and watched what was happening.

Two officers were searching Nina's car. They opened the trunk, moved seats, checked the glove compartment, the engine. Another went through their purses, examining each item. Nina's bag interested the officer the most. He pulled out several wee-wee pads that she carried for doggy potty stops and began ripping them apart, studying the contents.

"What in the world . . . ," Nina said from the far side of April.

One of them slid under the Chevy.

"What on earth are they doing?" Nina said, no longer kidding around.

"Searching for something," Gretchen said. "They aren't going to find anything, are they, Nina?"

"Other than a lot of dog paraphernalia? No."

"I don't think that's the kind of paraphernalia they're looking for," Gretchen said.

"Well, mumbo jumbo queen," April said to Nina. "You tell us what's going on."

"The police officers' auras are all orange. I'm pretty sure that means they don't know what they're doing."

"You're pretty sure?" April groaned. "You don't even know what the different colors mean."

"Sure I do. Most of the time. These are unusual circumstances."

"How long can this take?" Gretchen said, careful not to whine. She wasn't a Charlie's Angel. The Angels would have found a way out of this situation before they were locked up inside a squad car.

Being stuffed in a backseat with April, Nina, and three dogs wasn't her idea of a fun time. She watched the officers continue to search the Chevy. A blue car pulled up on the other side of the street, made a U-turn, and parked in front of the growing line of vehicles. Gretchen groaned. "What's *he* doing here?"

"I called him," April said with a big grin. "Would you look at those biceps? He can be my Charlie any day."

Gretchen tried to slink down in the seat. Matt strolled to the front of the squad car where they were imprisoned. Hands on hips, he shook his head. April gave him a wave and a giggle.

"I thought we needed help," she said.

"Do we ever," Nina agreed.

One of the officers approached Matt, and they went into a huddle. Matt looked surprised when he turned and stared at them. Then he made a phone call and paced back and forth in front of the Impala.

"What's he doing?" Nina asked.

"Arranging for jail cells?" Gretchen suggested.

"Oh, get outta here," April said. "He's our protector. They can't arrest us."

"Here he comes," Nina said.

The back door swung open. "I have to search all of you," Matt said, his eyes twinkling with mischief. "Then you're free to go."

"Me first," April said. "You're so naughty." Nina practically fell out of the car as April scooted toward her.

Gretchen rose from the squad car last. "Is this your idea of a joke?"

"What?" He grinned. "You think I did this?"

The officer who had stopped Nina's car walked over with their driver's licenses. "I'm letting you go this time," he said to Nina. "You're not getting a ticket, but get that brake light fixed." He nodded to Matt. "We'll be going."

Matt nodded back.

The cop's eyes shifted to Gretchen. "I'd watch this one," he said. "Yesterday we had a formal complaint filed against her. She had an altercation with a passerby not too far from here."

"Makes it hard for her to have been in Mexico, doesn't it?" Matt commented.

"We'll be going," the cop managed to say after mulling over the timeline.

Nobody said anything until the squad cars edged back into traffic.

"They can't stop us and search Nina's car without reasonable cause," Gretchen said.

"Yah," April said

"They had a tip," Matt said. "A car matching this description with three women inside was suspected of being on a drug run from the Mexican border."

"What?" Gretchen couldn't believe it.

"Rocky Point, to be exact," he said. "Did you snorkel in the Sea of Cortez while you were there? That's my favorite thing to do."

Gretchen stared. "Very funny." What was he, the class clown? She'd been smashed in the back of a squad car while all her personal belongings were searched. And he was making jokes.

"There aren't that many red vintage Impalas running around the city," Matt explained. "You weren't hard to find. The broken brake light gave them a legal reason to stop you and search the car."

"That's outrageous," Nina chimed in. "Where did this supposed tip come from?"

Matt shrugged, and from the firm set to the detective's jaw and his penchant for secrecy, Gretchen knew he wouldn't tell them if he knew. "You're free to go." He held the front passenger door of the Impala open for April. But his eyes never left Gretchen.

"Did you see him checking you out?" April said when they were back on the road. "He has the hots for you bad."

"Who knew all three of us were together?" Gretchen said, ignoring her friend's comment. "We didn't know until the last minute which car we were taking from the shop."

"The cops picked the wrong car," Nina said smugly. "I told you they were confused."

Gretchen shook her head. "I don't think it was a case of mistaken identity. Someone's been watching us," she said. It was the only logical conclusion.

By the silence in the car, Gretchen knew her friends were thinking over her last comment. They rode the rest of the way to Joseph's without speaking. All Gretchen could hear was the sound of dogs panting.

She wiped gooey drool from her leg.

16

Instead of the pink shirt and yellow shorts he had been wearing at the parade, today Joseph wore a purple polo shirt and khaki shorts. A pair of pink Crocs adorned his feet, and diamond studs glistened from both ears.

Nina and her canine entourage disappeared down the street under the guise of doggy exercise. Gretchen knew Nina really wanted to partake in her favorite pastime: window shopping.

"Miniature dolls are against the back wall," Joseph called to April when he saw her wandering around. With a backward wave, she hustled off in search of tantalizing little gems to lust over.

Gretchen couldn't believe the two Charlie's Angels investigators had abandoned her in pursuit of pleasure. She sighed. "Can we talk privately?" she asked Joseph.

"Follow me." He led her through the busy shop, offered her a seat in his office, and sat down beside her. "Wasn't it awful about Charlie?" he said. "I heard you were at Mini Maize when it happened, and I'd hoped to talk to you when I stopped by. Please tell me what you know."

Gretchen told him how the group of partygoers had discovered Charlie's body on the shop floor and the ensuing rush inside.

"Your mother told me your family is reorganizing her last room boxes," he said when she finished.

"The room boxes are ready."

She pulled out her camera phone. "There are four of them."

"The doll community has lost some real talent," he said wistfully. Joseph reached in his shirt pocket, pulled out a piece of square plastic, peeled the plastic apart, popped something into his mouth, and chewed.

Gretchen looked at the piece of plastic on the desk.

"Nicotine gum," he explained when he saw her watching. "I'm trying to quit smoking. Time number six."

Nicotine! Was nicotine gum potent enough to kill? Possibly. But how much? Could Joseph have known about its potential to kill? And if so, how would he have concentrated enough nicotine from gum to make it lethal? He couldn't have just plopped a wad of gum in her coffee. Common sense told her it was impossible.

"Let me see those pictures." He took the phone from her and hunched over it, chewing his gum and clicking through the photographs. "What's this?" He held it out so she could see the crudely constructed fifth room box.

"It was on the floor, along with the other room boxes."

April joined them, taking a look at the picture, then sitting on the corner of the desk. "We don't have any furniture or furnishings left to fill another room box. Looks like this one was barely started."

Gretchen had to force herself to concentrate on the conversation. She would worry about Joseph's nicotine addiction later. He wasn't the only person in Phoenix using the antismoking medication.

"It's the beginning of a kitchen." Joseph rubbed his goatee.

"A kitchen?" said Gretchen and April simultaneously.

"Don't you women cook?" Joseph said. "You know what a kitchen is? One of those places where meals are prepared and eaten?"

"It does have a rather flowery border," April said.

Gretchen looked closely at the room box photo. "Those are little apples and teapots bordering the ceiling."

April adjusted her reading glasses on the tip of her nose. "They are! Definitely kitchen wallpaper."

"The sink sketch would have tipped me off first thing," Joseph said, enjoying himself.

"Charlie was designing a kitchen?" Gretchen remembered the miniature peanut butter jar found under her body. A common kitchen staple, but a deadly one if you happened to have a severe peanut allergy. It didn't make sense. What had Charlie been up to? "Did you see a miniature refrigerator or stove when we were gathering things up?" Gretchen asked April.

"Nothing even close."

"Would you know what kitchen appliances looked like if you saw them?" quipped Joseph, the comedian.

"Very funny, wise guy," April said. "We would have figured it out eventually."

Nina reappeared with dogs and shopping bags just as Gretchen remembered the street signs and hauled them out of her purse.

"We found four street signs on the floor," she said, handing them to Joseph. "There's no way of knowing which one goes with which box. We'll have to guess. Unless you've heard of them."

"You found these on Charlie's floor?"

Gretchen nodded.

"I know one of the addresses."

"Which one?" Gretchen asked.

Joseph held up the sign that read Number ninety-two Second Street. "Is this a joke?"

"What are you talking about?"

"I'll never forget this street number, even though it's

been years. I did a paper on it in high school. Are you sure you found this at Charlie's?"

"Yes," Gretchen said. "What's wrong?"

"Number ninety-two Second Street is in Massachusetts. And I can even tell you that it belongs with the Victorian bedroom setting, the one with the mohair sofa."

"Spill it, Joseph," April said.

"That's the address," he said, "where Lizzie Borden allegedly used a hatchet on her parents. You remember the little ditty. It was a jump rope rhyme. 'Lizzie Borden took an axe and gave her mother forty whacks. When she saw what she had done, she gave her father forty-one.'"

"That explains the miniature axe," Nina said with a little shiver. "We put it in the wrong room box."

"The reality was," Joseph continued, "that her mother had been struck eighteen or nineteen times and her father eleven."

"You can't tell from the photographs, but there are blood spots on the sofa and on the wall," April added.

"I have a feeling," Nina said, using a dramatic tone, "that the discoveries here today are very important."

"Not one of your feelings again!" April said.

Nina's chin came up a few inches, a sure sign that she'd taken April's comment to heart. "The room box where the Bordens were murdered and the unfinished kitchen are clues. You have to believe me." She frowned at April.

"Thanks for the information," Gretchen said to Joseph, taking back the signs. "I'm not sure why Charlie would make such a morbid scene."

"We'll never know now," Joseph said.

Nina was pulling away from the shop when Gretchen remembered what she wanted to ask Joseph. "Wait, Nina," she said quickly. Nina hit the brakes. Gretchen rolled down the window, catching him about to reenter the shop. "I forgot to ask," she called out. "Were you at Charlie's shop Saturday morning?"

"No," Joseph said. "Last time I saw her was early last week. What makes you think that?"

"Weren't you invited to her party last Saturday?"

"Yes, but I couldn't make it, which I'm glad about, considering what happened. Seeing her like that would have been devastating for me."

"I thought I saw you at the parade," Gretchen pressed on.

Joseph shook his head. "No," he said, firmly. "I wasn't there."

"Break in traffic," Nina chimed in. "Got to go."

"Toodles!" April called as they cut into traffic.

Gretchen rolled up the window and felt the chill of the Impala's air-conditioning already kicking in. Or maybe the goose bumps on her arms were caused by something else. "He was lying," she said as they left Joseph's Dream Dolls behind.

"It really *is* a kitchen," April protested on his behalf, misunderstanding Gretchen. "Once he pointed it out, I could tell. It's definitely a kitchen."

"Gretchen's talking about the street sign," Nina said. "Why would he say it was the Lizzie Borden murder scene if it wasn't?"

Gretchen tried to clarify her statement about Joseph's lie. "That's not—"

What was the use? Nina was only interested in mothering dogs and reading tarot cards. April's main ambition in life was blowing one diet after another and gossiping with the doll club members.

"There's a sub shop," April shouted, pointing to the left, her finger almost in Nina's face. "Stop."

Gretchen's aunt blasted right by, pretending not to hear.

17

Joseph enters the church and crosses the lobby, hoping the meeting is almost over. He considers going in and joining them. What if he shared his problem with the entire group?

Too dangerous.

Joseph dips two fingers into holy water and crosses himself.

He's a wreck.

Gretchen Birch saw him! She can place him at the parade, within several blocks of Charlie's shop. He can't think of anything else.

What a fool he is. In more ways than one.

Charlie had it right all along. You can't fight your genetic makeup. Bad blood, she said, the outcome is inevitable. You'll self-destruct.

Thanks for the encouragement, friend.

He remembers the anger churning inside of him like a whirl of dust. "Look at you," Charlie had said as she watched him suck his life out through a menthol cigarette. "You have an addictive personality. Face it. You can't change. You can't stop the motion."

He still feels the hurt.

Tough as nails, the brassy broad had lost her perspective on humanity. She'd lost her compassion, and she'd given up on people after Sara died. That crackhead son of hers didn't help her view any, either.

Joseph enters the church interior, bends a knee, makes the sign of the cross, and slides into a pew.

A derelict from the street is the only other worshipper in this house of the Lord.

The church is soundless. The air smells like the bum two pews ahead of him.

Joseph tries to pray but can't. He kneels on the riser, folds his hands, and squeezes his eyes shut. Nothing.

He has dressed carefully to come here, curbing his appetite for attention. He's wearing all brown. Different shades. The same khaki pants from earlier today, a shirt the color of Phoenix gravel, brown sandals. His propensity for loudness is what got him into this mess. Those big, look-at-me colors. *Here I come,* he likes to say without words.

You can't help what you are.

Stop with the excuses. Isn't that part of recovery? No more excuses?

The clothes didn't do it. You did. Six months without a drink, and now this.

Joseph hears a murmur of voices outside the lobby, near the meeting room. Carl will stay behind to make sure the room is in the same condition he found it in before the meeting. He will turn off the lights and lock up for the group. Responsible Carl. Solid, perfect, example-setting Carl.

Believe in the power of God. Sit quietly when in doubt.

Joseph reviews the principles of Alcoholics Anonymous. The Twelve Steps.

But his mind wanders, and he tries to remember the night before Charlie died. He wants a cigarette so badly his entire body is trembling. He can't remember. More minutes of his life unaccounted for.

Wasn't it the blackouts that finally scared him enough to seek help for his drinking problem? He could live with the morning-after sickness, but not remembering . . .

The massive church doors open and close several times, and the voices die away.

He has the list in his pocket, one of the steps. It contains every person he has harmed with his actions.

One more to add.

But there will be no making amends this time. The woman is dead.

Joseph rises slowly and moves back up the aisle like an old man.

Carl turns from the meeting room door, and their eyes meet.

Joseph thinks his sponsor can see right into his very soul. Carl's face is a sea of tranquillity and, for a moment, Joseph hates him for it. "Joseph." Carl acknowledges his existence, then waits.

Joseph almost breaks and runs. Sweat seeps into his shirt. He's come this far, might as well finish what he started.

"Help me," he says. "I'm in trouble."

· 18 ·

Contests: How could the doll community exist without awards for excellence? Collectors and dealers alike anxiously await these announcements. Competition is friendly but fierce. Judges with scorecards move among the exhibits. The crowd's excitement builds while the contestants covet the grand prize. Winning means recognition, blue ribbons to display, prize money. Sometimes the top award leads to a feature in a reputable doll magazine seen by thousands of readers.

—From *World of Dolls* by Caroline Birch

Gretchen took a deep breath, savoring the fresh, early morning desert air. She wore hiking boots, a baseball cap, and binoculars strapped around her neck. She had already added many of Phoenix's local birds to her list: rock wrens, roadrunners, black-throated sparrows, and the elusive Gila woodpecker that builds its nest in saguaro cactus holes. She wanted to burn off her tension with a rigorous climb up Camelback Mountain. If she discovered a new bird, it would be a bonus.

The morning was still too chilly for snakes to be slithering about, and that suited Gretchen just fine. Bugs and snakes creeped her out, especially the poisonous kind that dwelled in the Sonoran Desert.

She strode along the footpath to the trailhead, past a creosote bush in full yellow bloom and a thicket of teddy bear cholla dominating a rocky slope. The teddy bear cholla looked furry and cuddly, but Gretchen had learned the hard way that it wasn't as huggable as it appeared. She had been careless and brushed against one of these silvery, tall cacti. Its spikes had reminded her that only those with very developed defense systems survived the harshness of the Sonoran Desert. It was always best to admire desert beauty from a safe distance.

February was a marvelous month in Phoenix, she decided, veering to the left and following the path to Summit Trail. Spring rain showers cleansed the desert dust away, blossoms sprouted from the tips of the different varieties of cacti, and the sun hadn't yet baked the earth hard and brittle.

She lost track of time as she began to maneuver over slippery rocks. The incline became steeper, and she dug in. At last she stood at the summit, looking off over the awakening city. This was the top of the world for Gretchen, a place to hide and think.

She sat down and studied the sheer, red cliffs, vegetation cropping out in the most unlikely places.

Her thoughts turned to Charlie Maize's death and the people involved in the doll shop owner's life. Why had Joseph lied about attending the parade? What was the story with Charlie's druggie son, Ryan? Did the craggy old man, Bernard, have designs on Charlie's shop? And Britt? What about her? Something about that woman seemed weird.

A roadrunner watched boldly from a few yards away. When Gretchen remained motionless, it went back to its task of hunting lizards. The answers to her questions didn't come to her on the top of the mountain, as she thought they might, not even a whisper to calm the disquiet she felt.

Gretchen hiked back down the red clay mountain and joined Nimrod and Wobbles for breakfast, opening cans of dog and cat food for them, toasting a bagel and pouring coffee for herself.

Then she went to work on a client's antique doll. Gretchen fished through a drawer and found a white leather glove. After studying the doll's kid body, she set about preserving the doll's original body as closely as possible: stuffing sawdust into the doll's ripped torso, carefully cutting a piece of the glove into an oval and gluing it on.

She was putting away the repair supplies when she heard her mother call out a greeting.

"Hey," Gretchen raised her voice. "I'm in the workshop."

"You're up early." Caroline plopped down on a stool. "It's good to be home. I'm staying put, no more book tours for a while." She picked up the doll that Gretchen had just finished. "Nice job on the kid body."

"Thanks."

"Evie Rosemont called yesterday. She wanted to know how the room boxes were coming along."

"Do I know Evie Rosemont?" Gretchen asked, trying to place her.

Caroline laughed. "You'd remember if you did. She's a hoot. Never stops talking. Wears enormous hats. She must have hundreds of them, all displayed on her walls. And antique shoes everywhere. Rooms of hats and shoes, a massive collection. Want me to take you over? It's worth seeing."

"Yes, I'd like to meet her." Gretchen remembered a woman outside of Charlie's shop the day of the parade, the day Charlie died. The woman had worn a big straw hat and had been the first one to speak to Bernard about unlocking the door. He had called her Evie.

Gretchen retrieved the street signs from her purse, which was on the floor with Nimrod cuddled inside. "Joseph knew the location of the Second Street sign," she said, relating the details.

"Charlie was really acting out her frustration with her sister's death," Caroline said. "Lizzie Borden was acquitted of the most brutal double murder of all time. The crime was never solved. Did you know that?"

"No. I thought she killed them."

"We'll never know."

"That's exactly what Joseph said when I wondered why Charlie would put together such an awful scene."

"Let's find the dolls that go with the room boxes today and finish up. I'm taking a camera along for the after pictures. Your camera phone takes okay pictures, but the colors aren't as vivid as they could be."

Right, Gretchen thought. *Make sure you can see all the blood splatters.*

She watched her mother head for the kitchen, trailed by the pint-sized puppy and Wobbles, who was trying to remain aloof but failing. Gretchen was sure her mother fed table scraps to the pets when she wasn't looking. Why else the intense devotion?

Gretchen took a quick shower and was drying her hair when her cell phone rang. The caller introduced himself as the manager from Gretchen's bank. "A courtesy call really," he said. "We aren't required to do this, but your mother is a good customer, and we realize you are new to our banking services."

"Is something wrong?"

"You're account is overdrawn."

"Impossible!"

"By quite a lot."

"That can't be right."

"I'm afraid it's correct."

"Well, how much?"

When he gave her the amount, she almost dropped the phone.

"Would you like to transfer funds from your savings account?"

"Yes, please," she said weakly. She'd have nothing left to her name after that transaction.

"Maybe you'd like to stop in and go over your account. You were fine until you wrote a substantial check recently."

"Who did I make it out to?"

The bank manager gave her a name. A name she knew. She'd get her money back if she had to beat it out of him dollar by dollar.

And she knew exactly where to find him.

Gretchen stomped across the street, dodging traffic, intent on the building ahead. She heard a wolf whistle behind her but refused to turn and look. Men! Sex-starved animals, chasing anyone in a halter top. She wasn't in the mood.

"Gretchen," she heard coming from the same general vicinity as the whistle. She flung around. Matt Albright bounded toward her with a big flashy white smile. Even in her anger, she appreciated his devilish good looks and replaced her scowl with a small smile. He was just the man to help her.

"I need you," Gretchen said. "Right now."

"Really?" he sounded surprised and hopeful. "I thought you were an Amazon woman, treading fearlessly through this wild jungle called life. But you *need* me?" He puffed his chest like a he-man.

"Not like that, Tarzan."

"We hardly know each other," he feigned shock. "But if you insist, we can go to my place."

"This is a criminal problem. You have to arrest someone."

"Oh," he pretended to deflate with disappointment. "Who are we arresting?"

"Follow me."

She spun through the revolving doors of Saint Joseph's Hospital, inquired about a room number at the front desk, found the elevator, and punched the Up button.

"Are you going to clue me in?" Matt said when she finally came to a stop while waiting for the elevator.

"I dropped my checkbook at Mini Maize the day Charlie died. A horrible old . . ." Gretchen could hardly speak she was so upset.

"Take a deep breath. Relax."

"A horrible old man found it and returned it to me."

"Horrible? He sounds like a Good Samaritan."

"He returned it *after* he wrote himself a big, fat check. My bank actually paid it, even though the transaction overdrew my account. I had to use my savings to cover the overdraft. Why didn't they let it bounce? Now I've lost everything." Gretchen should have told the manager that the check had been forged. Wasn't that the right thing to do? Yet, she hesitated. Forgery was a serious offense, and he was so old. All she wanted was her money back. Turning him in would be a last resort.

Matt scowled. "I still don't quite understand. The guy's in the hospital?"

The elevator arrived. Gretchen, still in the lead, pushed the floor number. "He deserved everything he got," she said, hands on hips.

"He deserved what? Please don't tell me that you put him in here?"

Gretchen gave the detective a narrow-eyed look. "Of course not. He was concocting something called bug juice, and it blew up in his face."

"I see."

She could tell he didn't see at all. "Follow me," she said.

"Don't I always?"

That gave Gretchen pause. Maybe he *was* always following her.

When they found the hospital room, Bernard looked like an extra from the movie *The Mummy*. His face was completely swathed in bandages. Gretchen knew it was him by the visible mop of white hair, though his mustache was hidden by the bandages. His name on the chart at the foot of the bed helped, too.

"He's sleeping," Matt said, still sounding puzzled. "I'm really lacking enough background information to handle this properly."

"Not for long." Gretchen thumped the patient's shoulder.

Bernard's eyes flew open.

"You stole my money, you old buzzard." It took all her control to keep her hands off his neck. "I want it back."

"You said you never use your account."

That's not exactly what she had said to him when he dropped off her checkbook. She had meant that she hadn't missed the checkbook because there was so little money in the bank. "So you thought you'd keep it active for me?" she screeched.

"Hold on." Matt said, trying to step into the middle of the scene and direct traffic.

"She called the cops?" Bernard's eyes grew wide when he saw Matt. "I only borrowed the money. Honest. I was going to return it long before she even knew it was gone."

"Surprise, I checked." Gretchen said. "And I want it back. Right now."

"Sir," Matt said, managing to squeeze between them. "Is that correct? Did you forge her name and remove funds from her account?"

"He sure did."

"I'm asking *him*, Gretchen."

Gretchen watched the old man's eyes. He wanted to deny it, she could tell, but he'd already admitted it. "I thought I deserved a reward," he said. "You know, for finding the checkbook and returning it to its rightful owner."

"Read him his rights," Gretchen demanded. "Arrest him."

"Where is the money?" Matt asked Bernard with a cold, hard stare. Gretchen never wanted to be on the receiving end of *that* look.

Bernard's eyes slid to a metal cabinet next to the bed. "In there. In my wallet. You can have it back."

Gretchen lunged for the cabinet, found the wallet, and counted out a large wad of bills. "All here," she said with a huge sigh of relief. It was all the money she had in the world, and she had almost lost it.

Bernard watched through slits in the bandages.

"What exactly happened to you?" Matt asked him.

"Explosion. Someone's trying to kill me." He nodded in Gretchen's direction. "Might be her, for all I know. Did you ever see anybody that mad before? I think she has an anger management problem."

Gretchen wanted to shake the scrawny weasel.

Matt glanced at Gretchen. Now that the confrontation was over, he had a hint of sparkle back in his eyes.

"You screwed the cover on too tight," Gretchen told him. She looked at the quizzical expression on Matt's face. "Britt Gleeland told me about it."

"I can't stand that woman," Bernard said. "She doesn't know anything."

"At least she came and visited you." Gretchen thought Britt must be the only one in Phoenix who liked the man well enough to care. What a disagreeable personality.

"That woman better *not* show up here."

"But I thought—"

"I know better than to close the lid tight," Bernard said, interrupting. "I left it loose. I've been making juice for years, and I know I didn't do it wrong. Someone added in another chemical to give it more power."

"Why would anyone try to kill you?" Matt asked.

"Because. That's why. Just because." Through the white wrapping, Gretchen could see his lips tighten down. Bernard wasn't talking to them anymore.

"What's going on in here?" a nurse said from the doorway.

"This police officer and young lady are bullying me around. I want them to leave."

Nimrod chose that moment to peek out of Gretchen's purse. The nurse glared. "I'm calling security if you aren't gone in thirty seconds."

Matt didn't even challenge the nurse. He apologized for the intrusion and escorted Gretchen out of the room.

"Don't you outrank a nurse?" Gretchen wanted to know on the way down in the elevator.

Matt chuckled. "No one on the police force would think of tangling with a head nurse. And I lost my advantage when the mutt made his appearance."

"Bernard Waites should be on your list of suspects."

"He seems to think someone's trying to kill him."

"Yeah, right."

"He took quite a hit. I checked his medical records earlier. He's lucky to be alive."

Gretchen stared at Matt. "You knew he was here all along."

"I knew about his condition, not about the theft."

"Were you following me?"

"I was leaving the hospital when you came up. I thought you were following me." Matt grinned at her.

"Did you interrogate him?"

"I questioned him right after Charlie died."

"That's how he knew you were a cop."

"He lied in the original report he gave Brandon Kline. He said he hadn't seen Charlie since the day before, but he had. Several witnesses saw him at the shop very early that morning."

"Ahah!"

"Another witness saw Charlie alive and well afterward."

"Oh."

"Bernard's in worse shape than you seem to think."

Was that true? Had she really bullied a severely injured old man? But look what he had done. "Why didn't you stop me if he's so sick?"

"And spoil the fun?"

Gretchen cracked a weak smile. "I was awful, wasn't I?"

"Out of control."

"I'm pressing charges."

"You should."

"Does that mean he's on the top of your list of suspects?"

"Everyone's on my list."

"Even me?"

Matt grinned. "Especially you."

· 19 ·

When Gretchen and Caroline arrived at Mini Maize with Nimrod, April was waiting in her car. She wore a loose, white sundress covered with yellow sunflowers and really did look thinner.

Nina and Britt swooped in right behind them with Tutu and Enrico. All the dogs ran off playing. Gretchen picked up the crude, unfinished room box that they had originally rejected and added it to the others in the display.

"It doesn't exactly fit," Britt remarked. "I'd throw it away."

"Nina thinks it's an important component. We'll see what we can do with it."

"I'm off," Britt announced, hugging Nina. "Any word yet on Charlie's funeral?"

Caroline answered her. "The police are still holding her body. They haven't said when they will release it."

After Britt left, Nina clapped and called out. The three dogs appeared in the room. Nina pulled a pink hatbox from one of her many totes. "I'm so excited," she said. "I could hardly wait to come in today. Wait till you see."

Gretchen exchanged glances with her mother. Something silly was up. They could tell.

Nina danced in anticipation. "Bonnie Albright has been working on a new venture."

"She's been very secretive about it," April said, dusting

dolls on a shelf. "We've been trying to get the details out of her at Curves, but for the first time in her life, she's not talking."

Nina jiggled the box. "She's been creating wigs."

Gretchen grimaced when she thought of the stiff, red wig Bonnie wore to cover a bald spot on the top of her head. She was the last person on earth Gretchen would consider qualified to create realistic wigs. Gretchen's eyes slid to the pink box. "You bought a wig from her?"

Nina bobbed her head in glee. "I've always thought about this concept, and she went out and did it."

"Let's see," Gretchen leaned in as Nina pulled off the little round cover.

"Tutu, come here," Nina called. The schnoodle bounded down one of the aisles in full anticipation of another treat. Nina had her hand over the box, concealing the contents. "At first, I couldn't decide between the two styles. Should I get the CleoPetra with bangs, or the Barky Braids?"

"CleoPetra?" April shouted. "For heaven's sake, will you show us what you have?"

"Eventually I decided on the Barky Braids." Nina extracted a wig and reached out for Tutu, adjusting it on the dog's head so that two braids hung down in front of Tutu's ears.

"The wig is for your dog?" April said, failing to hold back a full-blown roar. "I thought it was for you. It's for Tutu?"

Gretchen laughed along with April and her mother. It felt good after all the tension surrounding Charlie's murder and her own financial problems. Leave it to Nina to lighten the moment.

Nina grinned. "It's a perfect fit, isn't it?"

"How does it stay on?" Caroline asked.

"Elastic."

"I absolutely love it," Gretchen agreed. "Tutu looks ravishing."

"The wig is exactly the same color as Tutu's hair," April pointed out.

Nina preened at the compliments. "That's right. Bonnie's a miracle worker. I could have picked any color I wanted. She makes them to order. Nimrod and Enrico should have doggie wigs, too."

Gretchen glanced at the tiny teacup poodle and the aggressive Chihuahua, who were playing tug of war with a knotted rope. "Enrico's just beginning to fit in," she said. "Let's not traumatize him unnecessarily."

"Enough play," Caroline said. "Help me find the dolls that go inside the room boxes. I should have asked Britt more about them before she left."

They rummaged around on the storage room shelves without finding anything useful. Gretchen pulled open each of Charlie's desk drawers until she found a box filled with dolls.

"You're not going to like this," she said to the others after she opened the cover and peered in. "This is so sad."

The women gathered around. Miniature room box dolls were arranged in a row. Six of them. Three women and three men. Two of the dolls' skulls were bashed in, one had slash marks crisscrossing her tiny body, and two had gaping holes in their heads. The only one that appeared undamaged was a distinguished-looking male doll. Instead of holes and slashes, his face was contorted in the semblance of excruciating pain.

No one said anything for several minutes.

"Well," Caroline finally said. "I don't think we will be displaying the room boxes at the funeral after all."

"Wise decision," April said.

"We're done then," Gretchen said with relief. Charlie's

obsession with death, culminating with her own, was disturbing. Gretchen closed the cover. "The police must have seen these when they investigated."

"What would a few mutilated dolls mean to them?" Caroline said.

"It would be interesting to discuss them with the police," Gretchen said, deciding to take the dolls along with her.

"I'll get photos of the room boxes for Charlie's brother," Caroline said. "Without the dolls."

After her mother had taken the promised photographs, Gretchen helped Nina pack up dog supplies.

A window shopper stopped in front of the shop. Enrico the Enforcer lunged at the window, snarling and showing his teeth. The pedestrian took one look at the foaming, frothing creature and moved on.

"Poor Enrico," Nina said.

"Poor Enrico?" April said, incredulous. "He seems to have the upper hand."

"The poor little orphan."

Gretchen groaned silently. She saw it coming before April did. "Enrico is looking for a new home," Nina said as if on cue.

Her aunt couldn't resist taking in abandoned canines. That's how Gretchen had ended up with Nimrod. Not that she was complaining. The tiny pup was a perfect match for her. But Enrico and April?

Nina looked sadly at April, then peeked at Enrico, who still guarded the window. "His owner can't get used to—"

An explosion drowned out Nina's next words. Gretchen saw the shop window blow apart. One second, it was there. The next second, it was gone. Shards of glass flew everywhere. The noise was deafening.

Gretchen moved as fast as she could, but it still felt like

slow motion. She lunged for the space where the tiny Chihuahua had stood a moment before and saw only emptiness. She frantically turned left and right. Nothing.

Enrico was gone.

Another explosion.

Gretchen dove for the floor as the display case filled with recently furnished room boxes tipped toward the women. "Get down," she screamed. The other women crouched down behind her in a tight embrace.

Gretchen covered her head with her hands and curled into a ball. Some of the miniature doll furnishings shot across the room, others rained down on them. She stayed on the floor until the air assault ended.

She saw April's feet, encased in white socks and sandals, move past, glass crunching underfoot. Gretchen lifted her head and wiped off loosely embedded glass from the side of her face that had been against the floor. Blood oozed from small puncture wounds on her arms.

Flames licked at the room boxes, and a line of fire also ran along the windowsill. She caught the strong odor of gasoline and sprang up in time to see April pull off her sundress. Stripped down to panties and bra, April began to beat at the display case with her dress.

"Should we call for help?" Nina said through ragged sobs.

"Yes," Gretchen shouted to her aunt. "I'd consider this an emergency."

Nina looked dazed. Caroline rose from the floor.

"The dogs," Gretchen added, scanning the store, relieved that the women were on their feet and appeared to be unharmed. "Mom, help find Enrico."

That did the trick for Nina. Cell phone in hand, she sprang into action, pounding on its keys as she ran along the front of the shop searching for the tiny Chihuahua. With a breaking voice, she gave their location before scurrying off into the back room to check for the animals. Caroline was right behind her.

Gretchen looked for a fire extinguisher but didn't find one. She yanked a tablecloth from under a miniature display table and set about helping April smother the flames.

Judging from the power of the blasts, Gretchen thought all of the women should be plastered with glass shards, but she had been front and center, and the cuts on her arms appeared to be superficial, sustained mostly during her lunge for the floor. "Did a bomb go off?" Gretchen asked, beating at the fire with the tablecloth.

"That, or someone shot through the window," April answered, winded from the physical exertion. "You shielded us from most of the debris, Superwoman. Are you all right?"

Gretchen nodded. "We're fanning the flames rather than smothering them," she said. "We better get out of the shop."

"Help is on the way," Nina said, hustling toward them with a bucket of water. "The emergency operator said the fire truck will be here momentarily. Stand back." Her aim was flawless. The flames died back a little. April grabbed the empty bucket and ran for the back room.

"Don't let the dogs out," Nina called after her, watching the underclad woman charge away.

Gretchen tried to put out a line of fire along the windowsill with the cloth. It caught fire. She threw it on the floor and stomped out the flame.

April returned with the bucket and flung water on the remaining flames. "We should join the fire department," she said. "We'd be a great team."

"Nimrod and Tutu are in the storage room," Nina said. "I closed the door so they wouldn't get hurt on the glass or run into the fire. But I can't find Enrico anywhere."

Smoke still rose from the display case, but the flames along the window had been completely extinguished. Gretchen noted a thick, black substance where the fire had died away. April took another swipe at the display case with her dress.

"We'll have company soon. You better put on your dress," Gretchen advised her. The street was already filled with people. Gretchen heard a siren approaching, a few blocks away.

April flung the dress over her head, lumbered to the open window, and spread her legs in a no-nonsense stance. Her sundress, covered with black soot and burn holes, wasn't white anymore. "Everybody stay put right where you are until we figure out what happened in here. Did anybody see anything?"

A kid with a red ball cap raised his hand. "I did. I heard a kaboom and glass flew all over the street."

"Some guy threw something," another observer said. "He was wearing a do-rag on his head."

Ryan! Gretchen thought with dismay.

"Anybody out there hurt?" April called, sliding a knowing glance at Gretchen. She had thought of Ryan, too. No one spoke up. "Okay, then. I'm taking that as a 'no.' Anybody see a little brown dog?"

Gretchen stiffened, expecting someone to find Enrico's mangled body lying on the pavement. The glass shards would have acted like shrapnel, piercing the tiny dog's hairless body. And the fire! Had he burned alive?

A few people on the street shook their heads. Enrico must have been swept up in the force of the explosion and flung away. The poor thing. Nothing that small would have survived.

Nina cried into a tissue. Caroline wrapped her arms

around her sister. "Everything's going to be okay," she said. "Shhh."

"We have to find Enrico. He has to be here somewhere."

"We will," Gretchen assured her. "He could have jumped out the window and run away." She didn't believe her own reassurance for one second.

A fire truck pulled to a stop outside, and the siren died away. Several police officers arrived at the same time. Brandon Kline was one of those who responded. Nina and April told the tale, while Gretchen barely listened to the officer's questions and the women's responses.

The professionals went about their business. Gretchen stared at the window, or what was left of the window. All their work ruined. But did it matter anymore? The whole point of the exercise was to prepare the room boxes for display at Charlie's funeral, and they had already abandoned the idea after finding the macabre dolls.

Why attack the shop window and destroy the display?

What if the answer was inside the room boxes? Not in the intricate details they had so lovingly constructed, but in the simplicity of one of the boxes—the unfurnished kitchen. What if the kitchen and the miniature peanut butter jar held the solution to Charlie's and Sara's deaths?

Gretchen felt a hand on her shoulder and looked up to see an expression of concern on Detective Kline's face.

"Detective," Gretchen said. "We meet again."

"I'd like to inquire after your health. It appears to be in constant jeopardy."

Gretchen gave him a weak smile and introduced him to Nina.

Other emergency workers converged on the window, and Gretchen looked at the opening.

The detective followed her gaze, and his face hardened. "Not a rifle shot from the street," he observed.

"No." Gretchen had already deduced as much. Whatever had blown through the shop window cast a wider path of destruction than a rifle would. She studied the ruin that had once been a display case. Burned up. The room boxes were charred beyond recognition.

"A jar of gasoline?" she asked. "Or two? There were two explosions."

"We'll find out."

Red tape, yellow tape, crime scene experts, reports, interviews. The next hour was lost in speculation and repeating details of the blast.

Matt arrived, striding quickly through the debris. "Did anyone call for an ambulance?" he asked the technicians working the scene.

"We aren't injured," Gretchen answered for them, hiding the cuts on her arms by crossing them.

"I want to make sure," he insisted. "You should be examined."

April grinned widely behind him, smudges of soot on her round face. Gretchen could almost hear her offering to go first, but she remained silent. In a less stressful situation, she wouldn't have missed *that* opportunity.

"I'll refuse to get into the ambulance," Gretchen said firmly. "I really am fine."

"How about everyone else?"

"We're fine," Gretchen insisted. The other women nodded.

Matt opened his mouth to argue but must have decided it was a hopeless cause, because he walked away to confer with the firefighters instead. Gretchen noticed that he avoided looking directly at any of the doll cases.

Every few minutes Nina checked on Tutu and Nimrod, then nervously paced on the sidewalk outside the shop. "Enrico!" she shouted. "Come to Momma."

Detective Kline walked over to the open window where Gretchen was standing. "You can go now," he said. "We'll let you know what we find."

"You must have suspicions," Gretchen said. "What caused this?"

He ran a finger over the black substance on the windowsill that Gretchen noticed earlier. "Poor man's hand grenades." When he saw the questioning look on her face, he explained. "This is tar, one of the ingredients sometimes used in a Molotov cocktail. Tar causes the gasoline to stick to whatever it hits. Then the effect is broader when it ignites. Someone filled bottles with gasoline and tar, made crude wicks out of rags, lit them, and threw them at the window."

"Do you have a witness?" Gretchen remembered the discussion on the street. The bomber had worn a do-rag on his head.

He nodded. "And a potential suspect."

"You work fast."

"Just doing my job as quickly as possible."

She watched him approach a weeping Nina, place a hand on her shoulder, and lean in to listen. Matt was consulting with the other professionals on the scene, seeming to have forgotten her for the moment.

She went in search of her purse.

Now where did I leave it?

"I think I saw it under one of the dollhouse displays," April said when Gretchen asked her to join in the search. "*Not* under that freakish Victorian. Look by the English Tudor. You need to keep better track of your things, girl."

Gretchen spotted her white cotton bag under a table, leaned down, and pulled it out.

Nina was still moping. "Do you think Enrico is dead?" she sniffed. "We can't leave without knowing what happened to him."

Gretchen straightened up and checked the contents of her purse. She felt tears forming in her eyes, the first since the attack. "I know for a fact the little devil is just fine."

A warning snarl erupted from the depths of her purse.

· 20 ·

Frozen Charlotte has a fascinating and mysterious history. Her story was immortalized in a poem by Seba Smith, then set to music in a folk ballad that spread far and wide.

A beautiful young woman and her lover set out on a sleigh to attend a ball miles away from home. Her mother warned her to wrap up in a blanket, for it was a bitterly cold night. But the young woman refused the cover, and away they went. During their journey, Charlotte complained only once about the extreme cold. Then she fell silent. When the sleigh arrived at the ball, her lover held out his hand to help her down. But all that was left of Charlotte was a frozen corpse.

In remembrance of Charlotte's folly, dolls were produced in Germany and called Frozen Charlottes. Some were bath toys, others were bits of doll-shaped porcelain that were baked into cakes. The lucky recipient of the piece of cake containing the doll received a special prize.

—From World of Dolls *by Caroline Birch*

Once home, Caroline clattered over Gretchen like a mother roadrunner, as though just recovering from the shock of the explosions. She brushed shards of glass from Gretchen's hair.

Gretchen picked up a six-inch naked porcelain doll and

noted the doll's painted black hair and white body. "A Frozen Charlotte," she said.

"Poor, vain Charlotte. If only she'd listened to her mother's warning and wrapped herself in the blanket." Caroline examined Gretchen's shoulders and arms.

"If you're comparing me to Charlotte," Gretchen said. "I'd like to remind you whose idea this was in the first place."

"I know. I regret ever suggesting that we restore Charlie's display. Do you think her son threw the bomb?" Caroline's face was a study in sorrow.

"Stranger things have happened." Gretchen remembered Ryan's remote eyes and the way he'd struck out at her.

"Into the shower with you," her mother said, breaking into her thoughts.

Every bone in Gretchen's body ached. She stood under the hot water for a long time. "You have a visitor," her mother said when she came out of the bathroom toweling her hair. "He's on the patio. I set out two glasses and a bottle of wine."

Wine?

Gretchen peeked through the window. Matt Albright sat by the pool with Nimrod on his lap. Dusk settled over the desert. Camelback Mountain was a dark outline in the sky. The lights around the patio lit up.

"I hope you don't mind that I let him stay," Caroline said, whisking away without waiting for a response.

Gretchen stroked Wobbles, who sat on the window ledge next to her. "What do you think?" she said to the tomcat. "Is this business or pleasure?" Wobbles rumbled a deep purr and licked her finger. Gretchen pressed her head against his side to listen to his soothing inner machinery, keeping one eye on the unaware detective. "We think alike," she told Wobbles. "I agree. It's business."

It turned out to be a little of each.

"This case has more twists and turns than a desert dust storm," Matt said as soon as she walked onto the patio. He poured two glasses of white wine.

Gretchen glanced at the glass in his hand. "Off duty?"

He nodded. "I need a break. I've been working this case every waking hour. After I leave you, I'm getting some sleep."

She sat down on the chair next to him and ran her fingers through her wet hair. "Tell me what you've learned."

Matt sighed. "Joseph Reiner came in today accompanied by his Alcoholics Anonymous sponsor. He had a troubling setback in his recovery program last Friday night. He fell off the proverbial wagon and doesn't remember anything about the evening. And he didn't remember a thing about the next day until you told him you saw him at the parade. Seems you prompted a return to reality for him, but before that . . ." Matt shook his head in disbelief. "Nothing. Or so he claims."

"Interesting," Gretchen said.

Matt scowled at her. "You should have told me you saw him at the parade."

She shrugged an apology. "I didn't think it was important."

"You'd never accept that excuse from me."

True. But Gretchen wasn't about to admit it. "Joseph really didn't remember until I reminded him?" she asked.

"A total blackout."

"Did you arrest him?"

"I can't book a man for murder simply because he can't remember where he was."

"I thought you brute cops were all-powerful and could do anything you wanted."

"Ah, but we're confined by foolishness like laws, rules, and regulations."

"I might have evidence you can use."

"Tell me."

Gretchen picked up her glass of wine and took a sip before answering. "Joseph was chewing nicotine gum the last time I saw him."

Matt stared at her. "Well," he said very slowly. "That's certainly the worst circumstantial evidence I've ever heard." He grinned.

Gretchen giggled. "You're right. It is." *Quit acting like a teenager, you dope.* She tried to straighten her expression— more serious, more professional, more adultlike—but it was hard. The night lights, the wine, and relief that she and the others were still alive and unharmed made her giddy.

Nimrod scampered down from Matt's lap, dove into the pool, paddled around, jumped out, and shook himself dry in his favorite spot—right next to Gretchen.

Matt laughed while wiping water from his legs. Tan, muscular legs, Gretchen noticed. He had a smile like a strong magnetic force. It pulled her in.

"Do you have a suspect in the attack on us?" Gretchen asked. She *really* hoped it wasn't Ryan.

"We've eliminated Bernard Waites, as much as you'd like to see him behind bars," Matt said, not exactly answering her question. "He's still in the hospital."

"Maybe he snuck out when no one was looking, threw the bomb, and ran back to the hospital before the nursing staff missed him."

Matt raised a brow. "Nice try. You really dislike that guy, don't you?"

"He stole from me. And he has creepy eyes."

"Creepy eyes, huh. Another bit of evidence to explore, another break in the case." Matt leaned over and slid his hand under her chin. He turned her head toward the light. "You have abrasions on your cheek."

"A little shattered windowpane, is all," Gretchen said, like glass in her face was an everyday occurrence. "It'll heal."

He released her and leaned back. "You could have been killed today. Personally, I'm relieved your work at the shop is over. Although I would have preferred that you go out with less of a bang."

"We had finished the room boxes. In the end, the scenes weren't anything we'd want to show at Charlie's funeral. But we did get pictures for her brother before the blast destroyed them."

"Did you find any connection to Charlie's murder in your work?"

"That's an odd question." Gretchen glanced at him quickly, but his face was in shadow.

"I'm a detective; it's my job to ask questions. Well? Did you find anything?"

"We found bloodstains painted in two of the boxes and discovered tiny weapons on the floor. We realized that one of the street signs was a replica of that of Lizzie Borden's home, where she was accused of axing her parents to death. And today we found mutilated dolls in a desk drawer."

Matt sipped his wine. "Macabre. But it only proves that Charlie had a few emotional issues."

"One unfinished room box appears to be a kitchen."

"So when you consider the miniature peanut butter jar." Matt paused to sip his wine. "Things begin to add up."

"Yes."

He leaned forward, piercing her with his vivid eyes.

She took a sip of wine and turned away, focusing on what she wanted to tell him. "I think Charlie planned to reveal her sister's killer when she unveiled the display. I believe the incomplete room box scene could be a replica of the killer's kitchen where the poisons were concocted.

That particular room box's walls were hastily wallpapered with a full-sized paper, not a miniature rendition, like it was assembled in a big hurry."

Matt's dark eyes locked onto hers again. He didn't look convinced.

Gretchen continued. "I think all five room boxes were ready for the showing. After poisoning Charlie, the killer must have tried to rip apart the fifth room box, then picked up the incriminating pieces."

"But overlooked the jar because it was under Charlie's body," Matt finished.

"Exactly. All we have to do is find the room with the same wallpaper, and we have the killer."

"Except the kitchen room box went up in flames."

Gretchen struggled to keep her mind on the case instead of the man seated next to her. His body was emitting some sort of sexual energy, and it was affecting her. She wondered if he felt it, too.

Matt poured more wine for her. "The destroyed evidence presents a problem," he said, handing her the glass.

"Not as much of a problem as you might think," Gretchen answered, taking a small sip. "You see," she leaned closer, "I took a picture of the room box with—"

Matt slid his chair closer and leaned in as though he was having trouble hearing her. "—my phone," she croaked. *That was really a sexy voice.* He was still moving toward her. Slowly. Closer. Coming into her personal space.

His lips met hers. Longingly.

Gretchen knocked over her wineglass.

"You did that on purpose." Matt whispered, his lips close to hers.

"I . . . really . . . didn't . . . mean," Gretchen stammered, sitting upright and realizing she'd spilled the wine into his lap. She reached for a beach towel on the back of a lounge, stood up, and leaned over to blot the front of his shorts. She stopped just in time.

You almost stuck your hand in his crotch. Geez. Gretchen blushed, grateful that the darkness concealed her discomfort.

He laughed and took the towel from her hand. "I won't need a cold shower now," he said.

"I'm really, really sorry."

"Come here," he said, taking her arm and pulling her down. "Make it up to me."

"How?" But she knew the answer. Wasn't she a member of a well-established psychic family?

She pressed against him. Her lips found his.

Daisy, future Hollywood star and current member of the Red Hat Society, trudges along the edges of crumbling adobe walls, pushing her shopping cart filled with all her worldly possessions: sleeping bag, bits of food, knickknacks picked out of trash bins, clothes.

Graffiti and iron grates scar what's left of this once-flourishing side of the city. The streetlights flick on.

From the shadows, she looks both ways before turning sharply and slipping down an alleyway. The smell of rotting garbage doesn't bother her a bit. Why should it? She's seen and smelled far worse things than decaying waste.

Like that transient last month, new to the streets, beaten until every rib was shattered, blood seeping everywhere. She smelled fear while she watched him die. That smell is worse than a few whiffs of garbage . . . Well, she doesn't allow herself to think of things like that for too very long.

It can drive you insane, thinking too much.

Once the talent scouts find her, she's out of Phoenix but fast.

Daisy misses Nacho, her lover and friend. Has he abandoned her for the San Francisco streets, or will he return to the desert? Her life is like a soap opera. He'll come back; he always does. At least he found her a safe place to stay while he's away. An old storage shed behind an abandoned building. Nacho even installed a lock inside the shed so she'd be protected from the elements. The human elements, that is.

The young druggies are the worst. They are far more dangerous than anything Mother Nature can throw her way. Ready to beat you and stick you in the heart with knives just to steal the smallest bit of spare change. Anything for their next fix. So many threats on the streets: gangs, crazies, cops, druggies.

She has flyers in her shopping cart, pictures of the most deadly ones, circulated by the homeless, for the homeless. Stay away from that one, the posters say: like wanted posters, only these people *aren't* wanted by Daisy and the others.

Daisy is at the hub of the action, as always. She knows everything that happens on the street, and she's extremely wary. That's why she's still alive while most of her old friends are dead.

Maybe it's time to pay her good friend Gretchen a visit, clean up, sleep in a real bed, get the jitters under control. The doll repairer was a real find, her and her aunt, and all those little doggies.

But what about her career as a Hollywood star? The street is where it's happening.

Glad it isn't July. How many of her kind died last summer from exposure to extreme heat? No water, the pavement steaming at one hundred and thirty degrees, burning her feet right through her shoes. She swam in the irrigation canals to survive.

Daisy jerks her head around at a sound behind her.

A moan. Coming from the Dumpster, or behind the Dumpster.

Get inside the shed and bolt the door. She hears this in her head and knows it for what it is: good advice.

But . . . what if? What if it's someone in distress?

It's only the sound of despair. You hear it every day.

But . . . what if it's Nacho?

Daisy pulls an aerosol can from her pocket. Pepper spray. She refuses to carry a concealed gun or knife. Wouldn't the cops love that? They're more interested in finding an excuse to arrest the victims than in solving all the homeless murders.

Another moan.

Leaving her shopping cart by the side of the shed, she edges along, flattened to the walls, always in the darkness, hiding from the streetlights and the rising moon.

She hears another sound, but it's only a coyote in the distance.

A dark shape on the ground behind the Dumpster shifts slightly, and Daisy catches the movement. She has night eyes, cat eyes, she likes to think. Another reason she beats the odds.

The pepper spray acts as a buffer between Daisy and whoever is crumpled on the ground. She already knows it isn't Nacho.

"Help me." The whisper is so low and weak she almost misses the words.

A hand reaches out for her, and she sees who it is.

The man writhing in pain is Ryan Maize.

Gretchen overslept and almost missed her workout group at Curves. She rushed through the house, throwing on exercise garb as she went. "I fed Wobbles and Nimrod," her mother said, ready to go and holding out Gretchen's purse and a cup of coffee. "You needed the extra sleep."

When Gretchen and her mother arrived at Curves, most of the doll club members were in full throttle on the machines. "He's missing," Bonnie said in a stage whisper when Gretchen jumped onto the abductor. "Born to Be Wild" boomed from an overhead speaker.

"Who's missing?" Gretchen asked.

"Ryan Maize, that's who." Bonnie's feet did a tiny tap dance on the platform. Her red wig had extra starch today, every hair shellacked into place. "Matty knows Charlie's son tried to blow up you girls. Witnesses identified Ryan from pictures, but the police can't find him. He's not at that drug house."

"The do-rag did him in," April said, stomping up and down on the stepper. "He should have disguised himself better if he was going to pull a stunt like that. He could have killed us. Then it would have been murder one instead of attempted murder."

"Matty will get him; don't you worry."

"That poor drugged-out kid," Gretchen said, shaking her head.

April grunted. "First he knocks you out," she gasped, sweating profusely. "Then he tries to blow us up. And you feel sorry for him? I don't. If I get my hands on that little punk, I'll squeeze his scrawny neck until his eyes pop. He made me ruin my best dress."

"Change stations now," a preprogrammed voice announced. The circle of flab fighters moved to the left.

"You're lucky that's all he ruined," Caroline said. "It could have been so much worse."

"He demolished Charlie's shop," April said. "It's a mess."

Gretchen decided to pursue the idea she had explored with Matt. *That's not all we explored,* she thought with a hidden grin before saying, "The walls of one of the room boxes were covered with wallpaper. If I describe the design to you, maybe one of you will know who it belongs to."

"Is this a clue to the killer?" Rita, the Barbie collector, asked.

"Maybe." Gretchen ran in place while she considered how much to share with the group.

"Tell us, tell us," Bonnie said, licking her lips in anticipation.

"The wallpaper was tan, and it had an apple and teapot border."

Bonnie looked thoughtful. Her penciled brows edged closer together, and her red lips puckered.

As she often did when spending time with Bonnie, Gretchen tried hard to find any family resemblance between the woman next to her and the hunky police detective, but she couldn't find a trace of physical evidence that established their genome connection.

"I don't know anyone with wallpaper like that," Rita said.

"We'll keep an eye out," Bonnie said with a crafty expression. The doll club president was a woman on a new mission.

Gretchen would take any help she could get. She was determined to find that kitchen. Someone had tried to hurt her and her friends. What was that person planning next? Gretchen's life, or someone's close to her, might depend on moving quickly.

"Where's Nina?" Gretchen asked after watching the door for her aunt's arrival.

"She came in early and left already," Ora, the manager, called out. "Something about breakfast with a new friend."

"Britt," Gretchen and April said simultaneously.

"She thinks you are crowding her out," Rita said to Gretchen.

"Out of what?" April asked.

"Change stations now." Everyone moved in unison.

"The threesome," Bonnie said. "Threes don't work. Everybody knows that."

Gretchen didn't have to pretend to be confused. "What?"

"I get it," April said, looking at Gretchen. "She thought of you as her best friend. Then I came along. She feels displaced."

"That's ridiculous," Gretchen said. "She's my aunt, and I love her."

"Maybe you should tell her that," Susie of the Madame Alexander collection said.

"I will. But I thought everything was back to normal."

"Apparently not in Nina's eyes," Caroline said. "I haven't been around much to give her attention. She counts on you."

"Change stations now."

"How's your submarine sandwich diet going?" Rita asked April from the abductor.

April beamed. "I was measured this morning, and I lost three inches."

Ora piped up, "That diet will kill you."

April twisted from side to side on a platform, swinging her arms like clubs. "To tell you the truth, I can't stand the thought of eating another sub."

"See," Ora scolded. "Next you'll starve to death. What kind of a diet is that! You should get into my diet class. Curves teaches you to eat small portions of a lot of different things."

"We'll see," April said, but Gretchen thought her resolve was slipping. Ora might win.

"Tell us about that one room box," Bonnie said. "April said it was the Lizzie Borden murders."

"I researched the murders on the Internet this morning," Caroline said. "It's called parricide when parents are murdered by a child. Except Lizzie was tried and acquitted. Her father was sleeping on a sofa, and her mother was found on the floor in the guest bedroom. Each had sustained multiple blows to the head with a hatchetlike instrument. After viewing photographs on multiple Web sites, I can tell you that Charlie replicated the scene right down to the color of the mohair sofa."

"And we found dolls," April said, "that looked like murder victims."

"Gretchen brought the dolls home," Caroline added. "One of the male dolls wore a morning coat like the man in the online photographs. One of the female dolls wore a white dress, exactly like the dead Borden woman."

"And," Gretchen added, recalling the smashed-up dolls, "both dolls had bashed-in heads."

After Gretchen showered, she found Nina and Caroline in the doll repair workshop showing Britt Gleeland some of the work in progress.

Britt greeted her more warmly than she had in the past.
Gretchen still had her own reservations about the miniature
doll maker. First impressions really were hard to change if
they started out wrong.

Nina motioned toward the kitchen, and while Caroline
and Britt talked shop, Gretchen followed her aunt.

"I think you saw Matt last night," Nina said slyly, pouring a coffee refill for herself.

"Mom told you."

"She did not."

Gretchen thought of their intimate scene on the patio.
She remembered every last detail. "He's a great kisser,"
she said, unable to contain herself any longer.

Nina squealed impulsively, then quickly lowered her
voice so the others wouldn't hear. "I knew it. Today my an-
tennas are receiving at peak performance. I have to con-
fess, my aura abilities have been misfiring lately, but I'm
back on track." She squealed again. "I just knew it."

"Don't get too excited. It was only one little kiss."
Gretchen smiled at Nina. "Or maybe two."

"I won't tell a soul," Nina promised. "My advice is to
lay claim to that man as soon as possible. Other women
look at him like hungry she-cats. Look what he does to
April!"

"Is it a mistake to get involved with him?" Gretchen
chewed the inside of her cheek. "He's still married."

"You have the color of love surrounding you. You're
positively pink. See what love does?"

"Whoa. Back off. You're moving way too fast. Are you
listening to anything I just said?"

"No, I'm not. I'm tickled as pink as you are."

Gretchen appraised Tickled Pink, who actually was
wearing pink silk pants and a matching pink top.

Nina sat down next to Gretchen at the kitchen table.

"Thanks for telling me about Matt." She gave Gretchen a shy look.

Her aunt had given her the perfect opening. "You know, Nina, I really like April. She offered her friendship to me when I moved to Phoenix, when I didn't know anybody other than you. She made me feel welcome."

"That's right. She did. But then she took over, and all of a sudden, there she was, all the time. I think you prefer her company over mine."

"That isn't true at all. I love you."

"As a relative." Nina managed to make her voice sound dejected.

"No! I love you as a friend. You are absolutely my very best friend."

"Really?"

"Really," Gretchen assured her. "What about Britt? You seem to have found a new friend in her."

"She's really nice. Don't be mad, but I started out being friendly with her to make you jealous."

Gretchen knew exactly what to say next. "Well, it worked. I thought you'd abandoned me."

"Never, dear. We're adults, and I like Britt. You and I should be able to handle other people in other lives without letting it affect our friendship."

Gretchen nodded. *Finally! Great words of wisdom.*

"There you are." Caroline led Britt into the kitchen and offered her a seat and a cup of coffee. Britt held the box of dolls in her hands. "We were talking about the dolls," Caroline said, pouring coffee, "and thought you'd like to be part of the conversation."

Britt's face was flushed when she said, "I don't understand who would do this to my dolls. Surely not Charlie."

"She created the room boxes," Gretchen replied. "And at least two of them are murder scenes, the one we've identified as Lizzie Borden's home and another one of a backyard where there's blood on the ground and on the steps leading into the building."

"Tell Gretchen what you told me," Caroline said.

Britt inhaled, a ragged breath, and blew it out. "Charlie was very specific about the dolls she wanted. I remember her instructions to the letter. One male: tall, thin, white-haired, middle-aged; one female: same age, short, slightly obese."

Gretchen and Caroline exchanged looks. "The Bordens," Caroline said.

"And the other dolls?" Gretchen asked.

"She gave me more leeway. A male with the dignity of the clergy, a woman who would pass as a woman of the street, a choir girl, and the last one."

She glanced up at her waiting audience. "The last one would be male, well-heeled, powerful. And he must, she insisted, have a look of extreme anguish on his face. Other than that, I could sculpt him however I wished."

"A look of anguish?" Nina said, perplexed. "Why?"

"I asked her that. She said it was a surprise." Britt's fingers skimmed across the damage to her dolls. "I wanted to get these back as mementos of my last work for Charlie. But why would I want them like this? This is the only one that is still intact, and look at him!"

Britt held up the male doll she had created for her friend. The excruciating pain on his face was unmistakable.

Britt and Nina went off together, leaving Gretchen and her mother alone in the workshop. "I have an idea," Gretchen said, arranging the street signs in a row next to the computer they used for their doll repair business. "Let's search the other signs and see what comes up."

She keyed in one of the addresses. "Twenty-nine Hanbury Street. A London address." The search engine gave her a list of possibilities. She clicked on the first one, while Caroline looked over her shoulder.

"Jack the Ripper's second victim was killed at that address," Gretchen said, not sure whether to be proud of her sleuthing abilities or saddened by Charlie's obsession. "Look! The dilapidated backyard."

Without a word of explanation, Caroline hurried from the room. Gretchen was about to go after her to see if she had broken down in tears and needed comforting, but she returned as quickly as she left. And she had Britt's dolls in her hands. "This must be the one." She selected the slashed woman. "And the bloody knife must be part of that display."

Gretchen keyed in another address, the one on Elm Street. "Arsenic Anna."

"I'm not familiar with that murder," Caroline said. "Although I've heard the name."

Gretchen read aloud. "In the 1930s, a woman named

Anna Marie Hahn posed as a nurse as a way to care for wealthy, elderly men, who had no living relatives. Each of them died from arsenic poisoning. Four in all before she was captured and convicted."

"That's horrible," Caroline said. "And explains the facial features on the male doll. Death by poison."

Again Gretchen entered a street name. De Russey's Lane.

"The Hall-Mills murders," Caroline read over Gretchen's shoulder. "An Episcopal priest and a choir girl were found dead under a crab apple tree. Both had been shot in the head. Torn-up letters were found between them."

"The ripped pieces of paper we put in the unknown pile," Gretchen said.

Caroline held up two more dolls while she read the victims' descriptions. "Eleanor Mills wore a blue dress with red polka dots and black stockings."

The doll was dressed exactly as the description of the poor murdered girl.

"A blue velvet hat lay beside her."

"Another unknown piece placed." Gretchen remembered the little hat.

Charlie created four room boxes to represent famous murder scenes. Why would she do that? What did she hope to accomplish by inviting guests to view such horror?

"What do these murders have in common?" Caroline asked, puzzled. "How did she pick her settings? Jack the Ripper and Lizzie Borden are very famous murders. Arsenic Anna not quite as well known, and I've never heard of the Hall-Mills murders."

"Let me check each one again." Gretchen did additional searches to read the cases more thoroughly. Caroline worked on a cracked bisque doll at the worktable. Nimrod dozed on the floor, while Wobbles graced them with his presence for a few minutes, licking his coat.

"I've got it!" Gretchen shouted, startling both animals. "Charlie chose unsolved murders—Lizzie Borden was acquitted, Jack the Ripper was never identified, and the priest and choir girl's murderer was never found."

"And Arsenic Anna?" Caroline asked.

"Was electrocuted for her crimes. But she was the only one who used poison. Maybe Nina's right," Gretchen said. "She thought the kitchen was very important."

It was time to take a peek at a few kitchens. But Gretchen didn't say it out loud.

Bernard Waites lived on Twelfth Street in a brick ranch with white wood trim.

"That's his truck in the carport," Gretchen said. "He was driving it the day he came to return my checkbook." She noted that the sun was rapidly setting and checked her watch. A little after five o'clock.

Nina stopped the car across the street. "Why did he steal a check, then cash it and return the checkbook? Wouldn't he have been better off just keeping your checkbook or throwing it away?"

"He claimed he was borrowing the money and was going to return it to my account before I noticed."

"He decided to take out a loan?" Nina shook her head. "Is the entire world crazy?"

"Looks that way."

"What if he's home from the hospital?"

"He isn't. I called the hospital. He's still there."

Nina swung her head toward the house. "What's the plan?"

"I thought you might have one."

"Search his house and take a look at the kitchen."

"Let's go."

Nina tipped her head toward the backseat. "I'm the puppy sitter. You're the investigator."

"You're making this up as you go."

"You bet."

"Mom will kill me if she finds out what we're doing."

"I'm not going to tell her."

There wasn't any sign of activity at the house. Bernard had taken an ambulance ride after the bug juice blew up, which accounted for the parked truck. All Gretchen had to do was slip around to the back of the house and peek through the kitchen window. How hard could that be? "Okay," she said. "I'm not breaking and entering, but I'll look in the window. That's all."

Nina nodded in approval. "How hard can it be?" she said, echoing what Gretchen was thinking. Her aunt was starting to scare her. Maybe there really was something to all her quirky psychic beliefs. *No. Impossible.*

Gretchen opened the car door, eased it closed, and trotted across the street.

She had forgotten about Phoenix's passion for privacy walls. No one in the enormous desert community wanted snoopy neighbors spying on them, so they built walls to keep them out. Walls also kept snakes and wild animals from appearing on doorsteps.

Bernard's property wasn't any different than that of the rest of the populace. His privacy wall was made of concrete. Gretchen trotted back to the Impala. "I can't get over the wall. You'll have to give me a boost."

Nina rolled her eyes in mock exasperation. "The things I have to do in the name of family and friendship."

"How am I going to get out once I'm in?"

"There must be a gate on the other side," Nina said. "Every backyard has a gate."

They crept along the outside of the wall. Gretchen stuck a

foot in Nina's cupped hands, scaled up the side of the wall, and peered over the top. The coast was clear. She swung a leg up, scooted on her belly, and carefully edged the other leg over. She dropped to the ground on the other side.

The backyard looked like a lumber yard, only not as tidy. Piles of wood and cast-off remnants of lumber were scattered along the side of the wall where Gretchen crouched. Near the house, she saw a small wrought-iron table and four chairs. A vase filled with mixed flowers was in the middle of the table.

Gretchen mustered up her courage and strode boldly to a window on the right side of the table. She peered inside, shading her eyes with her hand for a better view.

And came nose to nose with an old woman on the other side of the glass. The woman had a face like a Cabbage Patch Kid.

Gretchen stifled a startled yelp.

The woman, however, let out a bone-chilling scream. It sounded more like a war cry than a fearful reaction.

The vase of flowers on the outdoor table should have clued Gretchen in. How careless could she be? Bernard Waites, the cranky thief, had a wife.

Since Gretchen was already in position, she took a moment to look past the woman and get a good look at the kitchen. She strained to make out the kitchen walls.

The woman on the other side of the glass got Gretchen's total attention when she waved something above her head. It looked like a meat cleaver. Looking solidly determined, the woman marched for the back door.

Gretchen quickly revamped her hastily laid plan to present herself at the back door and apologize. She broke for the wall, realizing halfway there that she couldn't get over without Nina's help.

There must be another way out. She turned in a circle

looking for an exit. Where was the gate? There wasn't one. It was either over the wall or through the house.

"I'll just let myself out," Gretchen called, whirling to face her adversary. "I didn't mean to scare you."

Bernard's wife snorted like a bull. "I belong to the neighborhood watch," she said, stalking toward Gretchen with the cleaver clenched in her fist. "The rest of the committee will be here any second, and we'll take care of you. Yes, we'll take care of you but good."

Gretchen saw that she meant it. Bernard's wife might not be Gretchen's physical match, but she had a look in her eyes that put the fear of death into Gretchen.

The woman waved the cleaver with menace.

"We're coming as fast as we can." Someone shouted from a nearby house.

Would Gretchen be hacked to death by a gang of blockwatchers? She eyed up one of the tallest woodpiles. If she could get a running start, she might make it.

Bernard's wife marched at her, raising the cleaver.

Gretchen took off as fast as she could and ran up the pile. A loose board underfoot almost tripped her up, but she maintained her balance and hurtled at the wall, digging her fingers into the top of it. Raising herself up through sheer desperation and fear, she launched over the wall to freedom.

Gretchen ran in a crouch to the side of the house, staying behind the straggly Arizona shrubbery. Two women stomped past, headed for Bernard's front door. Each carried a baseball bat. For the first time, Gretchen noticed a warning sign with an enormous watchful eye posted in Bernard's yard.

When the two gang members disappeared through the front door, Gretchen ran to the car. "Get down. Now," she croaked, gasping for breath. Several houses ahead of the Impala, another woman carrying a baseball bat hiked across the street. Gretchen could see the lines of determination in her face, and the excitement. This group had been waiting for an opportunity like this to wield their clubs of justice.

"Was it the room box kitchen?" Nina asked, ducking low.

Gretchen chanced a glance at the house from her slunk-down position in the seat. "No, it's not the one," she answered. "But please get this car moving."

Nina pulled out more slowly than Gretchen would have liked. She watched Bernard's house, expecting the women to rush out and attack Nina's car at any moment.

"See," her aunt said, not the least bit ruffled. "That wasn't so hard, was it?"

· 24 ·

Trolls: Thomas Dam, a poor Danish woodworker, carved the first Troll doll in the 1950s. They were an instant success. As the doll's popularity continued to increase, Thomas began making them from rubber filled with wood shavings. A family business was born. Sales continued to grow through the 1960s, when rubber was replaced with vinyl. Other companies copied Thomas Dam's Trolls, producing cheap imitations that never met the fine craftsmanship of the Dane's dolls.

Trolls are said to have magical powers. Bug-eyed and grinning with long, wild manes of hair in every color of the rainbow, they bring luck to their owners. But trolls are only lucky if they are the original, classic Thomas Dam Trolls.

—From *World of Dolls* by Caroline Birch

Early Saturday morning, long before the tourists and snowbirds descended on the popular hiking mountain, Gretchen climbed Camelback Mountain.

It had been over a week since the Scottsdale parade and the death of the miniature doll shop owner. Gretchen had very little to show for all her efforts and misadventures: a bombed-out doll shop and a tiny lead on a kitchen, which might not even be a real connection.

She climbed easily to an enormous boulder overlooking Phoenix to watch the sun rise over the Valley of the Sun.

Later in the day, tourists would be perched on this same boulder with cameras and binoculars, but for now she had it all to herself. She sat down, tucked her feet against her body, and cradled her legs between her arms, thinking of her growing obsession with the case of the dead doll maker and the seemingly endless lineup of potential suspects.

Charlie's drugged-out, missing son was as good a place to start as any. An alleged bomber, suspected of trying to blow up his mother's shop while people were inside where they could have been seriously injured, if not killed. What was his motive? Drug-induced psychosis? Gretchen still couldn't imagine that he would've killed his own mother.

Next suspect: Charlie's thieving business associate. Bernard's cleaver-crazy wife was as disagreeable as her husband and had probably tampered with his bug juice after a domestic argument. The woman was a militant vigilante with a bad temper. And to think, she'd mistaken Gretchen for . . . um . . . for an intruder. Okay, not really a mistake on her part, but her reaction was definitely excessive.

What could have been Bernard Waite's motive for murdering a business associate? Did he want Charlie's store desperately enough to kill for it?

Gretchen stood up on the boulder, hopped down, and began the steepest part of the ascent to the mountain's peak. The trail fell away. She gripped red boulders and continued up, keeping a sharp eye out for a new bird to add to her life list.

What was Joseph's story? He was a flamboyant alcoholic who claimed that he couldn't remember anything about the night preceding Charlie's death, or anything about the next morning when Gretchen spotted him at the parade. Was he telling the truth? Or was he hiding a sinister secret?

She grabbed a firm hold in the rocks and continued her climb. Birds chattered around her, and she saw several cactus wrens in a mesquite bush.

One of the main reasons Gretchen chose early mornings to hike her favorite mountain was to avoid rattlesnakes and other poisonous creatures. She'd had enough uncomfortable encounters with creatures in the past. The February air at this time of day was cool enough to keep them in their holes.

Arizona's list of creepy crawlers was endless: snakes, scorpions, Gila monsters, black widows, tarantulas, lizards. And the larger varieties: coyotes, mountain lions, and javelinas, the wild pigs with razor-sharp tusks.

Gretchen paused to catch her breath and take in the scenery. A chipmunk munched on the buds of a barrel cactus below and to her right. She'd heard that barrel cacti always leaned to the southwest, something to remember if she was ever lost in the desert.

She continued up until she stood at the very summit of Camelback Mountain. The air seemed clearer, affecting her entire view of the world. She sat down and felt her heart pounding from the exertion of the steep climb.

She told herself that once she started the trek back down the mountain, she wouldn't think of anything but the wonder of life. Maybe she would spot a hummingbird, her favorite bird. Hummingbirds were the gold medalists of the bird world, able to hover motionless in midair. They could stop faster and perform more acrobatics than any other bird.

Yes, she thought as she sat at the top of Camelback Mountain, on the way back, she'd research life. But for now she'd study death.

What about Britt Gleeland and her daughter, Melany?

Gretchen hadn't spent much time with Britt, but in the short amount of time she had, she didn't really like her. Was her inability to warm up to the doll maker a jealous reaction to Nina's friendship with her?

What a mess. Not to mention her personal life and the sexy but still *married* detective she was dodging. She had ignored two calls from him yesterday, listening to his voice messages urging her to return his calls. Gretchen didn't have to have a degree in psychology to suspect that she was running away more from her mixed-up feelings than from him.

One last look out over the city she called home, and she started her descent. Usually the mountain gave her a positive outlook on life, but this time when she put it all together it didn't seem like such a great morning after all.

On the way down, even the birds eluded her.

Her mother hadn't forgotten about her offer to introduce Gretchen to Evie Rosemont. She announced the plans when Gretchen walked in the door.

"Get ready," she said. "We're going calling."

Evie Rosemont's home was painted bright and bold. Splashes of red, green, and yellow popped from the small ranch.

Caroline watched Gretchen's face when they parked in the driveway. "Wait until you see the inside," she said.

Evie was short and squat and greeted them wearing a purple dressing robe and a matching beret with sequins and beads. Treating them as though they were long-lost friends, she proceeded to carry on a one-sided conversation that never ceased.

"Come in, come in. I have tea brewing. Girls, you must

see my remodeled hat room. Come this way. I couldn't fit everything into the room anymore, so I redid this and redid that, decorating skills from my dear departed Nana . . ." Evie rattled on while Gretchen and Caroline followed her down a narrow orange hallway.

Pictures of Evie at different stages in her life lined the hallway. She wore a hat in every photograph, starting with a black-and-white photo of her as a baby in a bonnet and ending with a current shot of Evie wearing a gold hat with purple and yellow feathers jutting from the top like water-works.

"This one is from my days in New York, high society you know, and this one is me, and this one . . . Here we are. Wait until you see. Hats make the person, don't you think?" Evie ran on, addressing her hatless guests. "You can tell everything, simply everything, by a woman's col-lection of hats."

They trailed Evie into a fuchsia room. It was filled with antique hats and shoes: black lace vintage bonnets, Victo-rian cream leather boots with lace closures, an orange feather hat. The hats were displayed on hooks, the shoes on numerous small platforms mounted on all four walls.

". . . is my latest acquisition, found, if you can believe it, in a dusty old attic when I visited poor Mama when she was on her deathbed. Mama had quite a few life-threatening health problems throughout her brief time on this earth. First there was her female trouble when she was only twenty-five, then . . ."

When Gretchen had seen Evie Rosemont at Mini Maize she had been wearing a large straw hat with sunflowers. Gretchen had heard Evie address Bernard right before he had opened the door. A bad heart, she'd said at the time, thinking Charlie might've suffered a heart attack. "I was at Charlie's shop the day she died," Gretchen said.

Evie's round, dimpled face turned to Gretchen. "Quite a series of unfortunate events. Where did I hear that expression before? No matter. Anyway, it all happened so fast, you know, Charlie had to watch it because of her heart, that's what I thought it was all along, but then those two detectives started digging deeper. Do you know anything more? The police won't say a thing, but why else would they be holding poor Charlie's body without a funeral? I hope you know why, because we can't let this go away, not if it really was foul play. I remember back about ten years ago when . . ." The woman chattered on.

Evie Rosemont, Gretchen decided, could benefit from medication.

". . . and Sara's death, bless her heart, almost destroyed Charlie. Did I mention that Charlie was like a sister to me . . ."

They were back in the hallway, heading for the last room on the left.

". . . and was it just yesterday I said to Carla, Carla's my neighbor, I said . . ."

Caroline gave Gretchen a look over the top of Evie's head and stood back to let Gretchen follow Evie in. "Wait until you see this," Evie said. "I painted my home, inside and out, to reflect the contents of this room. Here we go . . ."

Gretchen inched in behind her and clapped her hands in delight. Trolls, trolls, everywhere trolls. Evie had a special room totally dedicated to the grinning, impish dolls. Gretchen picked up one of the miniature trolls. The Dam marking was stamped into the underside of the troll's plump bare foot.

Evie stopped talking long enough to allow Gretchen to examine the doll. A brief moment of silence, then she started in again. "That's a baby boy in a Halloween costume.

This one is a caveman, this is a man in a suit. I've collected Thomas Dam Trolls for thirty years. I attend every doll show within driving distance looking just for them."

Gretchen returned the mini to its designated place in the display. Her eyes lit on two familiar trolls. A wedding couple. The groom had purple hair and a black tux, the bride had pink hair and a white wedding dress with a veil. Gretchen peeked under the bride's dress. "She's even wearing a little blue garter."

"Oh, my, yes. Aren't they darling little things?"

"I had this same pair when I was growing up," Gretchen said, looking at her mother. "Whatever happened to them?"

"They're in a box with your other childhood dolls," Caroline said, beaming. "I thought you'd never ask. I hoped one day you'd want them."

"Tea time," Evie called, fluttering from the room. "Do you take sugar? I like mine the European way with lots of cream. I remember when . . ."

Evie served tea on a patio in a small courtyard. Gretchen helped her carry things out from a brightly painted yellow kitchen, not a hint of wallpaper anywhere. No apples or teapots on Evie's walls.

"We put some of Charlie's room boxes together," Caroline said. "They turned out to be murder scenes."

"Charlie said to me, 'Evie,' she said. 'I'm working on horrible murders. It's therapeutic,' she said, if you can believe that. 'I think I'll show them at my party,' she said. I tried to talk her out of it, but her mind was made up, and it's her shop after all, she can do what she pleases. Charlie showed them to me the afternoon before it happened."

"Did others see them ahead of time?" Gretchen asked.

"I assume so, what with well-wishers in and out. She had plans for dinner with Britt, and she was expecting Melany to drop off tiny flower arrangements. Deliveries, customers, and whatnot."

Evie paused for a sip of tea, holding the cup with both hands. Gretchen noticed the cup was shaking slightly. "I did the books for Charlie," Evie said. "But you must know that."

Evie was nervous. The endless chatter and shaking hands gave her away. Gretchen was starting to suspect that she had something to hide. "How was the shop doing?"

"Small businesses really struggle, especially doll shops," Caroline said. "But Charlie was a shrewd business-woman. She must have been in the black."

"That's right," Evie agreed, setting the cup down and hiding her hands under the table. "She watched the cash register and never bought anything unless it was a super good deal. That's why I couldn't believe she'd cover up the way she did. It wasn't my fault. I can't be held account-able."

"We've been friends a long time, Evie," Caroline said. "What's bothering you?"

Evie's eyes grew wider. She began to wring her hands. "I knew it was a mistake to go along with it. I should have resigned on the spot, the minute I found out, but I didn't think it was my business. After all, I warned Charlie, held the spreadsheet with the proof right under her nose. Pointed right at it, even had his signature on the checks. He didn't even try to forge her name. The oaf used his own. But she already knew. Like I said, she watched the cash register, added things up, corrected my numbers once in a while. She could do the math in her head, while I needed a calculator."

"Evie," Caroline said. "What in the world are you talking about?"

"The first time, I thought I had made the mistake," Evie said, distraught. "I spent all day trying to figure out why the numbers didn't work. Then I realized that someone was stealing money from the shop. I took it to Charlie right away, but she told me to ignore it. Can you believe that? 'Look the other way,' she said. 'Fix it any way you like, but don't say a word.' She let the man keep doing it, and I'm telling you, the numbers were off every single month."

"Bernard," Gretchen guessed. She already knew that he had a bad habit of taking money that didn't belong to him. "But why? He has a comfortable home in a nice neighborhood."

"Charlie said he can't help himself."

Evie resumed her nervous chatter. "Charlie said he was getting professional counseling for it, so I went along. Last week, I finally gave him an earful, told him he should apologize to Charlie for taking advantage of her. I remember a time when something like this wouldn't happen. I used to work for . . ." And away she went.

When she stopped for breath, Gretchen clicked through the pictures on her camera phone until she came to the unfinished room box. "Does this look familiar?" she asked.

Evie barely glanced at it. "No, why should it?"

"Look again," Gretchen urged, putting the phone in her hand. "Was this part of Charlie's display?"

"What horrible construction. Charlie was better than that, much better. I've never seen that room box—if you can call it a room box—in my life."

At an appropriate gap in the conversation, Caroline said, "We should go. Work's waiting."

Gretchen practically ran for the quiet of her car.

"Please, don't say a single word," Gretchen pleaded with

her mother before she pulled out of the driveway. "I need a moment of silence."

That glorious moment was interrupted by an urgent phone call from Nina.

"Daisy's missing," Nina said.

"Daisy's always missing," Gretchen reassured her aunt.

"I have a bad feeling this time," Nina said. "Get in."

Gretchen boldly removed bewigged Tutu from the passenger seat of the Impala and climbed in. The pampered pet, wearing her Barky Braids, snorted at Gretchen from the backseat and turned her head away in disapproval.

"Tutu's miffed," Nina said, driving off. "Why can't you simply share the seat with her?"

Gretchen gave her aunt a withering glare. "You should know the rules better than I do." Gretchen began to tick the points off on her fingers. "Don't feed your dog before you feed yourself. Don't let the dog sleep with its head on the pillow next to you. Don't treat the dog like a supreme being."

"Okay, okay, already. Of course, I know that. I'm a dog trainer. It's just hard for me to apply the same set of rules to Tutu. After all, she was a rescue dog, the poor baby."

Gretchen glanced at Poor Baby and thought she saw the schnoodle grinning smugly back at her. Nimrod wagged his tail, perfectly happy to ride in the back.

"Tutu's spoiled rotten," Gretchen said.

"I know you don't mean that," Nina said, handling the car like a woman who loved to drive. "You're just crabby today."

"Where's Enrico?"

"He's been accepted into a temporary home to see how it works out."

Wonderful! No more snarling and growling from the pint-sized handful every time he didn't like something, which was pretty much all the time. Someone else could deal with his unruly, challenging behavior for a change. Hurray. Nina glanced over. Too late to appear compassionate.

"Don't look so happy," Nina said.

"There's a good reason you charge more to train Chihuahuas, and Enrico is a perfect example of why. Now, tell me about Daisy."

"She was supposed to meet me on Central Avenue. She agreed to help out with a new client, but she didn't show up. I had to cancel. The owner wasn't happy with me."

"That's not like Daisy," Gretchen said.

"If nothing else, she's reliable," Nina agreed. "And I know she needed the money."

"Maybe she's sick."

"She never told me where she was staying. It's a good thing you know," Nina said.

"Turn here."

Nina followed her directions, making several more turns and coming to a halt in the middle of a block when Gretchen instructed her to pull over. They stopped in front of an abandoned house marred by gang symbols. A weed-infested empty lot was next to it.

"The shed is behind this building." Gretchen had been in this neighborhood recently. "Ryan Maize lives close by," she said.

"Scary neighborhood," Nina said. "Why would Daisy choose this over a comfy room with you?

"That's a good question."

"I'm locking the pups in the car. They wouldn't be safe on the street. Do you have anything to protect yourself?"

"Like what?" Gretchen got out and waited for Nina.

"Take this." Nina came around the car. She had a silver lipstick case in her hand.

"Lipstick? We're primping before visiting Daisy?"

"Pepper spray disguised as lipstick. I bought two of them online."

Gretchen took the disguised weapon and chuckled. Leave it to Nina to have a custom pepper spray. She opened the cover and tested the spray by pressing on the bottom of the tube. A long, thin line of fluid shot out.

Gretchen walked along the side of the boarded-up house, picking her way past a pile of discarded junk until she came to a shed in the back. Nina followed at a distance, her "lipstick" at the ready.

Gretchen tried the door, but it was locked. She peered into the shed through a dirty side window, wiping away some of the grime for a better view. Daisy's shopping cart, bulging with all her worldly possessions, was stashed inside. An unfolded sleeping bag was tossed in the corner. "She isn't here," Gretchen said.

Nina, standing near the door, let out a screech. "Gretchen, come here. Blood!"

Gretchen rushed to join Nina. Streaks of red ran along the door frame as though someone with bloody hands had leaned on it for support.

"We have to get inside," Gretchen said.

"We should call the police."

"What if Daisy's in the shed, breathing her last breath? There isn't time. Let's break in, find out if she's there, then decide whether to call for help."

"What about fingerprints?"

"Don't touch anything. I'll be right back."

Gretchen ran to the pile of junk, pulled out a discarded metal table leg, and returned to the shed. She swung her makeshift club at the window, then quickly turned her face away to protect her eyes. The window shattered. She hit at it until she had removed all the shards of glass.

"Windows seem to blow out whenever we're near," Nina observed. "You climb in. You're younger and more athletic. I'll cover you."

Gretchen peered inside the window. What would she do if Daisy was in the shed? What if her homeless friend was dead? The would-be actress with the red hat held a special place in Gretchen's heart. She couldn't be dead. She just couldn't.

"Go!" Nina commanded, managing the operation from a position well out of the way. She fingered the lipstick while scouting for danger from all directions.

Gretchen went through the window with the table leg in her fist. She was careful not to touch anything with an open hand, which wasn't the easiest thing to do.

In spite of the sunny, cloudless day, the interior of the small building was dimly lit. But not dark enough to keep her from spotting more dark stains on the floor of the shed. She couldn't tell if it was blood.

The shed smelled of dirty clothes. Glass crunched under her feet as she stepped hesitantly to the shopping cart.

"Hurry up," Nina called in a stage whisper. "We don't have all day."

Gretchen used the table leg to lift off the top layer of worn clothes. Nothing.

"There's blood on the side of the cart," Nina noted from the window.

"Shush." Gretchen scooped out several layers of old clothes, before turning her attention to the corner of the shed.

"Wait." Nina cautiously climbed in and stood beside her. "Daisy could be under the sleeping bag."

They studied it.

Please, Daisy, don't be under there. "You look," Gretchen said. "I can't."

Nina was pale in the light from the window as she took the table leg from Gretchen and lifted the sleeping bag with the end of it. "Gretchen."

"Yes." A lump formed in Gretchen's throat. She squeezed back tears.

"It's just bedding."

Just bedding. Gretchen's legs threatened to give out. She leaned against the wall of the shed for support, feeling weak. This was too personal. Daisy was part of her life. "Let's get out of here," she said.

"What about all the blood? Shouldn't we call the police?"

"I don't know," Gretchen said, swinging through the broken window. "Let's try to find her first. She wouldn't be happy if she thought we had sent the police after her."

"What about her things?" Nina said, eyeing the cart. "I can't imagine anyone wanting to steal from her, I mean, what's worth taking? But she treats them like treasures."

"Let's put everything in the trunk," Gretchen said, grabbing a pile of clothing.

They checked out the soup kitchen and questioned people on the street who knew her. Two women feeding crumbs to the pigeons from a bench on Central Avenue didn't know where she was. No one had seen her.

A phone call told them she hadn't been admitted to a local hospital. At four o'clock they gave up and went home.

Daisy had vanished from the homeless community of central Phoenix, leaving behind her precious shopping cart and a trail of blood.

· 26 ·

Gretchen walked along the sidewalk leading to April's home in Tempe with Nimrod in her purse. She had learned to accept April's green Astroturf lawn and weeds forcing their way merrily along the edges wherever a bit of dirt existed. She appreciated the woman for her internal beauty rather than for her external environment. The inside of the house would be just as unkempt.

She heard an eerily familiar snarl when she knocked on the front door. *Please don't tell me Enrico's inside! It can't be true.* Nimrod perked up his ears in recognition. His tail beat in puppy glee. "How can you like that little devil?" Gretchen asked the fluff ball, bending close. Nimrod gave her a kiss on the nose.

April opened the door holding Enrico, who emitted another threatening growl.

"He knows who I am," Gretchen complained in exasperation. "Why is he growling? Look at him, his teeth are bared."

"He likes to put on a show," April said. "He's a scaredy-cat underneath the bravado. Come on in."

Gretchen thought back on her conversation with Nina. Her aunt had been intentionally evasive about Enrico's new home. She wouldn't want to be around when Gretchen learned that the monster menace might be a permanent member of the group. "I can't believe Nina talked you into taking him."

"He's kinda cute, and I can always send him back if it doesn't work out. This is a trial run for both of us. Have a seat."

Gretchen sat amid April's miniature dolls and told her friend about the visit with Evie and the discovery that Bernard had been embezzling from Charlie Maize.

"Charlie knew and didn't stop him," Gretchen finished.

"That sounds just like Charlie," April said. "She had a big heart when it came to her friends."

"Some friend."

"Let's move him to the top of our suspect list."

"He's number one on mine," Gretchen said. "Charlie showed the room boxes to Evie the day before she died. Evie says she never saw a kitchen scene. Charlie must have left it until the end as a surprise to all of them. The killer had to have found out what Charlie was up to."

"What about Daisy? Nina told me what happened. She's a tough cookie, and she's streetwise. I bet she's okay."

"I keep telling myself that." Gretchen let Nimrod down. He trotted off to investigate the kitchen floor, knowing April's floor always produced tasty morsels.

April stroked Enrico's tiny ears with her large hand. They both looked contented. Who would have guessed they'd hit if off?

"Any news on Ryan Maize?" April asked. "Have the police found him?"

"Not that I've heard."

"And that hunky detective? What's with you and Matt?"

Gretchen shrugged.

"That's one very scary female he's trying to get rid of. She has her hooks so deep in him, he'll never get away."

"My thoughts exactly." Gretchen remembered the kiss, how sweet it was.

"You aren't giving up on him, are you? You aren't going to let her win?"

"I can't get involved with a married man."

April covered her ears. "I can't stand hearing you say that one more time. The man is getting a divorce. He'd be available right now if she wasn't fighting it. He hides from her. Believe me, the love is gone."

Leave it to April to put the situation in perspective. Was she using Kayla as another excuse to run away? Was she more frightened by the possibility of a close relationship than by a crazy wife? Gretchen hadn't exactly excelled at choosing men in the past. Was she relationship phobic? Everyone else seemed to have some kind of phobia—Matt with his dolls, April and clowns. Was it so far-fetched that she might be too afraid to open up her heart again?

"Bonnie said a court date is coming up," April said. "She has great hopes for this one. Matt will be a free man."

Gretchen wasn't going to hold her breath. "Nina, Britt, and I are going to the rodeo tonight," she said. "I'm inviting you to go with us."

April's eyes widened. "But—"

"I know you're afraid of clowns. You don't have to go, I'll understand. But I want you to know you're welcome to come along. Besides, at the rodeo, clowns are helpers. They protect the riders. They aren't the scary ones. It's the bulls you should be afraid of."

"I'll come," April said a little hesitantly. "Maybe I can beat this thing. Yes," she said, with more confidence. "Count me in."

The Parada del Sol rodeo was in full bucking motion when they arrived. The women entered the arena without any pets. The noise and commotion, Gretchen had reasoned, would scare the dogs. April thought it over and sided with Gretchen, as did Britt, leaving Nina with the only vote to bring them along. She reluctantly left Tutu in the company of Nimrod and Enrico. Caroline agreed to dog-sit and protect Wobbles from the small gang of miniature instigators.

"Why spoil your fun?" Gretchen had argued with her mother. "They can stay alone. Wobbles doesn't need protection from the dogs. It's the other way around."

"I know that," Caroline replied. "But I don't really like rodeos ever since I saw a cowboy gored by a bull." She shuddered. "The man almost died. It's not fun anymore. I'd rather work. I've started my second doll book, and it's moving along nicely."

Tutu had watched Nina leave with such baleful eyes that her aunt almost broke down and took her along. Gretchen whisked her aunt away before she could cave in to the manipulative animal.

Wearing western gear like everyone else in the arena, the three women found places on the metal bleachers. April's cowboy hat had an enormous brim. Nina wore a snappy white cowgirl hat and a sequined jean jacket. Britt had even toned down her severe style by wearing jeans with a blue blazer.

Gretchen and Nina kept April between them so she couldn't panic and bolt. They weren't sitting five minutes before a clown popped out of a barrel. April screamed and crammed her knuckles in her mouth. With her free hand, she grabbed the red bandanna around Gretchen's neck and squeezed.

"It's going to be all right," Gretchen reassured her, trying to break free before her airway was damaged. "Focus on something else. Look over there."

A cowgirl rode into the arena, lasso swinging over her

head. The crowd cheered when she roped her calf. April's grip loosened, and her eyes lit up. "I've never been to a rodeo before," she said. "This is kind of exciting."

"What a deprived childhood you had," Nina said.

"I couldn't go because of the clowns. But this isn't so bad. As long as the clowns stay way over there, I should be fine. This is much better than a parade where they come right up to you. They aren't going to come right up to me, are they?"

"Nope," Gretchen readjusted her bandanna. "You're safe here." She loved the excitement of a rodeo, the danger, the feeling that she'd time traveled back to the past. "Cowboys are sexy," she said as one of the riders dusted off his pants with his hat and strode from the ring.

"Yummy," April agreed. "Good enough to eat."

"Look at that one!" Gretchen said, getting into the swing of things. Why not? She was single. She could ogle as well as any man. Although she didn't think any of them compared to Matt Albright. He was in a class of his own.

April pointed across at a group of cowboys getting ready to ride. "They could *all* eat crackers in my bed, all at the same time."

The women warmed up to the game, evaluating the rugged cowboys. Suddenly Nina gasped. "Don't look," she said harshly, leaning across April and squeezing Gretchen's knee.

"What?" Gretchen glanced at her aunt. Nina was full of drama most of the time. Tonight wasn't an exception.

"I said, don't look." Nina's eyes swung across the arena.

Gretchen craned her neck. At first, she didn't see anything unusual. Then she spotted Matt Albright sitting on the other side, slightly to the right and a few rows below them. She was surprised that Nina had been able to pick him out of the crowd.

She was even more surprised when he leaned over and

whispered to a blonde woman sitting beside him. The woman laughed. He laughed back. Then he put his arm around her and pulled her in to his chest.

April saw, too, because she sucked in air loudly.

Gretchen squeezed her eyes shut, opened them, and saw the same thing.

"I told you not to look," Nina said.

"What's going on?" Britt said.

"Gretchen's boyfriend is over there with another woman," April said, raising her arm.

"Don't point!" Nina hissed.

"What's the big deal," Gretchen said lightly, although she felt a shooting pain in her chest. A wave of nausea washed over her like the onset of flu. "It's not like we've made a commitment or anything."

Stolen kisses in the moonlight obviously meant much more to her than they had to him. Granted, she'd been avoiding him and hadn't returned his phone calls, but he could have tried harder, waited longer.

The discovery was hurtful, not to mention embarrassing. The entire doll community was expecting fireworks from Matt and Gretchen. They'd get fireworks all right, but not the kind they expected. Next time she went to Curves, they'd know all about tonight.

"What a rat," Nina said. "Two-timing Gretchen."

"He doesn't . . ." Gretchen began weakly, trying to keep her voice steady. "He's only . . ." What was he? And what did he mean to her? "Nothing," she decided. "He's absolutely nothing to me."

I sure know how to pick them! Her last relationship had ended when she caught the snake cheating. This one was over before it even got off the ground.

"Let's get out of here," Nina said. She stood up and sidestepped to block Gretchen's view of Matt and his new beautiful blonde. Another pencil-thin Arizona woman guaranteed to shatter Gretchen's self-esteem.

"Not so fast," April said, grabbing Gretchen's arm before she could rise. "We have a mission to accomplish. We're the Mod Squad."

"We have a mission?" Nina asked, echoing April. "We're the Mod Squad? Nobody told me."

"What mission?" Britt said, completely confused.

"You're helping me overcome my clown phobia. Besides, he must have an explanation."

"April's right about staying," Gretchen insisted, finding her voice. "We came to enjoy the rodeo, and I, for one, am going to enjoy it."

If it kills me.

Gretchen inhaled and exhaled slowly. She blocked the cozy couple from her mind. "I see a few people working here that I recognize from the homeless shelter," she said, watching a man empty a garbage can. "We can ask them about Daisy."

April's giant cowboy hat swung with her head. "Let's walk around, get something to drink, and see what we see." April struggled upright and adjusted her hat. "Don't kick any paper cups," she warned. "It's bad luck and could spook the horses."

"I thought you said you've never been to a rodeo before," Gretchen said.

"I haven't, but I read a lot. Horses are easy to scare. Just like me."

"You're tougher than you think," Gretchen said, hoping her words made April stronger. *But how tough am I?*

As they walked to the concession area, a cowboy riding a bull broke into the center of the arena, waving an arm and plunging back and forth while the bull did everything possible to unseat its load. The crowd went wild as the seconds ticked by. The cowboy catapulted from the animal and scrambled for safety. A clown drew the bull's attention away from the rider by running in front of it, waving a red flag.

"See," April said, sweat glistening on her face. "My immersion plan is working. I'm not afraid." But she hadn't taken two more steps before she grabbed Gretchen and Nina for support. "Oh, Lordy, I lied. I feel real weak like I might faint."

"Sit down for a minute," Gretchen said. They guided April to an open spot on the lower bleachers. "I'll get you something to drink. That'll make you feel better."

"I'll get it," Nina said, hurrying off. Her white cowgirl hat bobbed through the crowd.

"I'll go with her." Britt ran to catch up.

"I'm really sorry." April wiped her forehead with her sleeve.

"I'm proud of you for making the effort. You're doing great."

April's eyes bulged. She stared down the aisle. "Here comes one. Oh, no."

"You'll be fine." Gretchen didn't believe it for a second. April looked like she was about to have a fatal heart attack.

"I'm going to faint."

"Put your head between your knees."

April complied. The big woman's upper torso swung down. Her cowboy hat fell to the ground. The clown approached. He stopped in front of them. "Don't look," Gretchen warned April. "Stay where you are and take deep breaths."

"Word on the street," the clown said, "is that you're looking for Daisy."

Gretchen saw April turn her upside-down head to the side just enough to see the clown's big, red feet. "You're okay." Gretchen patted her back reassuringly.

Without a word, April heaved forward and crumpled facedown between Gretchen and the clown. No one in the stands seemed to notice. All eyes were focused on the cowboys.

"Too much to drink?" the clown asked.

"You need to leave before she opens her eyes and sees you again," Gretchen said, squatting beside April, wondering what to do.

Just then, the crowd seemed to part. Gretchen looked up and saw Matt Albright weaving toward them. Nina and Britt appeared next to her, carrying trays filled with food and drinks. April started to move.

The clown trotted away. Gretchen watched him until he stopped at an exit door and looked back at her. "Help April," Gretchen said to Nina, rising from her prone friend. She was afraid to take her eyes off the clown for fear of losing sight of him. "I'll be right back."

She followed him out the door and into the darkness. He moved quickly, heading away from the lights of the parking lot. Gretchen hesitated under a light, aware that she would become vulnerable to an attack if she continued. She was putting herself in a position that she'd been careful to avoid her whole life. Her mother would flip if she knew Gretchen was chasing a man through the night without protection. So would Nina. But she had to know what had happened to Daisy.

Wait. She still had Nina's lipstick pepper spray. It was buried somewhere in her purse, where it wasn't doing her a bit of good at the moment. Next time, she'd have it ready.

All Gretchen could see in the darkness was the clown's white face paint. He'd stopped moving. "Where is Daisy?" she asked.

"Daisy sends a message."

"Tell me." Gretchen was constantly amazed at the home-less community's communications network. She wondered how it worked.

"Meet her at midnight."

"Tonight?"

"Yes."

"Where?"

"Nacho's."

"How did she know where to find me?"

The clown's teeth flashed when he smiled, but he didn't answer.

Gretchen relaxed slightly. He wasn't going to attack her. "What if I hadn't been at the rodeo tonight?"

"Then we would have found you tomorrow. Daisy says come alone."

The clown turned his white face away and faded into the night.

Gretchen used her cell phone to contact Nina. Matt was still attending to April. "She's playing it for all it's worth," Nina said. "She's drooling all over him."

"Tell her to snap out of it," Gretchen said, walking to-ward the car. "Meet me outside. I'm not coming back in." The last thing she wanted was an introduction to Matt's lat-est conquest.

Gretchen stood in the darkness under a viaduct. Cars roared by overhead. Even at this late hour, the city was alive with activity. Streaks of light from passing cars exposed graffiti on the sides of train cars parked on the crisscross of tracks nearby. Ten minutes to twelve. She had worried about her safety at the rodeo. That was nothing compared to where she found herself now.

If she screamed, no one would hear, no one would come to her aid. If she was murdered tonight, her body wouldn't be found for days, or weeks, or ever. Yet Daisy was at home in this isolated corner of Phoenix where shadows constantly shifted and social outcasts roamed.

Gretchen didn't see any signs of life at the base of the massive concrete supports. Nacho's home. She remembered her surprise at that. A homeless person with a home.

The destitute man usually lived inside his head, inebriated more often than sober, but Daisy loved him. They had a better relationship than Gretchen had ever had. She put her personal problems out of her mind. There would be time later for self-pity.

Nacho had reconstructed his home several times. He called it upgrading. When weather conditions destroyed one of his makeshift homes, he built again in the same place, risking flash floods to live here instead of in one of the shelters where he would have to abide by someone else's rules.

His house consisted of cardboard walls framed around an enormous steel beam, secured with duct tape and painted steel gray to blend into the surrounding concrete. His home cleverly fooled the eye. Unless Gretchen looked very carefully, she couldn't see that it was there.

She stood motionless, unwilling to approach the cardboard house. Whose blood had stained the shed and Daisy's shopping cart? That was the thought that kept going through Gretchen's mind. Was Daisy hurt? What about Nacho? Had he returned from his trip to San Francisco?

Sensing someone behind her, she whirled, preparing to release a blast of her pepper spray. Daisy stepped forward.

"I was worried about you," Gretchen said with relief, reaching out for the homeless woman. She hugged her close, ignoring the ripe odors.

"Why worry about me?" Daisy drew back, uncomfortable with Gretchen's display of affection. "I get by just fine."

"I went to the shed and found blood on the door and on your shopping cart. I took your belongings to protect them. What's going on?"

"I'll show you. Follow me." Daisy moved out ahead of Gretchen, in the direction of Nacho's house.

Inside, newspapers were taped on the makeshift walls and on the ground, serving as insulation to keep the chill of the desert night from seeping inside. The small room had enough space for several rolled-out sleeping bags, an old propane camp stove, and a few boxes of miscellaneous items.

"Watch where you step," Daisy advised when they entered. "I'll get us some light."

Gretchen waited while Daisy fumbled around in the

dark. The homeless woman struck a match and touched it to a lantern wick. Low light played against the cardboard walls, illuminating the women and casting gigantic shadows on the walls. Someone slept on the ground inside one of the sleeping bags.

"It's him," Daisy whispered. "I found him in the alley, and I thought he wasn't going to make it."

"Nacho?" Gretchen blanched. "Oh, no. What happened to him?"

Daisy shook her head. "Not Nacho. Ryan Maize, the crazy druggie."

"You're kidding." She hadn't expected that. She drew closer but couldn't see any signs of life from the sleeping bag. "Is he alive?"

"He almost wasn't. I found him hiding behind a Dumpster two nights ago. He was in bad shape. He spent yesterday in the hospital."

"What's wrong with him?"

"Plenty." Daisy sat down on a sleeping bag next to Ryan. He didn't move.

Gretchen bent over him and checked for life. The dirty sleeping bag moved slightly with his shallow breath. He didn't react when she placed her fingertips on his neck and felt for a pulse. "His pulse isn't very strong," she said.

"I had to break him out of the hospital yesterday. The place is more like a prison than a place to fix people."

"I thought you didn't associate with drug people."

"I don't. But I'm the one who found him. He's my responsibility now."

Daisy felt responsible? That was a switch. Gretchen knew that most of the homeless were on the street because they couldn't accept society's constraints. Responsible wasn't an adjective commonly used to describe the indigent.

Yet here she was, claiming responsibility for a fellow human. Maybe Daisy was on the right path after all.

Gretchen knelt beside Ryan. "Why didn't you leave him at the hospital where he was getting professional care? He looks very, very sick."

"If they had found out who he was, it would have been jail for him. He didn't even want to go to the hospital, but he was too weak to run away."

"What's wrong with him? An overdose?"

"I told them I was his mother. The doctor said Ryan snorted some toxic drug. He burned it, inhaled the gases, and it caused horrible hallucinations. Ryan thought demons were slicing him into pieces. He fought them off with a knife but ended up cutting himself. They sewed him up at the hospital, but it's the drug that hurt him the most."

Gretchen recalled her first meeting with Ryan and his bizarre behavior. "He must have been high on the same drug when he hit me."

Daisy nodded. "He's been in one long, ugly nightmare. The doc said he's taken the stuff more than once or twice based on the amount they found in his blood. He might have permanent physical and mental problems and be disabled. There's no way to tell."

"What a messed-up kid."

"Whoever sold him this stuff," Daisy said, "had to know how bad it was."

"Dealers don't care what happens to their customers," Gretchen said. "They're sociopaths without a conscience."

"This dealer *really* didn't care."

"What makes this one any different from any of the others?"

"Ryan took something called ep . . . I can't remember the name of it. The doctor wrote it down." Daisy dug around in her layers of clothes, searching through her pockets. She handed a crumpled piece of paper to Gretchen. "That's the thing he inhaled."

Gretchen couldn't believe her eyes. It couldn't be possible. "Epinephrine?"

Daisy snapped her fingers. "That's it."

"Are you absolutely sure that's what the doctor said?"

"It's his writing. The doc wrote it down for me."

"And he said Ryan inhaled it?"

Daisy nodded. "That's exactly what he said."

"Are you sure he didn't say Ryan injected it?"

"No, he inhaled it."

Gretchen rubbed her eyes and studied the dirty paper again. "His aunt died from a severe allergic reaction," she said. "Sara might have lived if her epinephrine wasn't missing. That's the medicine she needed to overcome the reaction. Without it, she died."

"I didn't know anything about that," Daisy said. "You think Ryan stole it from her so he could get high?"

"I don't know. I've never heard of such a thing," Gretchen said. She remembered saying almost the same thing when she learned that Charlie had died from a nicotine overdose.

"Drug addicts will try anything to get a rush," Daisy said. "The doctor said the same thing you just said. He'd never heard of it, either."

"What does Ryan say when he's awake?" Gretchen nodded toward the sleeping bag.

"He doesn't say anything. He was conscious enough to help me get him into a wheelchair at the hospital, but that's the last time he's been awake. Getting him to Nacho's wasn't easy at all."

"We have to take him back to the hospital. He's very sick." Gretchen pressed her fingers against his cold flesh again.

Daisy shook her head and crossed her arms. "Don't worry about him. He'll recover."

"You don't understand," Gretchen said. "I can't find a pulse."

· 28 ·

Daisy hadn't returned the wheelchair after abducting Ryan from the hospital. She had stashed the getaway vehicle behind a pylon. Gretchen and Daisy would have had a hard time moving him without it, and they were determined to change his location before help arrived. Nacho's carefully hidden home had to remain their secret.

After using Gretchen's cell phone to call in the emergency, the two women wrestled Ryan's limp body into the wheelchair and pushed it up the hill. He weighed very little. Ryan Maize must have used what little cash he was able to panhandle to buy drugs, not food. His face was drawn, with dark circles under his eyes; his body wasted away to the point of starvation. He didn't respond in any way when they lifted him. If he was alive, it wasn't by much.

"I thought I was doing the right thing," Daisy said with a catch in her voice. "I wanted to help him the same way you help me."

Gretchen nodded in understanding. An ambulance siren pierced through other night sounds. "Go away and hide," she said to Daisy. "I'll think of something to tell them."

What could she possibly say? What had compelled Daisy to take Ryan from the hospital? If he died and the police found out, they would blame the homeless woman for his death. Gretchen chewed the inside of her lip while Daisy ran back down the hill and disappeared into the night.

She maneuvered the wheelchair over the curb and followed along the edge of the street, traveling as far as possible from Nacho's house before the ambulance would find them.

She was tired of ambulances and police, and especially detectives. It took a special kind of person to do this sort of work every day, and she didn't think she had whatever it was. If Charlie's son died, she was finished, no more involving herself in things that she couldn't possibly understand or prevent.

From now on, she'd leave the dark side of humanity to people better suited to handle it. She'd follow the sun—climb Camelback, work out with her doll club group, and confine her curiosity to the finer points of doll restoration. No more running off into the dark, chasing cold trails into blind alleys.

Gretchen stopped the wheelchair and laid her palm on Ryan's chest. She felt for movement. Nothing.

A fire truck and an ambulance turned onto the street running parallel to the viaduct. Gretchen pushed the wheelchair toward them and flagged the vehicles down when they came close enough. The firemen had Ryan on the ground in a matter of seconds, starting oxygen and taking his blood pressure and pulse.

While Gretchen watched, she worked on a believable story. If she said she found him lying on the street, they wouldn't have his medical history. What if there was a drug to counter the effect of the epinephrine overdose?

Gretchen came forward. A woman hooking Ryan to a heart monitor glanced questioningly at her. "He overdosed on epinephrine," she said.

The woman looked startled, like this was the first time she'd ever heard of that. "How do you know?"

"Um . . . he told me before he lost consciousness."

"Thanks. We'll take care of him. He's stabilized," the woman called to another paramedic. "Let's get him on a cot."

Gretchen still stood close to the huddled group. "You mean he's alive?"

"He's alive. Could you step back, please?"

Gretchen stepped out of the way and watched them load Ryan into the ambulance.

Soon she was alone on the street, the darkness closing in around her. She hurried toward her parked car. She and Daisy had pushed Ryan three blocks from the enormous girders that supported Nacho's home. Her subterfuge had been unnecessary. None of the rescue workers had asked who she was or where she came from. Or why she was standing in this desolate spot in the middle of the night. Neither the firemen nor the ambulance crew had questioned her about anything at all.

Daisy was safe for the moment, Gretchen hadn't had to lie, and Ryan was alive.

Yes, everyone was safe for the moment.

Everyone, that was, except Gretchen. Because Detective Matt Albright's unmarked car was parked behind hers. The detective leaned against the hood of his car, waiting for her. The expression on his face was unreadable.

Gretchen didn't feel friendly. The night had been long and complicated, and she needed to sleep. "Detective Albright," she said as formally as possible, with enough frost in her voice to freeze his private parts. At least she acknowledged him. He didn't even deserve that after leading her on.

Matt arched one of his eyebrows. "It appears to be quite a night for you," he said. *And for you,* she wanted to say. *Where's your date?*

Gretchen unlocked her car. Did the man ever sleep? He seemed to pop up at all different times of the day and night.

"What's wrong with Ryan Maize?" Matt asked.

"Epinephrine inhalation."

"Ah," he said, like he knew exactly what that was.

"How did you find me?"

"I happened to be driving by and saw your car."

"Not a very likely story."

"You're a very suspicious woman. Want to go to the hospital with me and follow up on his condition?"

"It's two o'clock in the morning."

"I hadn't thought of that." Matt pushed off from the hood and strode around to the driver's side of his car. He opened the door. "I'll call you later with an update."

"You're going?"

Matt nodded. "I need to know how soon I can question him. He's an important link." *Or the final link.* She saw it in his eyes, even though he didn't say it. Ryan didn't have much hope of walking out of the hospital if or when he recovered. Steel bars and prison guards were in his future.

"I'll follow you," Gretchen said, swinging into her car.

What about her vow to follow the sun and forget about murder and mayhem? She'd start tomorrow. Right now, she wanted to make sure Ryan would survive.

All the way to the hospital, she tried to figure out how Matt knew where she was and what she had been doing. Earlier in the evening, he was at the rodeo with another woman, so he must be off duty. Why roam around Phoenix this late when you could be . . . ? Gretchen didn't want to think about what he could be doing with the other woman.

Matt couldn't have been following her, or she would have known sooner. He would have tracked her into Nacho's home or revealed himself when she and Daisy left with the sick man. She was absolutely sure Matt hadn't been near her car when she wheeled Ryan along the street.

Someone must have told him where she was. But who? She hadn't confided in Nina. She wouldn't have approved of her plan to wander alone in a questionable area of the city at night. She would have tried to talk her out of it or would have insisted on going along. She hadn't mentioned it to April after she recovered from her frightening clown incident.

Daisy must have known Gretchen would come looking for her, but the homeless woman wasn't exactly friendly with the local police force. She never would have talked to the detective.

Had Matt been driving around looking for her? If it wasn't so late, she'd call home and ask her mother if he'd been inquiring about her. Wait a minute. Why should she care? She didn't need or want another womanizer in her life.

Gretchen liked to think she learned from past mistakes. It might have taken her seven long years to catch on to a cheating boyfriend, but when she finally *did* figure it out, she corrected the situation and moved on. She'd never waste her time again in a one-sided relationship.

Men! They were their own brand of poison. Yet she couldn't help reflecting on Matt's buff bod as she trailed him into the hospital. And all the rest: thick wavy hair, darkly brooding eyes, and an intelligence behind them that fascinated her. Too bad.

She forced herself to be flippant, but she could still feel the hurt of rejection seeping through the bravado.

Sunday morning, Gretchen joined her mother and Nina at a table next to the pool. The air smelled as fresh as the coffee in her hand. She'd slept late. The morning was almost gone. "Any word on Ryan?" she asked immediately, quite surprised that she'd slept as long as she had.

"Matt called while you were getting your beauty rest," Caroline said. "Ryan's going to make it."

"That's great." Gretchen leaned back in the chair, turned her face to the sun, and closed her eyes. *What a relief.* "I should have stayed at the hospital, but the doctor didn't think there would be any progress until later today."

And she didn't want to be *that* close to the woman-chasing detective. Matt had produced a blanket and pillow for her before selecting a comfortable chair for himself and arranging his body for sleep. The twinkle in his eyes was certainly readable enough.

If she hadn't seen him with someone else last night, she might have enjoyed the attention. It was too late now. He had flashed a grin. No one else in the world could possibly have a smile that magnetic. She had bolted for the revolving doors, but she didn't miss the confused expression on his face as he watched her leave.

"It's time to have a reading done," Caroline announced. "Gretchen, would you like to go first?"

"No, thanks." She didn't open her eyes. The sun felt so good, warm and soothing after the harsh desert night.

"Pick three cards," Nina directed her mother.

"You dropped one," Gretchen heard her mother say.

"I keep doing that," Nina said. "They're a little slippery."

Caroline chuckled. "I seem to remember hearing that there's significance in all aspects of a reading, including dropped cards." *Two peas in a pod.* Leave it to her mother to know tarot trivia. The two sisters took hunches and coincidences very seriously. Would her mother start seeing auras and reading futures?

"I've never heard anything about dropped cards," Nina said.

"You really need to take lessons," Caroline said. "Can't you find a class on tarot reading? You go from one New Age concept to another without taking time to research your topics and truly learn the skills."

"That isn't true."

"What about your dreams? You aren't able to interpret them."

"I'm just not that interested in dreams."

Caroline scoffed. "And your auras. You see them, I'm not doubting you, but you can't interpret the colors you're seeing. So what's the point?"

Gretchen opened her eyes. The two sisters were about to have a disagreement, and there was already enough conflict going around.

"I've figured out a few colors." Nina picked up the fallen card and held them out for Caroline to pick. Gretchen saw a firm set to her lips. "Auras and cards and dreams are lifelong learning experiences," Nina said. "You should take more time to delve into your own spirituality."

Gretchen joined the conversation. "That, sweet Aunt, is exactly what *I'm* going to do. Lie back, do nothing."

"Gretchen's hiding her true feelings behind indifference," Nina said to Caroline. "And it's all because of Matt Albright. She finally showed interest in a new man, and then what happened? He dropped her for another woman."

Caroline gave Gretchen a sympathetic look, which she didn't like at all. The pitiful glances were already starting.

"I think you're marvelous," Caroline said.

"You're supposed to say that. You're my mother."

Nina looked over at Caroline, who had three tarot cards clutched to her chest. "You have to show me the cards. This isn't rummy."

Caroline slapped the cards down on top of the deck and gave Nina a miffed glance. "I think Gretchen needs a reading more than I do," she said. "Come on, Gretchen, draw the cards."

Nina nodded encouragingly, and Gretchen reluctantly went along with their wish if for no other reason than to diffuse an argument. "Not good," she said, after looking at her cards and laying out a ghostly, black-clad figure. "I drew something bad."

"The death card," Nina said with significant meaning.

Great. Just what I need. The death card.

Nina watched her lay out the remaining cards. "That isn't necessarily bad."

"But what can be good about dying? There isn't anything positive about it from my point of view."

"I'll tell you in a minute." Nina broke into a big grin when she saw the other cards. "I'm so glad you drew the two knights." She reached for her instruction booklet and paged through. Gretchen and Caroline exchanged looks, neither taking Nina as seriously as she took herself. After a few minutes, Nina set down the booklet and cleared her voice. "The knight of cups means an opportunity will soon arise. I'm thinking something like a proposal. A marriage proposal."

"Oh, come on. You made that last part up."

Nina looked offended. "The card holds the meaning; I'm simply the interpreter. I have to read the significance of the card. Don't think for a minute it's easy." She turned her attention back to the cards. "And the knight of swords signifies courage, so you will have the strength to handle whatever is coming your way."

"And the death card?"

"Means you must clear away the old to make room for the new."

Caroline clucked. "I like Gretchen's reading."

Nina nodded. "Me, too. It sounds like a romance is in your future. And you'll have the courage to overcome your fear of men."

"I'm not afraid of men."

"Or . . ." Caroline offered, "it could mean you are on the right path in your quest for the truth, and you will handle the outcome just fine."

"What about the death card in that case?" Gretchen asked her mother, keeping an eye on the blackness of the card. She had goose bumps on her arms in spite of the warming rays of sun.

"Nina's right," her mother said, dodging. "It doesn't have to be in a physical sense."

Nina glanced up from her booklet. "But sometimes it does mean death."

Wonderful! "I should take a vacation," Gretchen said.

"Why don't you go shopping with Nina?" Caroline recommended.

"Okay."

"And tomorrow you can help me in the workshop."

"Terrific idea." A day in the workshop with her mother always made Gretchen feel whole again.

"According to the cards," Nina stage-whispered to her,

still pondering the three cards, "you have to follow the trail of the incriminating wallpaper. It's the key to everything."

Gretchen stared down at the cards. "Where does it say that?"

"Nina," Caroline said sharply. "I've had time to think over Charlie's murder and the potential danger. We should let the police handle everything."

"Okay, okay." Nina scooped up the three cards and returned them to the deck. "Let's take the pooches to the Biltmore Fashion Park for doggy treats. We'll even pick up April and Enrico."

"We'll talk strategy after we pick up April," she whispered later, surrounded by an enormous amount of baggage in the form of two little, bitty animals.

Gretchen climbed into the passenger seat of the Impala, thrilled that April was back in Nina's good graces and all was as it should be.

Gretchen chuckled to herself as the trio strolled through the open-air mall with their pooches skipping along beside them. They weren't the only ones out with their dogs. A Great Dane sniffed curiously at Tutu, who stuck her nose in the air. Nimrod passed the enormous canine with great caution. Enrico snarled menacingly. Foolish, considering that the Great Dane could wolf him down in one gulp.

Nina headed into the doggie bakery and purchased cookies for the dogs.

"I'm buying Gretchen a new doggy purse at the boutique," Nina said.

"What's wrong with my old one?"

"Nimrod is growing. He needs his own carrier."

Nina selected a black carrier designed to look exactly like a purse. "See," she said, twirling with it on her shoulder.

"It has a removable bottom and mesh side panels, so he can go incognito anytime he wants to and still see out."

Gretchen scooped up the miniature teacup poodle and placed him inside the carrier. "He likes it," she said, when he stuck his head out the top and wagged his tail.

"It's yours then," Nina exclaimed, heading for the checkout counter. "Your purse can be free for your own things. No more sharing."

"You mean I need two purses now?" This wasn't good. Soon she would have as much to tote as Nina. Gretchen preferred being as unencumbered as possible.

"Of course," April piped up, feeding a doggie cookie to Enrico. "That's the whole point."

The white cotton purse with the embroidered black poodles had also been a gift from Nina. For the last few months she had carried all her belongings in it as well as Nimrod, so it was looking a little worn. "I think I'll buy a purse to match Nimrod's," she said. "Something small and black."

"After that," Nina announced, handing Gretchen her new puppy carrier, "I have a surprise. We're going over to Britt's house for coffee. She invited me, but I thought it would be fun to take you both along. She won't mind."

April clapped her hands in glee. "Oh, goody. I want to start making my own dolls. Britt's going to help me get started. This is exciting."

"Shouldn't you call her and ask if you can bring guests?" Gretchen asked. "We can't just barge in."

"Sure we can," Nina said. "Besides, we're investigating kitchens, and we haven't seen hers yet."

"That Maize kid did it," April said with conviction. "End of story."

"I'm not so sure," Gretchen said. "But I'm really through traipsing around. We didn't sign on to get blown to bits. Our job was over when the window exploded and the display disintegrated."

April laughed. "She's just as dramatic as you," she said to Nina.

Nina laughed along, considering that a compliment.

Gretchen glared at her friends. "And I was almost macheted to death by Bernard's wife."

"Macheted isn't a proper verb," Nina said. "But I get your drift. Some people aren't cut out for extreme adventure."

"You weren't the one facing that wacko, with no place to run."

"Trust me," Nina cooed. "We're only going to peek at Britt's kitchen while we visit. What's the harm in that?"

"If I recall correctly, you said the same thing right before Bernard's wife tried to butcher me."

"The cards were clear; the quest must continue," Nina said. "If you aren't up to it, I'll carry on without you."

"I'll help because we're friends." April said. "But the kid did it."

"I heard," Nina said, "that killers who use poison usually get away with their crimes unless they continue to poison victims. Then they start leaving trails."

"Like Arsenic Anna," Gretchen agreed. "I've been reading about her, and the psychology behind killers like her. Arsenic Anna was a psychopath, and according to what I'm reading, psychopaths aren't insane. They kill because they lack a conscience."

"That qualifies as crazy in my book," April said.

"Arsenic Anna maintained her innocence right up until the very end when they threw the switch. But she wrote letters that weren't opened until after the execution. In them, she explained how she killed those old men. Rat poison in oysters, in orange juice. She even tried to kill a woman who lived near one of her victims by poisoning an ice cream cone."

"Do you think a psychopath murdered Charlie?" Nina asked.

"I don't know," Gretchen admitted. "That's why we should stay out of it."

"Better yet," April said. "Don't accept any food or drink from anyone."

"Here poochies," Nina called. "Let's go. Should we drop you at home, Gretchen?"

Gretchen sighed, remembering that there was safety in numbers. "I'll come along."

"She's back in," April said, grinning.

30

Melany Gleeland has a truly horrible secret. It's almost bigger than she can handle by herself, which is why she has to get away from Phoenix—any way she can, by any means available.

Whatever it takes.

Melany fingers the knot of the black do-rag in her hand. Do-rags. Everybody's doing do-rags: cancer patients hiding bald heads during chemo treatments, hip-hop groups, bikers to prevent helmet head. Black is the hot color. You've seen one, you've seen them all. Her biker boyfriend wears one under his helmet. This could be his.

She can't get out of this city fast enough. She hates everything about it: the brown smog that hovers over Phoenix, breathing in toxins right along with oxygen, unbelievable pollen counts, new allergies assaulting her sinus passages daily. Then there's the blinding, unrelenting heat from the sun, no shade anywhere, the weather forecasters predicting a significant change in temperature, as if a drop of four degrees is national news.

And her mother. If she doesn't leave right now, she might do something to hurt the witch. Like set her hair on fire while she's bent over her precious kiln. Give her head a blast of flammable hair spray, and *whoof*. Up she goes. Problem solved in one big incendiary moment.

She really hates her mother's perfectly symmetrical face.

Melany is homely, according to Mommy Dearest, because her features aren't balanced properly. Look at Melany's face from one side, then the other, and you can see the problem. Symmetry is the secret to real beauty. Draw a line down the middle of your face. The sides should match.

How unfortunate for Melany.

Poor girl.

31

The first step to becoming a doll maker is deciding what type of doll to cast. That determines what mold to use. Modern dolls are created from sculpted molds. Then they are finished off with contemporary clothing and synthetic wigs. Antique reproductions are cast from existing antique dolls. Every effort is made to re-create the look of antique painting. Costumes for antiques are natural fibers such as silk or cotton, and wigs are mohair or human hair. Make your selection, and let the fun begin.

—From *World of Dolls* by Caroline Birch

Britt Gleeland had converted a wing of her home into a doll-making studio. Gretchen didn't see any dolls on display when she walked through the living area, which she considered unusual for a doll collector. She did manage to get a glance at the kitchen and saw wallpaper in colors that seemed to match the unknown room box, but she was too far away to see the pattern. She had to find an opportunity to get closer.

Nina jabbed her in the ribs and raised her brow. She'd seen, too.

"I'm so excited to be here," April gushed when she saw the doll-making workshop. She headed for a long table in the center of the room, which was filled with tiny projects in various stages of completion.

"My class meets every Thursday," Britt said. "I have seven students at the moment, but they are in the middle of their projects. It would be impossible for you to catch up at this point."

"When does your next class begin?" April plopped down and dreamily fingered the miniature pieces.

"In a few weeks. I like to have a full table of students before I start. Why don't I call you?"

April barely heard her. She was completely mesmerized by her surroundings.

Gretchen had to admit that the miniatures were extremely captivating. She'd devoted her career to restoration of full-sized antiques, but she understood April's fascination. Someday she might take a miniature doll-making class herself.

"Who would like coffee?" Britt asked. Every hair in her twist was right where it should be.

Nina cast a sly eye at Gretchen. "We all would love some," she said. "I'll help you in the kitchen."

"No need; it's right here. Come sit." Sure enough, a carafe filled with coffee and all the trimmings sat on a round table to the side of the worktable.

Gretchen and Nina exchanged warning glances. Now what? Britt would expect them to drink the coffee. Gretchen solved the problem by offering to pour, after which the women watched Britt take small sips. Once she had drunk half of the coffee in her own cup, the others joined in.

While they chatted, Gretchen tried to think of anything that might be missing from the coffee supplies so she could follow Britt into the kitchen to retrieve them. But the doll maker had been thorough, even including honey, rich cream, and raw sugar on the service tray.

Gretchen was determined to get a good look at the kitchen. "Excuse me, please," she said. "May I use your bathroom?"

"Of course; it's right over there." Britt waved toward the back of the studio.

Foiled again, Gretchen went through the motions now required of her and entered the bathroom. The room was starkly functional, designed for Britt's students, not for her personal use. None of the cabinets contained potions or poisons.

When Gretchen came out, the coffee klatch had moved to the kiln. "This kiln can reach well over two thousand degrees," Britt said to an impressed audience. "The control is mounted on the wall over near the door to keep it safe from the heat. I lock the kiln for safety when the class isn't using it."

"It looks like a big washtub," Nina said.

"Like an old-fashioned washing machine," April agreed.

Nina made a move to lift the cover.

Britt grabbed her wrist, striking out swiftly, as though she'd anticipated Nina's intent. "I have pieces cooling inside. If you open it, they might crack."

"Cool air meeting hot air," April said, picking up a pair of safety goggles with green lenses and trying them on. "Basic physics."

Britt's daughter Melany appeared in the doorway. "I'm going now," she said, staring at her mother, seemingly unaware that she had company. Britt hurried over and gave her a hug. Melany stiffened. She didn't move to return the embrace.

Britt's fingers fluttered to her French twist, nervously feeling for renegade locks.

Again, Gretchen noticed the contrast in the two women. Melany went for the no-makeup, rumpled look, almost in direct opposition to her mother's organized, proper appearance. Was she acting out? Was it a passive-aggressive stance?

Once Melany was gone, Britt moved her guests to another table. "These are some of my work in progress. I go through six stages of painting and firing. See these? The initial firing makes the porcelain pink, but not a flesh-colored pink like I want. I keep adding colors. They become richer and more natural looking with every firing."

"What if I make a mistake?" April asked.

"Then you use paint thinner to start over." Britt's voice had become tutorial. "Over here I'm cutting out eye sockets, and over here I've just cut out the crown of this doll's head."

"And you made earring holes," April exclaimed, beside herself with joy. So much for a working crime partner. One of Charlie's Angels had gone to heaven.

While Britt preened under the rays of April's worship, Gretchen studied Britt's doll-making tools. Gretchen didn't feel the same warmth for the doll maker as April did. What if Britt and Bernard were accomplices?

Gretchen felt a twinge of conscience for being mean-spirited. While Bernard had stolen from her, and she had a good reason to distrust him, Britt hadn't done anything remotely suspicious. She'd try harder to like her, *after* she got a good look at Britt's kitchen. She'd make more of an effort. That was, if the wallpaper didn't match.

Some of Britt's tools were familiar to Gretchen: stringing clamps, body paint to give a doll body's an antique look, hooks, and pliers. The studio was also well-stocked with supplies different from Gretchen's: modeling clays and a variety of molds.

When Gretchen needed to replace a part, she had to find an original from the same time period. Too bad she couldn't just whip up a copy in Britt's kiln. Her serious antique collectors would know instantly that she had cheated.

"That's an incising tool," Britt said, appearing next to her. "It's used to mark the creator's name on the doll. We have to be very careful that a reproduction isn't mistaken for an original."

Gretchen held up a scalpel. Nina, she suddenly noticed, was missing from the room. The bathroom door was open, so she wasn't in there. Her stealthy aunt had vanished into the interior of the house.

"I have all different sizes in the drawer below it," Britt said.

Taking that as permission, Gretchen opened the drawer. It was filled with scalpels and syringes. She reminded herself that Britt was a doll maker and that scalpels and syringes were important tools of her trade.

She opened the next drawer. More knives. "Quite a collection." She held up a knife. The handle bore the steel image of a feather.

"That's a Native American feather knife. It belonged to my grandfather."

Gretchen used the contents of the drawers as a distraction to cover for Nina. "What do you use this one for?" Where was Nina?

Finally she caught a flash of pink behind Britt.

Nina's jeweled fingers reached in and closed a drawer. "We should be going," Nina said.

"Thank you for stopping by." Britt said, showing them out a back door. "April, I'll call you as soon as I have enough students signed up for a class. And Nina, call me."

"Well?" Gretchen said when they were in the car. "Was it the kitchen?"

"Same general colors as the room box wallpaper, but the border isn't teapots, its grapes."

"Good work, partner," Gretchen said. "Another elimination."

"Check that Maize kid's house," April advised. "I'm sure he did it."

"The drug house is next on our list of kitchen stops," Nina said.

"Ryan Maize didn't kill his mother," Gretchen insisted.

"He's the most obvious suspect," April said from the front seat. "He was stoned out of his mind on drugs, he's violent—I *saw* him hit you—he threw a Mali-something cocktail and almost blew us up."

Gretchen scooted to the middle of the backseat and leaned forward. "If you had evidence that your son had killed your sister, would you make a room box and accuse him at an unveiling with a room filled with complete strangers? What kind of mother would expose her child that way?"

April humphed. "What kind of kid would kill his mother or his aunt?"

"Exactly!"

"Let's check him out anyway," Nina said diplomatically. "We should rule him out together. A unanimous decision, since we are a t-e-a-m."

"Go team," April said. "I could hardly drink the coffee after our discussion of Arsenic Anna and rat poison."

"Britt and I are becoming close friends," Nina said. "I shouldn't even be suspecting her."

"The coffee was fine," Gretchen said. "It came out of one carafe."

"That was smart thinking," April said.

"There's so much to learn about detecting," Nina said.

"Live and learn," April said.

"I think you mean," Gretchen said, "learn and live."

They should have saved the mission to Ryan's house for another day. "Look at the commotion," April said.

"Keep going right past," Gretchen said to Nina from the backseat. From now on, she was going to drive herself. She felt trapped in her aunt's car.

A police officer tried impatiently to wave them past when Nina slowed down. "I said, keep going," Gretchen repeated, raising her voice.

Matt Albright's unmarked blue car was parked at the curb. She saw Detective Brandon Kline standing on the broken-down porch talking to a cop. Brandon turned and shouted something to the officer near their car. The cop gave way, and motioned them to pull over.

Nina followed his direction. Gretchen moaned.

"The cops are searching Ryan's pad," April said, breaking into her version of street talk. "Look at all those strung-out crackheads." She pointed to a pathetic group of five huddled at the corner of the house. They were in varying degrees of undress. Only one wore a shirt, all were barefoot, and if the others hadn't been bare-chested, Gretchen wouldn't have been able to figure out which were males. The one wearing the shirt was still an unknown as far as sexual persuasion went.

Gretchen slunk down in the backseat and crawled onto her stomach. The dogs, always ready for a ripping good time, used her as a runway. Tiny, sharp claws raked her back as they ran back and forth.

"What are you doing?" Nina said with more than a hint of disbelief in her tone.

"Hiding."

"I can see that. But from whom?"

"I vowed never to have anything to do with that womanizer again. If you had driven by when I asked you to, I wouldn't be flat on the seat with little nails piercing my skin. I'll be able to wear studs in the holes by the time they're done with me."

Okay. Gretchen was pretty sure she was acting immature. That's precisely what the detective did to her and why she was avoiding him. When was the last time she hid out in a car? She remembered exactly when—fourteen years ago—her sophomore year in high school, right before Eddie Bremen caught her with another guy. She'd tried to break it off, but he wouldn't take no for an answer, so she had ducked down to protect her date. It hadn't worked. Eddie Bremen had really clobbered her date.

Slinking was justified that time, and it was justified this time. Hopefully, she'd have better luck than last time. "What brings the pleasure of your company?" she heard Matt say right next to the car door. "And why is Gretchen hiding in the backseat?"

April giggled.

Gretchen shot up. "I wasn't hiding. I was looking for my . . . uh . . . contact. It jumped out of my eye."

She didn't even wear contacts, but he couldn't possibly know that.

"I'll help you." Matt opened the back door and carefully edged in, his eyes on her instead of on the floor. "I lose mine every once in awhile. It's a real pain."

"I found it!" Gretchen exclaimed, pretending to cup the

lens between her hands. "Give me some room, and I'll plunk it back in. You have more important things to do."

Brandon Kline came up behind them. "We haven't found a thing. Not so much as a roach clip or dope pipe. The place is squeaky clean."

Matt shook his head. "Impossible."

"They insist this is a rehab house. Junior over there . . ." He pointed at the ragged group, "claims he's the sponsor."

"Let's make him prove ownership," Matt said.

Brandon's gaze settled on Nina. He smiled.

Nina batted her eyes. "I should do a reading for you as soon as you wrap up this case," she said. Gretchen would have to teach Nina the finer points of conversing with the opposite sex. *I should do a reading?* What an awful pickup line.

"I'd like that," he said, sounding like he meant it.

Nina eyed up his back end as he moved through the police officers, barking orders.

Matt winked at Gretchen.

She ignored him, glancing at the so-called homeowner and the pink stucco house. What if it was true? What if the house really was used for drug rehabilitation and not drug deals? "Ryan's bizarre behavior could have been completely due to the epinephrine," she said, thinking out loud.

"He certainly was full of the stuff," Matt said. "Heavy usage for at least a week, maybe longer, according to the physicians. He's lucky to still be alive. He must have a death wish."

"Did they find any other drugs in his system?" Gretchen asked, trying to overlook her personal issues with the detective. *Act grown-up. Drop the inner pout and move on.*

"That was the surprising thing," Matt said. "Not a trace of any street drugs."

"What does he say to explain his condition?"

"He's disoriented and lethargic. Says a goddess was serving him, according to the medical staff. I don't know when, if ever, he'll be lucid enough to give answers that make sense. His physician hasn't cleared him for questioning yet." He looked over at the house. "I better get back inside."

"We want to look at the kitchen," Nina said. "We're studying crimes and the effects on kitchens."

April giggled, which was all she seemed to be able to do when she was too close to Matt. Did Gretchen act that dopey around him? She hoped not.

"You can look through the window from the outside of the house," Matt answered, wearing a look of amused confusion. "But stay away from the tenants. By the way, Gretchen, you don't wear contacts."

"Busted," April said. "What tipped you off?"

Gretchen wished April would go back to giggling. So what if he caught her lying? Gretchen leveled Matt with a steely glare just in case he thought his approval mattered to her.

"A true contact wearer," he said, "holds a contact like this." He pressed his fingers together. "We don't cup them in our palms. And the terminology isn't 'plunk' it in. It's 'pop' it in. They don't jump out of our eyes, either." He grinned. "But I still like you, even if you aren't one of us."

"I'm a contact wearer," April giggled.

Gretchen marched behind him toward the house with Nina and April taking up the rear and, oh no, all the dogs. "Potty stop," Nina said when Gretchen scowled at her. "As good a place as any." Nina glanced at the trash in the weedy yard. "I won't have to clean up any doggie do. It'll blend right in." Nimrod and Tutu trotted with Nina. Enrico ran alongside his new owner, with his lip pulled up on one side to show his back teeth. He had a nasty gleam in his beady little eyes.

Matt shook a thumb over his right shoulder and addressed one of the officers. "They want to look in the window. Let them."

He entered the house with Brandon. A band of police officers maintained a circle around the motley bunch of tenants. The cops remained a respectable distance away, trying to appear casual and unconcerned. But they kept a sharp eye out.

Judging by the group's state of undress, no one was carrying a weapon. The most that could happen would be that one could run away. "Who owns the house?" Gretchen asked them when she was close enough. She kept her voice low.

"We don't have anything to say," said one with a shaved head. "We want an attorney."

"Have you been arrested?"

"No. But we aren't talking to any cops."

"Do I look like a police officer?" Gretchen said, suspecting that the bald one was the homeowner. She pointed at Nina and April. "Do they look like cops?"

"She's right," another one chortled. "What kind of cops would have dogs like that?"

Good reasoning. This one, at least, wasn't all drugged out. Up close, Gretchen could tell that they were all men, even the shirt person. "I'm a friend of Ryan's," she said. "I'm trying to help him."

"You're too late, he's totally whacked out. We should have thrown him out as soon as we found out he was doing drugs again," Baldy said. "We knew he was messing up. Now look what's happened, man."

"Nina and April, why don't you check out the kitchen?" Gretchen said. Her eyes scanned the group, then she asked, "Which window is the kitchen?" No one answered, but a few eyes shifted to a window. "Try that one there." She pointed.

The two women hustled over to the house. They grabbed

the bottom of the windowsill and tipped up onto their toes to peer in. "It's too high," April announced. "I can't see in."

"Boost Nina up," Gretchen called before scooting to the opposite side of the huddle. She didn't want to see what was going to happen next. Right before she turned her back, she saw April plant her solid legs and lace her fingers together.

"Hold the dogs," Nina said behind her.

"How can I hold them *and* boost you?"

"How can I go up with them? Put the leashes around your wrist, like that. Ready?"

"Ryan was doing drugs," Gretchen said to the tenants, a statement rather than a question. "But you still wanted to help him?"

"He dried out while he was here," one with dreadlocks said. "No alcohol, no drugs, but he slipped back. We hoped it was temporary."

"Don't talk to her," Shirt Guy said.

"She's a friend of Ryan's. How's he doing anyway?"

"He's alive," Gretchen said. "But barely. And he's hallucinating."

"He was doing good, and then all of a sudden, he was all screwed up. Nobody could talk to him. Everything that came out of his mouth was total garbage."

Gretchen tapped a piece of paper trash on the ground with her foot, thinking. "He talked about a goddess."

"We got that shtick, too. He claimed some fairy chick visited his bedroom at night."

"We never saw her."

"That's cuz she didn't exist."

"Duh."

"He said she flew in the window."

"He said a lot of dumb things. When was the last time you saw a fairy flying?"

"When was the last time you saw a fairy standing around?"

Gretchen heard a commotion behind her, then a shriek, then a thud. She tried to block it out. "Bad news, man," Shirt Man said, referring to Ryan. Or so Gretchen thought. Shirt Man was facing the kitchen investigators. She hoped the comment wasn't about Nina and April.

"Watch where you're falling," April wailed. "You could have killed Enrico."

"You dropped me," Nina screamed.

"I released you. There's a difference."

"Can you intervene for us?" the bald one asked Gretchen. "We really are running a rehab program."

Gretchen believed him. He and the other occupants were as much on the fringes of society as the homeless people she knew. But druggies? When she looked into their eyes, they were clean and bright, without the hopeless, empty gaze associated with drug addicts. They didn't have that hunted, haunted fear she'd seen in Ryan's eyes or the wasted away, thin bodies.

Nina stomped past carrying Tutu. April heaved off from the side of the house and made for the car with the other two miniature dogs.

"We're going to the hospital to see how Ryan's doing," Gretchen said to the bald one.

"Say hi. We hope he makes it."

Gretchen hustled after April. She peeked in the entrance to the house as she passed but didn't see the two detectives. Why was she even checking? She didn't care. Nope. Not one teeny, tiny bit.

· 33 ·

"Ryan did it," April insisted, pounding a plump fist on the dashboard to stress her point. "He killed his mother. I don't care about wallpaper. We're getting too wrapped up in kitchens. Forget the room box. He's the one."

"His kitchen was the most disgusting thing I've ever seen," Nina said, darting through traffic. She had recovered quickly from her graceless fall. "Crud everywhere. Men shouldn't be allowed to live in large groups. They're pigs. I can't even imagine how awful the bathroom would be." She shivered for effect.

"All I saw was your rear end," April said. "And then that lizard darted across the wall right next to us. He stopped and stared me right in the eye. Sorry I dropped you."

"Forgiven," Nina chirped. Their friendship had come a long way. A few weeks ago, Nina would have held a grudge against April much, much longer. This one was over within minutes.

The safest thing to do was to get them back on task before one of them had a chance to say the wrong thing and start another disagreement.

"The ICU staff wouldn't give me any details about Ryan's condition," Gretchen said. "They gave me the patient privacy protection speech. All they'll say is that he's on that hospital floor."

April shook her head. "You'll never get inside."

"*We'll* never get inside," Nina corrected her. "We are a t-e-a-m."

Gretchen visualized all three of them and the dogs attempting to sneak into the hospital. The Three Stooges, that's what they would be. They could stuff the canines inside their purses, even Tutu, who was a bit large for a handbag. She chuckled in spite of herself.

"How are we going to get into Intensive Care, boss lady?" April asked from her usual position of authority in the front passenger seat.

"Boss lady? Are you talking to me?" Gretchen asked. Starting tomorrow, Gretchen was absolutely, definitely driving her own car. No more of this backseat-with-the-animals traveling.

"You're the woman."

"I think one of us should go in," she said. "One will stand a better chance."

"You're the one, boss," April said. "You've established a bond with the kid."

"You have to be kidding. He thought I was a cop! He decked me. The next time, on his porch, he wasn't much friendlier."

"See, he's warming up, boss."

"If I'm the boss, why am I in the backseat?"

"We're your chauffeurs."

Gretchen looked around at her luxury ride. Goo dripping from the back windows and dog hair coating the seats and her clothes. Nimrod climbed up her chest and licked her face. Tutu sat as far away from Gretchen as possible, pretending she didn't exist. Enrico was getting used to her. He only growled now when she shifted her legs or made sudden movements.

"How come I'm the boss every time you don't want to do something?" Gretchen wanted to know.

"I'd go in," her aunt said. "I'd do it myself, but I'm recovering from my tramatic fall to the ground."

Nina pulled into the visitors' parking lot. "We'll keep the getaway car running."

"Thanks, t-e-a-m." How bad could it be? It wasn't like she was trying to break into a gated senior community. Or like she'd disguised herself as a nurse. She couldn't get busted for impersonating medical personnel. Was that illegal? "Anyone have a nurse's uniform?" she asked. "I could sail right through with the proper attire."

"Getoutadacar," April said.

The gangsta doll appraiser was starting to get on Gretchen's nerves. She got out, strolled casually into the hospital, requested the directions to ICU at the information counter, and took the elevator to the second floor.

So far, so good.

The roadblock came when she dead-ended at an imposing set of doors with a sign that said Restricted Area. A nurse passed her and pushed a button on the wall. The door swung out. The nurse walked inside.

Gretchen peered through the massive doors, studying the layout. The door swung shut. Easy enough.

"May I help you?" a different nurse said the instant Gretchen stepped over the threshold into intensive care. No tiptoeing past the guards, after all.

"I'm here to see Ryan Maize," Gretchen said.

"One minute, please." The nurse did something in a computer. "Are you family?"

"I'm his aunt."

"He's in room 220. It's down this hall."

Gretchen grinned all the way down the corridor. Detective

Albright should take a few lessons from her. *He* hadn't managed to get past the nurses' station with his impressive credentials and flashy badge. All she had to do was walk in and ask to see Ryan.

The patient looked like something out of a bad sci-fi movie. Tentacles jutted from the sheets on both sides of the bed, carrying colored fluids, some flowing in, some flowing out. Monitors hummed and beeped, displaying information Gretchen couldn't read.

His eyes were open.

"How are you feeling?" She stopped at the foot of the bed.

"Not so good."

"You're lucky to be alive."

"I'm not so sure." Ryan didn't appear to be delusional, certainly not catatonic. Then, "Where's the carnival man?" he said, crushing her optimistic outlook for him.

Gretchen realized he might mean the doctor. She wasn't very good at street slang. "Do you need something for pain? I can call the nurse."

"Yah."

"Talk to me first."

He looked at her without recognition, his eyes glassed over from either inner demons or the effects of medication, or both.

"What happened to you?" she asked.

"A little friendly connection gone bad."

"What does that mean?"

Ryan didn't answer. He closed his eyes.

"Did someone do this to you?"

He nodded and squinted up at her. "Fruit of the gods. The end is unclear. It's what happens when you buy in. Trust is elusive."

This was hopeless. Gretchen wasn't going to learn

anything useful from Charlie's son. He was too busy associating with goddesses and gods.

A nurse came in and adjusted a few tubes.

"He says he's in pain," Gretchen said to her.

"This will help." She injected something into an IV.

"How is he?"

"He's doing really well."

"Any signs of drug withdrawal?"

"No."

"Isn't that unusual for a drug addict? Not to have withdrawal symptoms?"

"Who said he was an addict?" she said. "Epinephrine was the only drug in his system when he came in." The nurse finished up and left. "He was sick enough with what he had."

So maybe Ryan was riding high on hospital drugs. Yet he had been living in a drug rehabilitation house. He was drug-free when he checked into the hospital (well, other than the epinephrine). Who ever heard of an epinephrine addict, anyway? "Who gave you the drugs that made you ill?" she said to him, noting that he was about to nod off.

"Carnival man. He came through my window every night. I tried to stay away, but he forced me."

"I thought a goddess came through your window," she said, remembering the conversation with his roommates. "Who is carnival man?"

"Bad dude. Green hair." He made a weak gesture with both hands. The IVs followed his arms. He placed his hands on the sides of his head, then shoved them away like he was saluting.

This wasn't getting her anywhere. But she had to try. "What else do you remember about him?"

Ryan's hands fell to the bed.

His words were slow. There must have been a sedative

in the injection the nurse gave him. "Bald around the top of his head, green hair on the sides, man, I don't know, sticking straight up."

Gretchen sagged against the bed. This guy had really gone insane. The epinephrine overdoses might have sent him permanently over the edge, but he'd been headed to the cliff long before this. She couldn't imagine the depth of his mother's grief at her son's state. How long ago had Charlie lost her son? How long had she tried to save him from himself before she realized she never would? That kind of heartache must live inside a person forever.

Ryan's mouth was moving, but the words came out too softly to hear. His eyes were shut.

Gretchen moved around the side of the bed and leaned closer, trying to catch his last words before the drugs eased him into a deep sleep.

"Big red nose," he whispered. "Big red feet." Then he was asleep with his mouth still open.

Gretchen's legs weakened when she realized what he had been trying to tell her. She plopped down on the side of his bed, carefully moving his arm to the side so she wouldn't bump the tubes. She watched his face relax.

The carnival man had come in through his bedroom window, so the others living in the house wouldn't know. Getting him to cooperate the first time would have been the hardest. Or would it? Hold the promise of drugs right under his nose, hand it to him, offer him just a little. He could have gone along. After the first time, it would have been easy to continue to poison him.

He was already a little overloaded with the first major dose of epinephrine, seeing things a little skewed. Every night, giving him another dose, making him appear crazed, focusing all the attention on him. Ryan Maize was the perfect murder suspect.

Based on information from his roommates, Ryan Maize had been on the road to recovery. Then suddenly, one day, he began hallucinating, seeing demons, fighting them off. That explained why he had struck out at her so viciously. What horror had he seen in her that day to provoke him into violence and into such fear? She'd read it in his eyes at the time. Unbelievable fear.

Gretchen rubbed her forehead with both hands, feeling a headache coming on. She was as crazy as he was. Why couldn't she let it go, let the police wade through all the lies and deceptions?

Because she could feel the truth, and she wasn't convinced that they would. She felt it strongly. Not that Gretchen would ever say that to her aunt. Nina didn't need any more fodder to fuel her belief in the family's psychic abilities.

This was plain old intuition.

Ryan Maize was as much a victim as his Aunt Sara and his mother had been. And he would have followed right behind them to his own grave, dying soon from an intentional overdose. They would have said he committed suicide because he had killed his own mother. That he didn't want to live after what he had done.

Gretchen knew who the murderer really was. She hadn't been paying attention at the time, because she was late and in a hurry. The crowds and the parade had distracted her. Yes, she'd had an encounter with the person who poisoned Charlie, and she'd had it right after Charlie had succumbed to the toxins.

Gretchen remembered looking up from where she had fallen at the parade, seeing the bald head and green hair sprouting from the sides in comic tufts.

The killer had been disguised as a clown.

· 34 ·

Gretchen didn't sleep much Sunday night. She spent the time going back over her encounter with the clown at the Parada del Sol, searching her memory for any clues to his identity. How could she possibly recognize anyone under all the layers of makeup and clothes? Perhaps the killer clown wasn't even someone she knew.

She went through the scenario for at least the hundredth time. They had collided in the middle of the street at the very tail end of the parade. Gretchen had fallen down. The clown hadn't made any effort to help her up or to offer an apology. That was about it. Wait . . . something else . . . the clown had spoken to her.

"Watch where you're going." That's what he'd said. He? Was it a man's voice? She hadn't been paying enough attention. She thought the voice had been gruff, but that didn't mean anything. A woman could easily lower her voice if she wanted to disguise it.

Remembering back, she thought the clown wasn't very adept with that white goo that clowns use on their faces. A rush job? Trying to remember more was fruitless. The interaction had been too brief and hurried.

In the morning Gretchen drove to Curves. She, April, and Nina had agreed to work out earlier than usual, before the other doll collectors arrived. After that, they had a meeting with Detective Kline. Nina had willingly taken that assignment, arranging the meeting the night before.

April had been incapacitated after hearing one brief, paralyzing sentence. "We're looking for a killer clown," Gretchen had said. That was it for April. All her words since had been inaudible croaks.

This morning, April looked closer to normal, greeting Ora, the manager, then bouncing onto a platform next to Nina and Gretchen. "Sorry about fainting again," she said.

"Good thing Gretchen caught you," Nina answered. "Otherwise, you could have really hurt yourself."

Gretchen didn't mention her bruised shoulder and aching hip where April had slammed into her. She hadn't exactly caught her. She'd accidentally broken her fall.

"You can't image how scary this is for me," April said.

"It's scary for all of us," Nina reassured her. "That's why we're turning it over to Detective Kline. We aren't going to get involved anymore, are we Gretchen?"

"Right," Gretchen agreed. "A killer clown fascinated with toxicology who poisons victims isn't exactly what we envisioned."

"Nothing in the world could be more horrifying," April said, thumping up and down on the stepper. "I'll do a lot in the name of friendship, but this has crossed the line. I'm going to the meeting with you, and then I'm through."

"What about the kitchen room box?" Nina asked. "Was I wrong to think it was important?"

"I don't know," Gretchen admitted. "At first, it seemed like the best evidence. But, even if it is important, the killer has had plenty of time to remove it. What is or isn't evidence doesn't matter anyway, because we're out of it. We'll share all our suspicions with Brandon and let him decide what to do with the information."

"What about Matt Albright?" April said, brightening

perceptibly. "Shouldn't we tell him what's going on, too?" She caught the look on Gretchen's face. "I know, you don't want anything to do with him, but you two didn't have some kind of agreement, did you? You weren't exclusive, right?"

"Change stations now."

Gretchen moved to the next platform, arranging her face to appear indifferent. With a little more time, she hoped it would come more easily and honestly. "We'll leave the information with Brandon, and he can share it with anyone he chooses," she said. "As far as a relationship, you are correct. We didn't have a verbal understanding. It was more like . . . uh . . . unspoken."

"Maybe he didn't hear it the same way you did."

"What's going on with Caroline?" Nina asked, tuning in to the conversation and realizing it was time to change the channel.

"She left early this morning for Apache Junction," Gretchen said. "She's looking at a doll collection. She'd be happy to hear that we're going back to our routine lives, only she didn't know we were still pursuing bad guys. I have a workshop full of dolls waiting for my attention, and I can't wait to get started on them."

"And I have a long list of clients to train. I'll need help catching up. I'll have to find Daisy."

They were on the sidewalk in front of Curves discussing whose car to take when Bonnie pulled up and parked. "Oh, no," April gasped, her solid frame blocking Gretchen's view.

At first, Gretchen thought April was overacting because of the killer clown. Maybe Bonnie's stiff red wig and painted face reminded April of her all-too-real fears. Matt's mother tended to look a bit clownish.

Gretchen watched the passenger door open and Matt's rodeo date step out. Gretchen heard Nina inhale sharply behind her. She felt her blood pressure rising.

Bonnie, who claimed she wanted Gretchen and Matt to get together, was parading his new woman right in front of Gretchen. And at Curves. The group's special place. What nerve! What a slap in the face!

"Hey," Bonnie called. "Are you girls done working out already? What's the story? You should have called me. We could have come earlier."

"We're in a hurry," Nina said with narrowed eyes and a reddening face. She was working up some steam on Gretchen's behalf. She sashayed forward with her hands on her hips, snorting fire. "And who might this be?"

"Let's go, Nina," Gretchen said, placing a hand on her aunt's shoulder. "It isn't important. We'll be late."

"Not quite yet."

April popped into the conversation. "I think we should go."

"Not quite yet."

"What's wrong with everybody?" Bonnie said, her penciled eyebrows in one big question mark. "Usually a workout puts everyone in a better mood. You sure are crabby."

No one answered. Nina snorted again while Bonnie searched their faces for clues. Gretchen risked a glance at the woman. She was blonde and beautiful. Not a blemish on her porcelain skin. Gretchen had dolls with worse complexions. The woman passed Gretchen and peered into the workout room.

"You go on ahead," Bonnie said to her. "I need to talk to my friends for a minute."

"Former friends," Nina said.

"*What* is going on?'

The model/Hollywood star opened the door and disappeared inside.

"Who is that?" Nina demanded, pointing a ramrod-stiff arm at the empty space where the woman had just been standing. "And why in the world would you bring her to Curves, of all places? You knew Gretchen would be here. Didn't you? Admit it."

"What are you talking about? Meggie—"

"That was *so* underhanded," April chimed in.

"Let's go," Gretchen pleaded. "This isn't worth destroying our relationships over."

"If someone doesn't tell me what's going on, I'm going to scream," Bonnie shouted.

"I'm leaving," Gretchen said.

Bonnie let out a scream so high and piercing, windows within two miles were sure to blow out. Nina and April had their hands over their ears.

The Curves door opened. Starlet peeked out, looking worried. "What's up?" she called loudly trying to be heard over Bonnie. She glanced at Gretchen apologetically. "She hasn't been herself lately. That's why I'm visiting for a while. Auntie Bonnie!"

Bonnie quit screaming.

Nina's mouth fell open.

"Coming, Meggie," Bonnie said meekly. "Sorry, ladies."

"This was all a misunderstanding," Nina said. She hugged the confused president of the Phoenix Dollers Club.

Gretchen couldn't help it. A big grin spread across her face.

"We're losing her," April said. "I knew I should have driven."

Gretchen was trying to keep up with Nina on the drive over to the Scottsdale police station. Her aunt drove like a NASCAR racer, darting and weaving through traffic without so much as a backward glance to see if her niece was still behind her.

The three dogs were in Nina's Impala, and Gretchen caught a glimpse of them in the backseat now and then. After running through several questionable yellow lights to stay behind Nina, Gretchen gave up. She used her cell phone to call the station and ask for an address.

Nina disappeared from sight after another acceleration and another yellow light. Gretchen didn't care. She was elated.

Model Girl, aka Meggie, was Bonnie's niece. That made her Matt's cousin. Gretchen couldn't see the family resemblance, but then she didn't see any between Bonnie and Matt, either. She should have guessed, or at least considered the possibility that the blonde woman was a family member.

Had Gretchen wanted to think the very worst of Matt? Was that how she planned to dodge commitment for the rest of her life? By being overly suspicious? She should have communicated her concerns to Matt instead of leaping to conclusions. It was apparent she still hadn't recovered from the residual effects of her last relationship. The scars ran deeper than she thought.

"Next time I'm driving," April announced. "I could keep up with her." Gretchen didn't say anything about the condition of April's Buick. It had more crumpled metal than a demolition car. No way was she *ever* riding in a car with April at the wheel. "I'm off my diet," April said. "Let's stop for food."

"That was a hard diet to follow. Why don't you try the Curves diet? Everyone says it works. Or try Weight Watchers."

"I lost what I wanted," Gretchen's friend said from the folds of a yellow muumuu. "Can't you tell?"

"I thought you looked especially slim and trim," Gretchen punted.

"The clown theory really bothers me. How can we trust

Ryan?" April said, abruptly changing the subject. "You can't believe anything that kid says. He's a druggie. They lie."

"What are the odds he would have described the same clown I ran into?"

April waved a dismissing hand. "They all look alike."

"No, they don't."

"By the way," April said, "You never told me how you got into the intensive care unit."

"I stealthily moved through the hospital like a Ninja shadow until I found the nurses' lounge. There, still stealthing, I discovered a uniform and cloaked myself in disguise," Gretchen said. "After that it was easy. I only had to take out one security guard before I completed my mission."

April laughed. "You walked right in, didn't you?"

"I'll never tell. Next time you'll have to come along if you want the details."

"You sure do have a silly smile on your face. Matt Albright's got to you good."

Gretchen grinned. Matt's cousin! What a great day!

Nina and April were talking at the same time. From a conference room chair, Gretchen listened to her friends' accounts of events relating to Charlie's murder while Detective Brandon Kline took notes and asked them to clarify details. It was a convoluted trail. Gretchen pitched in when she could get a word in, trying to keep the story on a linear path.

It began with the discovery of the unknown kitchen room box and the miniature peanut butter jar. "We found out what all the room boxes were modeled after," Nina said, using 'we' very loosely. Gretchen didn't remember much participation from her aunt. She was too busy reading fortunes.

"They were replicas of famous murder scenes. Except for one. At first we didn't think it belonged with the others. Then we decided it must belong to the person who killed Sara."

"An unveiling," April added, "in which the killer would be revealed."

"Dramatic," Brandon said, scribbling away.

"That's what I thought," Nina, the drama queen, agreed.

"The display case was inscribed with Sara's name," April said. "Murder scenes. Can you believe it! Very spooky."

"Then Ryan Maize viciously attacked Gretchen."

"And Bernard Waites was blown up with bug juice, and we found out he was a thief."

The stories went on.

"Since Evie covered up for Bernard's embezzlement," April deduced, "she might be part of the scheme, but as far as I'm concerned, Charlie's own son committed the actual murder, in spite of what Gretchen thinks."

Brandon glanced at Gretchen.

Nina jumped in with another plausible suspect. "Joseph chews nicotine gum, *and* he's an alcoholic who had a blackout, or so he says, right when Charlie died."

"Then the miniature shop window exploded," April cut in. "We were stopped by the police and wrongly accused of transporting drugs. The killer's way, I'm sure, of seeking revenge for our efforts to expose him."

"I can explain that one," Brandon said. "When the drug tip came in, the Phoenix police moved too quickly. They generally have to close in fast when they get a tip like that, but they ought to maintain some distance until they're sure of their facts. This one slipped past the normal channels."

"Any idea who made the call?" Gretchen asked.

"We know who made it."

Gretchen looked at him expectantly.

"I'm not free to divulge that information. Let's just say you were set up by someone who used to be very close to someone Gretchen is close to. The call was motivated by jealousy. I apologize for the misunderstanding."

He could only be talking about the Wife. *Kayla!* Gretchen fumed. *Of all the low things to pull.*

"Apology accepted," Nina said in her huskiest voice.

He smiled, and little lines around his eyes crinkled in a cute way. Nina blushed coyly.

"Anyone have anything more to add?" Brandon said.

"Oh, you might want to talk to Britt Gleeland," Nina said. "At the very beginning when I told Britt that Detective Albright suspected murder, she—"

"That was supposed to be a secret, Nina," Gretchen interrupted sharply.

Nina covered her mouth and glanced quickly at Gretchen. "I wasn't supposed to tell, I know. I'm sorry."

"You didn't hurt anything," Gretchen said, realizing Matt had told *her* in confidence. If anyone was to blame for spreading it around, it was Gretchen. "Everyone knows about it by now."

"Anyway," Nina said. "Britt figured it was Charlie's heart problem that killed her. But if it really was murder, Britt said she'd overheard the son, Ryan, threaten his poor mother enough times."

"Gretchen doesn't think Ryan killed Charlie," April said. "She thinks a clown did it."

This was Gretchen's cue. She told the detective about the incident at the parade and her conversation with Ryan Maize in which he described the same clown.

"So," Gretchen said to the detective when she finished, "what do you think?"

Brandon dropped his pen and leaned back in his chair. "I really can't discuss the case with you," he said. "I wish I could, but it's against policy. You've all done a great job. You know what I suggest at this point?"

"No, what?" April said.

"I suggest you go home and get back to your normal lives. You've played an important part in the investigation, but now that part is over. Detective Albright and I will take it home from here."

"That's exactly what I said," April chirped, making an effort to push her new, lithe body out of her chair. "Let's go, girls."

"Nina, can I speak to you for a minute?" Brandon asked. "Alone?"

Gretchen and April filed out.

Nina fluttered out a few minutes later. "He wanted my phone number," she said, glowing like the sun.

Through the conference room windows, Gretchen saw Detective Kline talking on a phone. He was all business. She would love to hear what he was saying. And to whom.

· 35 ·

To style a tangled mohair wig you need to learn about the hair fashions from your doll's era. Make sure you match the hairstyle to the doll. You can use small permanent wave rollers, hairdresser's end papers, hair clips, bobby pins, plenty of hairspray, and your imagination. A bit of warning though—of all the wig materials, mohair is the most difficult to work with. First practice on human hair or synthetic wigs. If proper care is taken, your new coiffed style will last another hundred years.

—From *World of Dolls* by Caroline Birch

Early Tuesday morning, Gretchen climbed Camelback Mountain at a brisk speed and stood at the very summit overlooking the awakening city and the rising sun. Back to normal. Back to her life. It felt good.

Today, she would set an original mohair wig in curlers. She reflected back on her first styling effort. She'd rolled all the curls away from the doll's face and had to redo the entire thing. Live and learn.

Learn and live. Isn't that the advice she'd given her friends? But she wasn't going to think about murder today. She'd hike, work in the workshop, and play with Wobbles and Nimrod.

The desert air was fresh and clean at this altitude, and she breathed it in with familiar appreciation. This was her favorite spot, up with the birds at the top of the world. No one else seemed as enthralled with the mountain as Gretchen. A few serious hikers came up this far, but it was a difficult, steep climb. Most people stopped at the enormous boulder just before the most grueling part of the trail began.

She saw a few ant-sized people close to the trailhead, but it was still too early for the tourists to be out. Gretchen started down.

Matt Albright was waiting for her at the boulder. He wore cargo shorts, running shoes, a Don't Worry Be Hopi T-shirt, and he was leaning against the rocks watching her descend.

"Don't run away," he said immediately, pushing off from the face of the boulder. "Talk to me."

"I'm not going to run away." *Far from it!*

"I thought you and I were making progress, then something happened." He took her hand, and she felt tingles up her arm, through her body. "We need to talk about it."

"There's nothing to talk about," Gretchen squeaked. "I was going through some old relationship burnout. I'm better now."

"Nina told me."

"Told you what?"

"That you thought Meg was my date when you saw us together at the rodeo."

Gretchen didn't respond. Good old interfering Nina with her big, blabby mouth. Kindhearted, but way too involved in Gretchen's life.

"Did Detective Kline tell you about the clown?" she asked.

"You're dodging."

Of course I am.

"Well, did he?"

"We've contacted all the local costume shops. None have a clown suit like the one you described."

Gretchen opened her mouth to ask another question, anything to get him off this uncomfortable topic.

He cut in.

"Can we start over?" Matt asked. The sun rising as a backdrop lit up the rocks. He squeezed her hand.

"Your pending divorce seems to be going on forever," Gretchen said. Finally, it was out in the open. "And your wife is stalking me. This isn't the best time to start something new."

"Ignore Kayla."

"That's not so easy. But that isn't the main problem. It's that you're still married, still going through the process. And I have a lot of baggage from my last relationship," Gretchen said, intent on talking him out of wanting her. "I need to resolve some issues. Otherwise I'll bring them right along with me."

"Don't you think I have a few of my own?" He laughed lightly. His teeth gleamed. His face was handsome and tan. He had a firm, tight body, and he was fun to be with.

What are you waiting for?

"Let's work together," he said.

"We can't start out with so many problems." *Whine, whine, whine.* Part of her wanted to go for it. The other part skidded to a stop.

"I tell you what," Matt said. "In two days I hope to remove one of the obstacles; it's my final divorce hearing. Truthfully? I've had this 'final' hearing several times before with one postponement after another. So I can't make any promises. To show you how much I respect your integrity, if it's postponed, I won't bother you again."

Yikes. Was he slipping away already?

"But . . ." He slipped a finger under her chin and waited until she looked at him, until their eyes met, "if the divorce is final, you give me a chance. Deal?"

He kissed her gently.

"Deal," she whispered.

Then he left her standing alone halfway up the mountain.

The rest of the morning passed in a cloud. Gretchen peered into her completed projects basket and was surprised to find it full. She was operating on automatic drive while her mind replayed the kiss and promise.

She sighed, fully aware that she was behaving like a teenager. It was wonderful to be in love. Or was it lust? Whatever. It felt great. She wished Matt were here. Then she remembered his doll phobia.

One more reason why this would be a difficult relationship to maintain. Heavy sigh.

Gretchen set down the antique German doll she was holding.

Nimrod raced past on his way to the doggie door. The tiny door had been a good investment. It allowed him to decide on his own when he needed to go out. Wobbles uncurled from a position on the edge of the worktable and stretched. A few pats from her, a little purring, and he plopped back down. What a life.

She found Caroline and Daisy on the patio, having iced tea and sandwiches.

"I spent the night, and you didn't even notice," the homeless woman said. She was scrubbed clean, and her purple dress had been washed. Nimrod was on her lap.

"Sit and have lunch," her mother offered.

"You should come more often." Gretchen joined them, pleased that Daisy felt comfortable enough to pop in.

"I hear Ryan's doing well," Daisy said.

"He's so lucky," Caroline said.

Gretchen poured a glass of tea. "Daisy, the other night at the rodeo, a clown told me where to find you."

Daisy nodded. "That was Andy. He works for the rodeo every year."

"Does he own the clown suit?"

"No," she said. "They supply it."

"Ever see a clown with green hair and a bald spot on the crown?"

"I thought you were going to let the police handle Charlie's murder from now on," her mother complained. "Let it go."

Daisy rolled her eyes skyward, thinking. "Can't say that I have. Why?"

"It's not important," Gretchen said, catching the fed-up look on her mother's face. She changed the subject. "Is Nacho back from San Francisco yet?"

"He's home. He didn't like California." Daisy held up her glass of iced tea. "Here's to love," she said, staring knowingly at Gretchen. They toasted.

How did Daisy know? Was it that obvious? Daisy, now that Gretchen thought about it, had her own glow since Nacho was home. The moment was idyllic—perfect weather, basking in the sun with two terrific women, the possibility of a serious relationship with Matt.

Gretchen's cell phone rang when she went to the kitchen for more coffee. "I think I made a terrible mistake!" Nina shouted on the other end.

"What's up?" Gretchen asked.

"I botched a reading."

Tarot cards again. "Did Brandon Kline ask you out yet?" Nina *had* to get a life.

"Don't patronize me. You have to listen. Are you listening?"

"You're shouting. I don't have a choice."

"Here it is then. Remember the reading I did for Britt? Well, I read the cards wrong."

"How do you know?"

"Because I'm down at Aurora's New Age Shop, and Aurora knows these things. Let me talk. Remember she drew the king of pentacles? And the hanged man fell on the floor? The card with the man hanging from a tree upside down? I thought the hanged man was for April because it fell at her feet, but it was really for Britt."

Gretchen entered the workshop and gazed out the window at Camelback. Nina really needed male companionship. Someone to take her mind off of auras and palm readings.

"But the hanged man means the reversal of the other cards' meanings. Instead of a person of character and a loyal friend, the opposite is true. Britt is corrupt; she'll use any means to achieve her end. She's ruthless, unfaithful, and extremely dangerous."

"That's what the cards say?"

"Right. She was capable of killing Charlie."

What would her aunt come up with next?

"Nina, what kind of concrete evidence is that? The police can't arrest her because the hanged man says so."

"But we can try to prove she did it."

"Call Detective Kline and get him onto her."

"You constantly make fun of me, don't think I don't know it. You have to believe me this time. We can prove it. Then you'll have to give me credit. I'm so tired of being mocked."

Nina hung up without saying goodbye.

Gretchen went back to work in the doll shop.

36

"Where's Nina?" April asked the next morning. Gretchen was bent over a restringing project in her shop. April had stormed in without knocking.

Gretchen looked up. "She's mad at me."

"She isn't home."

"She's probably shopping."

"Tutu's there."

"Sometimes she leaves the princess home. Rare, but not unheard of."

"I think she's been gone awhile. Tutu has doo-dooed and wee-weed all over the house."

Gretchen put the doll's arm down. "How long do you think she's been gone?"

"Judging by the canine evidence? Since at least last night."

Gretchen felt faint. Something terrible might have happened to her aunt. "We have to call the hospitals."

"I'm way ahead of you. Scottsdale Memorial has a Jane Doe admit. I'm headed over to take a look. Want to come along?"

Gretchen shook her head. "No, we'll be more effective if we split up. I'll try some of her favorite haunts. I'm sure there's a good reason. Maybe she connected with Brandon last night."

"She would never neglect Tutu."

April was right. "Don't tell my mother," Gretchen warned her. "Not yet. It will only upset her. But last night Nina called, babbling on about Britt Gleeland's tarot reading and reverse meanings, and that she'd decided Britt might be the murderer."

"What nonsense! I ought to throw those cards away."

April rushed out. Gretchen left her project where it was and grabbed her purse. Nimrod looked at her expectantly. "You're staying home today, bud."

What could have happened to Nina? Where was she? Think. Last night she hung up on Gretchen. Was she so angry she had an accident? Maybe. More probable? She had rushed off to prove herself. She certainly had total confidence in the cards. Okay. Work it out.

If the clown was the killer, and she was convinced it was, she could eliminate several people. Joseph, Bernard, and Evie couldn't have been disguised as the clown, because she had seen those three within minutes of bumping into the clown. Joseph passed with the crowd, and Bernard and Evie were at the doll shop. None of them would have had time to change.

That left Ryan, Britt, and Melany. The poison mixer could be anybody, but since she was making wild assumptions, she would assume that the killer was one of the remaining three people.

Could Nina be right? Britt wasn't the most likable women Gretchen had ever met. She had dinner with Charlie the night before she died. And she had been in the shop the night after Charlie's death. Cleaning up, Britt had said. Getting some of her things out of the shop.

Gretchen reached for the phone and called the Scottsdale police department. She asked for Detective Kline. Fortunately, he was in and came on the line. No, he hadn't seen Nina, but he had tried to reach her at her home the evening before. He was sure she was all right, but he'd keep an eye out for her car.

"Tell me," Gretchen said. "Did anyone have permission to remove items from Mini Maize on the Saturday that Charlie died?"

"Of course not."

"So no one should have been inside."

"Absolutely no one."

"I thought Matt Albright told me you were finished with the shop on Saturday."

"We were. But we didn't release it until you arrived the next morning."

What possible motive could Britt have that would drive her to murder? Charlie had been her best friend, or so she claimed. Britt didn't seem interested in taking over the shop like Bernard. She hadn't been stealing from Charlie as the old dollhouse maker had.

Yet, she had been a doll maker, too. She might have been in competition with Sara, her best friend's sister. Britt had made pretty weird comments about friendships.

Gretchen remembered her own challenges with Nina and April, the tiff they'd had because Nina felt Gretchen was spending too much time with April.

It had almost ruined their relationships.

Gretchen jumped into her car and roared away with no clear destination in mind. Almost subconsciously, she turned in the direction of Britt's house.

Nothing fit into a snug package. Gretchen tried to put herself in the killer's mind. *Pretend you just killed Charlie Maize. What would you do next?* She'd hope the police would buy into the heart attack. Charlie had had a bad heart, and if they didn't detect the nicotine, she would be home free.

Hadn't Matt told Gretchen the autopsy almost missed the traces of nicotine overdose? Nicotine traveled through the body quickly, so the evidence might have been easily overlooked. But it hadn't been.

After that, Gretchen had shared a secret with Nina, and her aunt passed it on to her new friend Britt. Charlie had been murdered.

The police would now look for the most likely suspect. The killer would have to throw suspicion somewhere else. Why not blame the burned-out drug addict son who had caused his mother so much grief?

One block from Britt's house, Gretchen stopped the car and thought about her next move. All her conjecture could be wrong. And she had no proof.

But what about Gretchen's missing aunt? She felt her stomach lurch and tried to calm her nerves. If Nina had barged into Britt's house, flinging accusations in her natural theatrical manner, and she was right, Nina might be dead this very minute.

If Britt was the killer. As April would say, there were a lot of ifs flying around. Gretchen tried to call April but got no answer. Then she realized April's cell phone would be turned off while she was inside the hospital. *Please, April, don't call and tell me Nina is the Jane Doe!*

She eased the car down the street and passed by Britt's house. The garage door was up. And it was empty. Gretchen parked around the corner, grabbed a handful of doll repair tools, and headed for Britt's house.

What was she thinking? For starters, she'd get a good look at the wallpaper that had been so similar to the wallpaper in the room box. And she'd look for her aunt.

Walking briskly into the garage, she knocked on the

door. After waiting for a response, she lowered the garage door. No sense flaunting her lack of break-in skills in front of the entire neighborhood.

Giving up with the tools, she tried to open the locked door with her repair hooks and her utility knife, but it wouldn't give. She reached up and ran her hand along the top of the doorframe. Hadn't she read somewhere that people like to stash keys near the door? Her fingers touched on metal, and she pulled down a key, stunned at her unbelievable good fortune.

Gretchen opened the door, made her illegal entry, and hurried to the kitchen. The house creaked, startling her. The refrigerator motor kicked in, and she almost fainted.

Get a grip, she scolded herself.

The basic wallpaper seemed to be the same color as that in the room box, but the border was different. Gretchen chewed on her lip, trying to remember more clearly. Too bad the room box had been scorched in the fire. She had a picture on her camera phone, but it was a little out of focus, and the colors weren't exactly right. Not to mention that she had left it in her car.

Gretchen pulled over a kitchen chair and stood on it. She reached up and tried to peel away the edge of the border. It wouldn't budge. She tried a different spot. What was the paper glued down with? Cement?

She moved the chair to a new spot and tried again. Any second, she expected Britt to come home and catch her. She was almost ready to give up, when she felt the border give slightly under her fingers. Carefully she inserted her utility knife under the wallpaper, working it loose.

She pulled the first layer away and stared at the underlying design: an apple. A teapot. The room spun. Gretchen leaned against a cabinet for support.

Britt hadn't had time to remove the wallpaper, so she'd just papered over it.

Nina had been right. But Gretchen hadn't believed her. She would never forgive herself if her aunt was dead. Gretchen replaced the chair.

She heard the garage door rising.

37

Gretchen quickly calculated her chances of getting out of the house before Britt came in and caught her. Slim to none, she decided, running for the doll-making studio. She'd go out the back workshop door, the same one she'd used when they had visited. Piece of cake.

Except the back door was deadbolted, and the key wasn't in the lock. She felt along the top of the doorframe. Nothing.

Gretchen heard someone enter the house just as she spotted another door she hadn't noticed when she visited. It was a walk-in storage closet. She slid in and held her breath, wondering how she would get out of this mess.

If it came to a physical confrontation, she was sure she could take Britt. Gretchen was a larger woman than Britt. This was the one and only time she had ever appreciated her size. Still, she hoped it wouldn't come to that.

It was dark in the closet, but as her eyes adjusted, she saw the outline of storage units lining the wall. If she scooted back far enough, she might remain undetected. Then what? She would have to wait until dark and sneak out.

Too bad she had left her cell phone in the car.

Smart thinking, Gretchen.

She edged toward the back of the storage closet. Her foot struck something soft, something unyielding. At that moment, she realized she wasn't alone in the closet.

She blinked, straining to see more clearly. Gretchen squatted and gasped. The clown suit! She slapped her hand across her mouth to stifle a scream. Gretchen could see the jutting hair and the shiny bald spot on top. And the big nose.

The most horrifying thing of all was that the suit wasn't empty.

Someone was crumpled in a heap, wearing the clown face: nose, wig, and white face paint. The paint seemed to glow in the dark. The rest of the body was clothed in a fabric Gretchen could identify even in the dark: her aunt's favorite pink pantsuit.

The lifeless body belonged to Nina!

Gretchen ran her fingers along the prone woman's neck, searching for a pulse. If Nina was dead, Gretchen would attack Britt and strangle her with her bare hands.

A pulse throbbed under her fingers. Gretchen felt tears of relief well in her eyes. She wiped them away and cradled her unconscious aunt in her arms.

She couldn't sit tight and wait until dark to get out. Who knew what Britt had given Nina? Her aunt might have enough poison in her body to kill her while Gretchen waited for the right moment to make her escape. She had to get help as quickly as possible.

When she peeked out of the closet, she found the room empty. With dawning horror, she realized she had left her tools in the kitchen in plain view. She had to be quick. Her best bet was still the back door. Or a window. Why hadn't she thought of that earlier?

The casement window opened easily enough, another stroke of luck.

"What are you doing?" Britt stood next to the kiln, her face twisted with rage—wild, angry eyes and a red, distorted face. "What are you doing in my house?"

Gretchen whirled. "What is Nina doing in your closet?" She steadied her voice. "What did you do to her?"

"Your aunt was distraught. I gave her something to calm her nerves. See how effective my potions are? I like to mix and match and watch the results. An old hobby left over from my lab assistant days. I love the way chemicals interact with each other, don't you? A little flour here, a little liquid nicotine there, a small dose of epinephrine—"

"I'm calling for help."

"No. You aren't."

With one experienced motion, Britt opened the firing kiln. "This was meant for my traitorous friend, Nina, but I'm sure it will accommodate you as well. Twenty three hundred degrees. Just the right temperature."

"But, why? Nina offered her friendship to you."

"Nina doesn't understand friendship any better than Charlie did. Best friends are best friends for life. Until death do us part. Just like wedding vows. Charlie wasn't a true friend, or she never would have cared about her sister more than me."

"You have that twisted." Did she ever! "You killed Sara and poisoned Charlie. What kind of person are you?"

"You'll never understand true love. You're as fickle as the rest."

She blazed with hate as she lunged at Gretchen.

Gretchen readied herself for the physical attack. If she could only get to the drawers that contained the knives.

She hadn't anticipated Britt's strength. Nor had she seen the hypodermic needle in the killer's hand. Until it was almost too late.

Gretchen grabbed her wrist and tried to snap it away from her, but she couldn't break Britt's grip on the syringe. They were locked together when they fell to the floor. Gretchen felt the sting of the needle pierce the skin of her arm. She wrenched away before Britt could release whatever evil potion she had concocted.

Britt struggled to her feet, panting, preparing for another attack.

Gretchen heard a scream from the doorway.

"Mother! What are you doing?" Britt's daughter, Melany, looked stricken.

"Tying up loose ends. You came just in time."

Britt's French twist wasn't perfect any longer.

Melany's eyes dropped to her mother's hand.

The firing kiln spewed raw heat.

"Nina is in the closet," Gretchen said, afraid to move, anticipating another rush from Britt. "We need to get help for her."

"What did you do to her, Mother?"

"Gave her something to calm her nerves."

"Tell me."

"You have to help me with both of them," Britt said. "You don't want your mother in prison, do you? Hold her for me, and I'll take care of the rest. We'll burn the clown suit right along with them. No one will ever have to know."

"My old clown suit? What does that have to do with anything?"

When Britt didn't answer, Melany moved toward them, close enough that Gretchen could see the indecision in her eyes. "You still talk in your sleep," she said to her mother. "Night after night I hear you apologizing to Charlie for killing her sister. You make excuses for yourself. Did you know that?"

"I'm sorry, baby. I never wanted you involved. Sara had to go. She was interfering with the love between Charlie and me. You know I always thought of Charlie as my best friend. If only she hadn't found out what I'd done. Why did she have to make that sloppy excuse for a room box?"

Melany looked stricken. "The room box with a sample of your wallpaper?"

"And a miniature peanut butter jar and a vial that was labeled as poison."

"You killed her because of the room box?" Melany looked like she might pass out. The girl started trembling. Tears welled up in her eyes. If Gretchen made a run for the window, would she make it? Would Melany let her mother burn Nina while she ran for help? Gretchen couldn't risk it.

Britt stared at Gretchen, every muscle flexed for combat. "I had no choice. She and I went to dinner the night before the party to celebrate. She was so excited about the room boxes. We stopped back at the shop. She had forgotten her house key, left it on the desk. I peeked under the display cloth while she was in the back room. I saw what she intended to do. To our friendship, to you and me."

"Mother," Melany cried, "I'm the one who put that room box in with the others. I was the one who wanted to expose you for what you really are."

"No!" Britt said. "It was Charlie. Not you. Help me now. We'll talk later."

"Please, Melany," Gretchen said. "Call for an ambulance. Save Nina."

"You're already an accessory," Britt said to her daughter. "You knew about the explosion at the store and didn't turn on me then. You're on my side. I'm your mother." Britt smiled sweetly.

Gretchen thought again of escape. Could she climb out the window before Britt plunged the syringe into her back? Even if she made it, her aunt would be a pile of ashes before Gretchen could get back with reinforcements.

Neither of them would make it out alive if Melany sided with her mother.

Melany came closer. "You pretended to be Ryan Maize. I

found the do-rag," she said, her eyes riveted on her mother. "You set him up. And all the time it was you."

"Clever, wasn't it?"

Gretchen edged away. She could see the raw terror on Melany's face.

Melany stared at her mother. Fearful. Uncertain.

Britt had a sharp eye on Gretchen. "He would have died peacefully while engaged in his favorite pastime, if she hadn't interfered. Charlie's murderous son, dead by his own hand." Her voice hardened. "Melany, grab her."

Melany was very quick. Gretchen stepped back, fear clamping down on her chest so she could hardly breathe.

Britt's eyes widened in sudden comprehension when her daughter turned toward her. Melany pushed her backwards. Britt stumbled once and almost fell down.

She recovered, but Melany was on her. Another push. Britt screamed as her back made contact with the hot metal of the open kiln. Melany was going to roast her mother.

Gretchen rushed forward and tried to pull Melany away. "*No!*" she screamed. "Let her go."

"She deserves it. Look what she's done. She's evil!" Britt screamed.

Gretchen pulled at Melany with all her strength and pleaded, "Don't become what she is. Let her go."

Melany hesitated.

"Don't become her," Gretchen whispered.

Abruptly Melany released her mother. Britt crumpled to the floor, moaning. Gretchen saw severe burns along her shoulders and spine. The clothes on her back had been burned away. Gretchen ripped her top over her head the way she had seen April remove hers to fight the shop fire. She wrapped the cloth across Britt's back to douse the few remaining sparks of fire and to protect her skin from further damage.

"Make the call, Melany. I'm going to check on Nina."

Melany stood as though paralyzed, staring at her mother. Then she dropped to the floor and buried her face in her hands. Britt moaned beside her.

Gretchen placed the emergency call, requesting more than one ambulance. She didn't leave her unconscious aunt's side until she heard the sirens outside the house.

· 38 ·

They were all crowded into Nina's hospital room: Gretchen, Caroline, April, and Brandon Kline.

The only one missing was Matt.

"Where was he while all this was happening?" Caroline said. "I'd asked him to keep track of you."

"That explains why he kept popping up," Gretchen said. "You gave him permission to follow me around?"

"He didn't need my permission. Besides, you didn't expect me to allow my favorite daughter to put herself in jeopardy."

"Britt isn't in this hospital, is she?" Nina said. "I won't be able to sleep if she is."

"You're going home today; you don't have to worry," Brandon said. "And I'm driving you."

Nina blushed.

"I owe you an apology," April said sheepishly to Nina. "I pooh-poohed all that psychic nonsense . . . I mean . . . well . . . I mean . . ."

"Spit it out," Nina said, grinning. "You believe me now?"

"I promise," April said, crossing her heart, "I'll never laugh at your mumbo jumbo again."

"I agree," Gretchen said. "Maybe there's something to it after all. But you really handled it the wrong way."

"I know. I wanted to prove myself so badly that I just rushed in."

"We might never have solved the case without you," Brandon said to Nina, laying it on a little thick, Gretchen thought.

Brandon looked around at his captivated audience. "Britt Gleeland was responsible for everything. She killed Sara because Sara didn't like her, and Britt worried that Charlie would stop being her friend. She killed Charlie when she thought Charlie was going to expose her publicly at the unveiling," he continued. "She rigged Bernard's bug juice to explode, plotting to keep him away from the shop. She wore a do-rag when she bombed the store to eliminate the evidence and throw suspicion on Ryan, and she shot him up with enough epinephrine, taken from Sara last year, to slowly kill him."

"She told you all this?" Gretchen asked.

"She made a full confession."

"All in the name of friendship," April said. "What a certifiable kook."

"Sometimes," Nina said quietly, "friends do crazy things, hurtful things."

April smiled at her. "I'm so glad you're safe."

"What's going to happen to Melany?" Gretchen asked Brandon.

"She won't be charged," he said. "She did what she thought she had to do to save you and Nina. Her mother's going to prison, and Melany feels responsible for Charlie's death. She thought she was doing the right thing by placing that box with the others. Instead, it triggered Charlie's death."

"I don't think Charlie even saw the extra room box before she died," Gretchen said.

The detective agreed. "Melany placed it with the others after Britt and Charlie left for dinner. Chances are good that she never got a chance to see it."

"At least," Caroline added, "Charlie never knew what Britt had done to Sara." She shook her head. "What possessed her to make those room boxes, I'll never know."

"Ryan's one floor up from you," Gretchen said to Nina. "He's making progress, but he needs time."

"That's more good news. Now clear out," Nina ordered them. "I want to get dressed and get out of here. Not you, Gretchen. You stay and help me."

Brandon, Caroline, and April dutifully left the room.

"Everything turned out," Nina said. "The only one who will be permanently scarred for life is the burn victim, and she deserves it."

"I think there will be some emotional scars for a few others. Ryan and Melany have a long way to go."

"Everything will work out for Ryan and Melany," Nina said with a knowing look on her face. "What about you? Where's Matt Albright?"

Gretchen sat at the very top of Camelback Mountain. She barely noticed the birds, or the beautiful sunny February day, or the spectacular view of the city below her.

She chewed her lip and waited. The inside of her mouth was raw from worrying it.

Late afternoon, and the lower cliffs of the mountain were crowded with inexperienced climbers. Groups of them sat on the big boulder, the same boulder where Matt had held her hand and kissed her.

She remembered his exact words. "Once my divorce is final, you have to give me a chance."

"I'd climb a mountain for you," he'd said when he called to remind her of the court date and time. As though she could forget. The divorce hearing had begun at one o'clock.

"I expect you to climb all the way to the topmost peak," she had said, laughing.

"The top!" he'd replied. "I'll never make it that far."

"The top," she'd insisted.

Neither of them had mentioned the other possibility—that the divorce would be postponed again.

Gretchen checked her watch. Four thirty. Three and a half hours since the final hearing was scheduled to begin. He wasn't coming.

Her cell phone rang, and she dug it out of her pocket, reading his number on the caller ID. Her dwindling spirit fell further. He was calling to say he wasn't coming. She didn't answer the phone.

Now what? Keep waiting? The divorce might never happen. Gretchen had to move on with her life.

She stood up. Her phone rang again. Him again. She sighed and answered it. "Hey, I know, it didn't happen. And I can't wait—"

"I'm a free man," Matt said. "Single. Dashing. Intelligent."

Gretchen glanced down the mountain. So why wasn't he climbing to meet her? Had he reconsidered, decided to give bachelorhood a try? Maybe he wanted another fashion-model Arizona woman like Kayla.

"You're wondering why I'm not crawling up the mountain on my belly, right?"

"It crossed my mind."

"If we're going to get our relationship off on the right path, we have to be willing to make an effort."

"Okay." Where was this going?

"Both of us."

"Absolutely."

"I thought," Matt said, "you should meet me halfway."

Gretchen grinned.

"I'm up past the boulder. See me waving?"

Gretchen *did* see him.

"This is as far as I've ever gone. Get your cute bod down here to meet me, woman."

Gretchen tucked the phone into her pocket and started down the mountain.